BLACK LIST, WHITE DEATH

ALSO BY STEVE HOCKENSMITH

BLACK LIST, WHITE DEATH

TWO HOLMES ON THE RANGE NOVELLAS

STEVE HOCKENSMITH

ROUGH
EDGES
PRESS

CONTENTS

BLACK LIST, WHITE DEATH

BLACK LIST

(APPETIZER: NOVELLA #1)

Urias Smythe
Smythe & Associates Publishing, Ltd.
175 Fifth Avenue
New York, New York

Dear Mr. Smythe:

In the spring, they say, a young man's fancy turns to thoughts of love…

Well, I'm hoping you know who "they" are, because I'd like a word with them. I don't think they know much about young men. Or old men. Or in-between men.

Your typical man has his fancy turned to love—or women anyway—year-round. In this regard—unlike, say, my exceptional good looks, charm, and storytelling ability—I admit to being typical. In fact, I've just spent an entire winter with my fancy turned to thoughts of one woman in particular: our friend and colleague Diana Crowe. As you know from the stories I've been sending you for *Smythe's Frontier Detective*, my brother and I have had the opportunity to work with her on a couple cases since we and she and her father launched the A.A. Western Detective Agency at winter's start. But far too often, she's been afield with one of the agency's other operatives, Percival Burr, leaving me to fancy from a distance (while Burr gets to do it up close, damn him). It made this young man's winter very, very frustrating.

I've long suspected that my brother's fancies are turned to Diana, as well, but he denies it. Loudly. Work is all he'll admit to fancying—the kind that'll pay the agency's bills and give him something to do with the big, complicated, *very* atypical brain he carries around in his hard head. So when Col. Crowe told us we had a job lined up in Kingman, Arizona, Old Red didn't even ask if Diana would be coming along.

I did.

"We've been asked to conduct 'a confidential inquiry' on behalf of a local lawyer," the colonel replied. "If you think that's something you can't handle, I'll send Burr."

"We can handle it!" my brother said. And he snatched away the telegram Colonel Crowe clutched in his little hand (our partner, you'll recall, being so small he practically needs a stepladder to see over his desk) and marched out of the Double-A's office.

I stifled a sigh and gave the colonel a smile.

"Where is Burr right now, anyway?" I said.

It wasn't really Burr I was so curious about, though.

Diana's desk was conspicuously devoid of Dianas. (There was an occupant—the colonel's dachshund, Capt. Zimmer, who was curled up on Diana's seat—but I saw no need to drag him into the conversation. He'd surely take the colonel's side anyway.)

"He is conducting a different confidential inquiry. With my daughter," Colonel Crowe said. "But I expect him back quite soon. He's not just discreet and dependable, he's efficient."

"We're discreet, dependable, and efficient," I said.

"Come on! Let's go! We got work to do!" Old Red roared from down the hall.

I cleared my throat.

"We're dependable and efficient," I said.

"Prove it," Colonel Crowe replied, and he shooed me out of the office with two quick, irritated flaps of the hand.

I stifled another sigh and left, and not two hours later, Old Red and I were on a train bound for Arizona Territory. Which I'm sure comes as a relief to you, being this far into my letter with no assurances so far.

Fear not: What you now hold in your hands is not forty pages of ruminations on love and ladies and a young man's fancy. It is an account of a new case—one I suggest you publish under the title "Black List." I know *Smythe's Frontier Detective* leans toward titles along the lines of "Six-Gun Showdown with the Vigilante Kill-Mob!" but I do hope you'll keep mine. For once.

We arrived in Kingman the next morning after two train changes, one mostly sleepless night in the Las Vegas depot, and a near-infinite number of growls, groans, and grumbles from my train-hating brother. Though Kingman has a bit more hustle-bustle to it than your average territory town—and a bit more of a skyline, too, thanks mostly to a marble-arched courthouse and the four-story hotel directly across from it—it was easy enough to find our destination. It, too, was directly across from the courthouse.

The law offices of Charles Burton Cornelius III, Esquire. Our client.

Who was busy, apparently. When we stepped in, we found ourselves in a waiting room with a very dark—and very closed—oak door to the left. We could hear the muffled voices of two men on the other side of the inner door, so we closed the outer one and took a look around.

It felt a bit like a wee little lending library with its two armchairs and walls lined with books. As you know, Old Red's been working hard on his reading lately: He started the year illiterate, but now, not even three full months in, he's already got his A-B-Cs down all the way through his X-Y-Zs. The words you mix and match those letters to form are coming more slowly, but my brother's pushing himself every day. So I wasn't surprised when he pulled one of the books off its shelf and took a look inside.

I also wasn't surprised by the puzzlement and consternation that came over his face.

I stepped up to the same shelf, took down one of the books there, and opened it to the title page.

THE PACIFIC REPORTER
VOLUME 14
Containing all the decisions of the Supreme Courts of
CALIFORNIA, KANSAS, OREGON, WASHINGTON, COLORADO, MONTANA, ARIZONA, NEVADA, IDAHO, WYOMING, UTAH, NEW MEXICO, OKLAHOMA, AND COURTS OF APPEALS OF COLORADO AND KANSAS
September 5 – November 7, 1891

I flipped to one of the decisions and saw what I expected: words words words words words. Long ones, in teeny type. With no fun illustrations of, say, Sherlock Holmes stretched out on the ground hunting for clues or lighting up his pipe or telling Doc Watson that he's blind as a bat for the hundredth time. It was a law book, after all.

I looked down at the words words words before me and began reading some out.

"Elder v. Rourke, Supreme Court of Oregon, October 12, 1891. In an action for services for cutting grain, plaintiff alleged that the work was done for the agreed price of $1.25 per acre. The defendant denied the material allegations of the complaint, and for a defense alleged that the work was performed at the instance and request of a third person and that the defendant, as cashier of a bank, guarantied the payment of plaintiff's services to the extent of the proceeds of the grain harvested when the same shall be sold and not before."

"Show-off," Old Red said, and he slammed the book in his hands shut, slid it back in place on the shelf, and slapped the dust off his hands. (The book I was holding was dusty and musty, too. Obviously they were there more as wallpaper—the kind that said, "Look at me! I'm a lawyer!"—as opposed to anything actually useful.)

"I wasn't showing off," I said. "I was showing you you're not missing much. Unless you're suddenly fascinated by whether fellas do or don't get paid for cutting grain."

"I ain't," my brother said, and he carried on around the room. He squinted at the book spines turned out toward him though all he'd see on them, if he'd paused to sound it all out, would be variations on BORING OLD GOBBLEDYGOOK VOLUME 9 and LEGAL MUMBO JUMBO VOLUME 127.

I didn't say it out loud, but I actually was a bit interested in the paying or non-paying of grain-cutters: Having clerked at a granary as a boy back in Kansas I'd observed first-hand a few knockdown drag-out fights over just that. But as I read more of *Elder v. Rourke*—silently now—I found that I couldn't even figure out which one was "plaintiff," which one was "defendant," which one I was rooting for, and which one won.

I closed the book and put it back on the shelf.

Old Red had turned by now to stare out the big window at the front of the office. It looked out on the courthouse steps—and the men dressed for business hustling up and down them in patent leather shoes.

Not everyone was in a suit or a hurry, though. A cowboy sat on the steps languidly rolling himself a smoke. And please note that I'm not one of those ignorant Easterners who call any man out West in a Stetson a cowboy. I know one when I see one, having been one myself not so very long ago. Everything from the crease of his hat (Montana-style) down to the heels of his boots (custom-crafted extra-long for hooking over stirrups) said "cowhand." He may as well have been twirling a lasso and singing "Bury Me Not on the Lone Prairie."

Except he wasn't atop a cow pony nursing cattle, of course. He was puffing on a cigarette on the courthouse steps. And staring, it seemed, directly at us.

It wasn't an accidental stare, either—not a glance that just happened to linger before moving on to something more interesting than a plate-glass window with "CHARLES BURTON CORNELIUS III, ATTORNEY AT LAW" painted across it. He was watching Cornelius's office and not bothering to be sly about it.

And he had a gun on his hip—a big, long-barreled one in a holster, probably a Colt Peacemaker or a Smith & Wesson American.

Aren't I observant?

"Shouldn't he be out chasing strays somewhere?" I said. "Or getting drunk?"

"Yeah. You'd think," said Old Red.

The cowboy took a drag on his cigarette, puffed the smoke from his nose like he was an idling locomotive, and went on staring.

"Maybe he needs a lawyer," I said. "He looks like the 'disturbing the peace' type."

"That he does."

The voices in the inner office grew louder, and when we turned toward the door, it swung open to reveal two men who looked very much like the ones striding in and out of the courthouse. Not that they were identical—far from it. One was tall and lean and clean-shaven and fortyish, the other short and stout and sixtyish with a walrus mustache so thick and white it could've been someone's lost mitten stuck to his upper lip. But they both wore the dark cutaway coats and gray vests and stiff-collared shirts and neckties of the men of means coming and going outside.

They took us in with a glance—me in a suit but topped with a Stetson (a look I've been experimenting with after deciding that bowlers and boaters are too small for my brawny form, like sticking a thimble atop a grizzly) and my brother, as usual, still dressed cowboy-style all the way. The older gent gave us a pleasant nod. The younger one widened his eyes and went pale but didn't pause the smooth patter he was directing at his companion.

"...see you in court this afternoon," he was saying. "And hopefully at Hervé's tonight...?"

The old walrus chuckled. "Oh, I'll be there! I hear pheasant under glass will be on the dinner menu. I've been wondering what the hell that is for years!"

Both men laughed—the younger one a little over-enthusiastically.

"Well, we're about to find out...and I'm sure it will be delicious," he said. "Thanks for coming by, Cliff."

"Always a pleasure, Charlie."

The men shook hands, and the older one went out the front door.

"That was Clifford Ball, presiding judge of the Mohave County Superior Court," said "Charlie"—a.k.a. Charles Burton Cornelius III—once the door was closed. When he turned around to face us, the smile he'd put on for the judge was gone. "And who would you be?"

I got the feeling he wanted us to know who the judge was as a way of saying, "You've been seen here by an unimpeachable eyewitness...so don't try anything."

"I'm Otto Amlingmeyer, and this is my brother, Gustav," I said. "From the A.A. Western Detective Agency? I believe Col. Crowe should've wired you we were coming...?"

Cornelius' smile returned—though now it was a smile of relief.

"Yes! He did! It's just..." Cornelius shifted his gaze from me to Old Red. "You're not what I was expecting."

"We are unique," I said.

Old Red nodded at the window. "You got cowboy trouble?"

Cornelius furrowed his brow and looked over his shoulder. Judge Ball had already crossed the street and was about to head up the courthouse steps—passing as he did the cowhand-looking fellow still sitting there with a cigarette in his mouth and his eyes on us.

"Oh. Him," Cornelius said. He turned to face us again. "No, it's not cowboy trouble. That's close to it, though. 'Cattleman trouble' is more like it. There's a certain local rancher, a powerful one, who…well, it's rather complicated. Shall we?"

He held a hand out toward the inner office, and my brother and I went inside.

The walls were lined with more bookshelves—and lots, *lots* more volumes of *Boring Old Gobbledygook*—except for a spot directly behind Cornelius's big mahogany desk. That was reserved for a portrait of a dark-haired, solemn-looking woman in a green velvet dress covered at the shoulders by a black lace capelet. She gazed down on us somberly as we sat—Cornelius directly beneath her, Old Red and I in the armchairs on the other side of the desk.

"The rancher's name is Clay Aintree," Cornelius said. "I came to Kingman to work for him, actually. Seven years ago. The cattle business here was booming, and there was talk of making Kingman the county seat. It seemed like the proverbial land of opportunity. What I didn't count on was how ruthless Aintree is. It turned out most of my job was trying to squash the smaller ranchers' land and water rights. Create legal trouble for them any way I could. They fought back, in their way, but that just brought them more legal trouble."

"They cut Aintree's wire and stole his beeves," Old Red said.

Cornelius's gaze flicked down to go over my brother's duds again. "A familiar story to you, I suppose."

Old Red and I looked at each other.

Colonel Crowe had stuck us in the middle of another range war.

Oh, joy.

"It's familiar to anyone living west of the Mississippi," I said. "But yeah—we've seen it up close more than once."

"I take it you're not on Aintree's side anymore," said Old Red.

Cornelius nodded. "That's right. Eventually, after I'd been here about a year, Aintree went too far. He was head of the local Cattlemen's Association at the time—he still is, actually—and he convinced the other big ranchers to pool their money and men and go after the nesters and rustlers with…more vigor. Not just blacklist them from Association roundups or pressure the big buyers—the Army, the reservations, the meat packers—not to deal with them. That was all being done already, of course, and Aintree said it wasn't enough. It was time to take action outside the law."

"Ah," I said.

"Mm-hmm," said Old Red.

The story was continuing to be very, *very* familiar.

Someone was about to get seriously dead. Maybe a bunch of someones.

"They drew up a list," Cornelius said. "Eleven men they marked for death. And they brought in an outsider to see the work through. A man named R.T. Mead. Have you heard of him?"

I shook my head and looked over at Old Red. He was shaking his head, too.

"He used to be in your line of work," Cornelius said. "He was a Pinkerton for a time. Then he went independent. Taking on the jobs even the Pinkertons won't touch."

"Like premeditated murder?" I said.

Cornelius gave us another nod—a sad one this time. "I wouldn't have touched it myself if I'd known. But Aintree made me his middleman. Almost his scapegoat, it turned out."

He sighed, steeling himself for his next words.

"*I* was the one who passed that death list to Mead."

Old Red put up a hand. "You're sayin' it was a *list* list? Names actually written out on a piece of paper?"

"That's right."

My brother gave Cornelius a dubious look.

I knew what he was thinking. I was thinking the same thing.

"If you don't mind my saying, Mr. Cornelius, that doesn't seem very smart," I said. "Evidence of a criminal conspiracy and all that."

Cornelius looked both impressed and depressed.

"I would've told Aintree the same thing if I'd known what was on that paper," he said. "But I'd been told I was passing along money and instructions, that's all. It was in a sealed envelope. I had no idea what those 'instructions' were until it was too late."

"So how far'd it go?" asked Old Red.

His real question: How many folks got killed?

"There was one death. One assassination. The uproar it caused brought the whole thing to an end. Mead was identified as the killer and arrested and put on trial." Cornelius heaved another sigh. "And I defended him. And did it well, because that was my job. Mead claimed he'd merely confronted the man about his ties to rustlers. The man pulled a gun on him—supposedly—so Mead shot him out of the saddle. Never mind that there was no proof of that at all. It planted enough doubt. Mead was convicted, but of manslaughter, not murder."

Old Red raised a hand again.

"But the list…," he said.

"Exactly," said Cornelius. "If the prosecution had had that piece of paper, things would've turned out *very* differently. I knew the list existed when we went trial because Mead told me about it. And I told him to hide it somewhere safe. If the trial went badly maybe we could use it to make a deal. But I wasn't going to risk it at first because it was proof of premeditation. Mead could've been convicted of murder in the first degree. Then he'd face the rope. As it turned out, he got six years at Yuma."

"Ah. Six years, huh?" my brother said.

I jumped in to show I'd been paying attention and could do math, too.

"So now he's out," I said.

I thought of the cowboy watching Cornelius's office.

"And Aintree wants that paper because it's proof he and his pals have blood on their hands," I went on. "So he's got his boys out looking for it."

"That's it exactly," said Cornelius.

I gave Old Red a gloating grin. Sometimes we Watsons are able to do a little deducing ourselves.

My brother ignored me.

"But it ain't everything, or we wouldn't be here," he said to Cornelius. "Something else happened."

"Yes. You're right," Cornelius said. "When Mead got out of

prison, he came back to Kingman. He came to see me, but he was…evasive about his plans. Cagey. Later, he was seen talking to Aintree—and very soon afterward, he somehow had the cash to buy a little house outside town."

"Blackmail, huh?" I said. "Dangerous game to play with a man you know doesn't mind killing."

"Dangerous indeed. Mead is dead."

Old Red sat up straighter in his seat. I wouldn't say he looked thrilled—he's a grouch, not a ghoul—but his eyes did light up. This was turning out to be more interesting than just another range war.

"Murdered?" he said.

"More or less."

Old Red quickly went back to looking grouchy. "What's that mean?"

"He was found out at his house. Beaten to death, it looked liked at first," Cornelius said. "He was bruised, bloody. But that wasn't what killed him. Not directly."

"Yeah?" my brother said.

He spun his hands in the air in a "Get to the point" way.

Cornelius—obviously unaccustomed to being rushed in his own office—gave him a little glare before complying.

"The coroner says he had a heart attack. Mead was only forty or so, but you know Yuma's reputation. It's a hellhole. He came out of it weakened. Damaged. So much so that one sustained beating was enough to trigger a massive coronary."

Old Red nodded slowly and sank back into his plush chair.

"And no one knows who doled that beating out?" I said.

Cornelius shook his head. "No. But there were tracks of multiple men, apparently. And Mead's house had been ransacked."

"'Ransacked' as in searched?" said Old Red. "Not just tore up or burned down?"

"*Searched*," Cornelius said.

"Ahhh." Old Red steepled his fingers and nodded again. "So it wasn't some old friends of the man Mead killed, out for revenge.

It was someone lookin' for something…and tryin' to whale where it was out of Mead. Only he up and died before they got it out of him."

"That's how I see it," Cornelius said.

"How do you know they didn't find it?" I asked. "This Aintree fella might've already tossed the list in a fireplace by now."

"I know Aintree's men didn't get it," Cornelius said, "because Clay Aintree is an arrogant, cruel son of a bitch who's hated my guts ever since I quit working for him. He's got to know that I want that list as much as he does—so that I can see that he finally answers for what's done. And if he had it, yes, he would destroy it…but he'd make sure I knew. So he could gloat. He'd send me the ashes, come here to taunt me, something. Instead he's had his cowboy thugs watching me day and night. No—the list is still out there somewhere."

"And we're here to find it," said Old Red.

"Before Aintree's boys do," I added.

"Precisely," said Cornelius.

The intrigued gleam had come back to my brother's eyes. This was the kind of challenge he lived for.

There was no mirror handy to check in, but it would be a pretty safe bet no gleam lit up my eyes. I would've much preferred the hunt for a missing slip of paper if a passel of "cowboy thugs" —ones who'd already punched someone all the way to a heart attack—weren't looking for it, too.

Oh, well. Beggars can't be choosers. And to hear Colonel Crowe grouse about the agency's bills lately, we were beggars (or soon would be). I just hoped we'd live long enough to bill Cornelius.

"I got just one more question for now," said Old Red. "Where's Mead's house?"

Cornelius gave us directions, and off we went. And by "we" I don't just mean me and Old Red. It was three of us who went off to the nearest livery: my brother, me and our new cowboy pal from the courthouse. He peeled himself up off the steps, followed us and waited outside while we rented horses and tack. He made no attempt to conceal himself as we mounted up and went trotting out of town. He just leaned against an awning post in front of the print shop across the street and rolled himself another cigarette.

"I guess that's as far as our friend's gonna follow," I said to Old Red.

"Looks that way."

I glanced back at the cowboy. He watched us another moment, puffed out some smoke, then turned and sauntered back toward Cornelius's office in no particular hurry.

"If they got a man watching Cornelius, they'll probably have one watching Mead's house, too," I said. "At least one."

"It's possible."

"Well...what are we gonna do about that?"

"Be sneaky," my brother said. "And keep these handy."

He patted the forty-five in its holster on his hip.

I was heeled, too, but not in the same way: I had my Webley Bulldog in a shoulder holster under my suit jacket. That didn't help me feel any better, though.

"I've heard better plans," I said.

"Oh? Let's hear one then."

"For this? I don't know. We don't go near the house till dark?"

Old Red snorted. "I've heard better plans, but I don't think I've heard worse."

"What could possibly be so wrong about creeping in after dark?"

"It's *dark*, that's what. We'd need a lantern to take a look around...and that'd make us easy targets for anyone watchin' when we couldn't see them at all."

"Oh. Well. All right, I'll concede ya that one. So instead we... create a distraction?"

"What kinda distraction? And how do we distract someone if we ain't sure where they are?"

"You just have to naysay everything, don't you?"

"I don't naysay *everything*. Just foolishness. If that means I'm naysayin' you all the time, well..."

Old Red looked over at me and rolled his eyes.

"I'm sick of all this talk," he said, and he dug in his heels and got his horse up to a gallop.

End of conversation. "Be sneaky and keep our guns handy" it would be.

Now, being sneaky is easier some places than others. The area around Kingman—that's one of the tough ones. Kingman's on the eastern edge of the Mojave Desert, so if you want a tree to hide behind it might take you an hour to find one, and when you do, it'll probably be a Joshua that couldn't provide decent cover for a jackrabbit. What there are plenty of is rocky buttes and canyon washes, so keeping out of sight is a matter of winding up and down and around while plodding along at an amble so as not to kick up extra dust.

Which meant Old Red had to rein up and slow down and suffer my company soon enough. I took mercy on him and let the conversation stay ended, though. I may enjoy talking as much as he doesn't, but I know another big part of being sneaky is keeping your damn mouth shut. So I did.

Eventually we hit upon the old mining road Cornelius had told us to look for, and we followed that (from a distance) into the foothills of the Cerbat Mountains. Mead's place was nestled in a little valley about a mile off the road, and we crept up to a bluff above it for a good, long look around.

"No way to get down to the house without being seen," I said. "You sure waiting till dark is such a terrible idea?"

Old Red moved his gaze slowly around the valley's upper rim. If any of Aintree's men were out there, they were pretty good at being sneaky themselves.

"No, I suppose it ain't so terrible," my brother conceded. "But the place has already been searched once. If the list is still hid down there somewhere, it ain't gonna be anywhere obvious or easy to see. We're gonna need light, and plenty of it, to look weren't it ain't obvious and easy. So let's go while we got some."

And we got back on our horses and rode down into the valley.

The spread was of the sort you'd expect for a small-time

rancher who'd hit hard times. The adobe walls of the little house were crumbling here and there, and half the fencing for the corral was gone entirely—probably taken down and chopped up for firewood. If there'd been any outbuildings, they'd suffered the same fate so long ago even their foundations were gone, covered over now by weeds and cactuses that crowded in practically to the front door.

"Not much of a retirement home," I said as we got up close.

"Nope," said Old Red. "But I reckon it beats Yuma."

"Getting thrown in a patch of prickly pear probably beats Yuma."

My brother grunted. (Often that's his way of saying, "Indeed, Otto, you are correct.") His gaze was locked on the house ahead —and the busted furniture and strewn clothes and upended bags and boxes and cans on the ground before it.

Someone else had wanted to do their searching in the light of day, as well.

We tied our horses at what remained of the corral and walked to the door for a look inside. There wasn't much there. Everything had been dragged out and kicked around, but the bed and that hadn't survived either. The frame was broken to pieces, the straw mattress ripped apart and emptied. There were holes kicked and hacked in the walls here and there, as well, and big gouges in the dirt floor.

Old Red turned away and went back to scanning the debris out front—and the tracks weaving through it. He pointed down at twin furrows in the dirt.

"They dragged him outside. A man on each arm," he said. He walked off a few steps, eyes still angled downward, then stopped. "Held him here while another man beat him. So at least three of 'em."

He crouched down beside a spot where the sandy soil was so roiled even I knew what it was.

"He fell there," I said. I nodded at the hoofprints nearby. "And stayed there till someone loaded the body on a horse."

"Yup."

My brother swept a hand through the disturbed earth. He picked up a clump, eyed it close, then tossed it back with a flick of the wrist.

"Not much blood. If they cut on him, they didn't get too far into it before he keeled over. Looks like Cornelius and the coroner have it figured right."

Old Red stood and headed back toward the scattered bric-a-brac—all of R.T. Mead's earthly possessions. There wasn't much. My brother prodded an empty lard can with his toe—its contents long since melted out into the dirt—and flipped over a half-shattered crate. There was nothing underneath but a scorpion.

"'Scuse me," Old Red muttered as it scuttled off.

My brother wisely moved in the opposite direction, eyeing more of the busted-up junk on the ground. He stopped before a large book that lay with its black leather cover splayed out.

"Hel-lo," he said, and he squatted down and picked it up.

As you know, up until this year Old Red couldn't have read so much as "OK" on the sign over a corral. But even if he hadn't been working on his letters lately, he'd have recognized that book straight off.

You don't need to read to know a Bible when you see one.

Old Red held this one out and gave it a shake. No loose papers dropped out. He flipped through it and still found nothing, then returned to a page at the beginning.

"Buh…eye…urr…tuh…huh…suh," Old Red said.

I came close and looked over his shoulder. But I didn't read out the word my brother was struggling with—the one printed in big, swirly text at the top of the page. I knew he'd get it soon enough.

"Births," he said.

It was a family Bible—the kind with a birth registry at the front. Old Red put a finger under the first handwritten line and began to slowly move it across the page.

"Juh…oh…suh…eee…puh…huh. No. P and h make fuh. Juh-oh-see-fuh. Joseph."

He skipped the middle name—being "Ezekiel" it was long and

odd-looking and probably deemed not worth the effort—and jabbed his finger at the word after it.

"Mead?"

"Mead," I said. "Joseph Ezekiel Mead, Greenwood, Indiana, January 12, 1851."

Old Red started dragging his finger slowly down the page over the other names on the registry. He stopped at the first one that began with R. The middle name started with T.

"R.T. Mead," he said.

"Yup. Robert Thomas Mead, Centralia, Illinois, August 5, 1859."

Old Red nodded and began dragging his finger down the page again. There were only five more names under Robert Thomas, all of them Meads born in Illinois or Iowa in the sixties except the last.

My brother tapped that last one but didn't sound it out.

I got the signal.

"'Logan V. Teller IV, Paso Robles, California, November 19, 1882,'" I read out. "My congratulations to Logan V. Teller III. He must've landed himself a Mead for a wife."

"But ol' R.T. ended up with the family Bible. Funny. Wouldn't have pegged a man like him for religion."

"Even a bastard can get sentimental for his family."

Old Red grunted his agreement, then closed the Bible and placed it back on the ground. I could tell from the slow, gentle way he did it that it didn't feel right leaving a copy of the good book out to bake in the Mojave sun. But it wasn't *our* good book, and it was too late to bury it with R.T. Mead. So we'd leave it where we found it—out with the scorpions. Who could say? Maybe one of them would end up saved. One of them seemed as likely as Mead.

My brother straightened up and headed for the house. I followed. When we got inside, Old Red began a slow walk around the interior, his gaze sweeping up and down over the walls.

"Well, don't just stand there," he said after a half minute of it. "Search."

"It's been searched."

"Not by us." He pointed up without looking back at me. "Start with that."

"The roof?"

"No, not the roof. Didn't see no ladder outside, and I don't think Mead could just jump up there or fly up like Santa Claus. I meant the ceiling. You like to remind me you're taller than me. Well, make use of it. Go over every inch of that thatch and make sure there ain't a slip of paper wove in somewhere."

I looked up at the rough ceiling of reeds, weeds, and yucca leaves.

"Every inch?" I said.

"You can bet the one you *don't* check is where that list is hid," Old Red said.

He didn't sound sympathetic. Which was typical, but I'd been hoping for an exception.

I spent the next thirty minutes bent backward, arms stretched up, fingers probing the thatch overhead. My brother, meanwhile, moved on to knocking on the walls looking for hollow spots, then inching across the floor on all fours.

I found thorns and spiders aplenty. Old Red found adobe and dirt. Neither of us found the list.

"Well," I said when I finished with the last inch of ceiling and could stop collecting scratches and spider bites, "now this place *has* been searched by us. And we still got nothing."

Old Red pushed himself up to his knees and sighed. "Had to try."

"So we tried," I said. "Now what?"

The answer came from outside.

"Come out of there slow with your hands up and empty, or you're going to get holes where God didn't intend them to be!"

Old Red and I looked at each other in surprise.

The voice was a woman's. An old woman's—warbly but strong.

"Where'd she come from?" I whispered to my brother.

"Never mind where I came from!" the woman snapped. She may have been old, but she definitely wasn't deaf. "You do as I say before all of us out here lose our patience and start blasting!"

I cocked an eyebrow at my brother. The message: "Do we listen?"

Old Red shrugged. "We was raised to mind our elders."

He put up his hands and trudged toward the door.

I reluctantly did the same.

"No need for impatience, ma'am. Or blasting. We're coming out," I announced.

The woman had to be close, or she wouldn't have caught my whisper a moment before. Yet when we stepped outside and my eyes adjusted to the bright desert light, I saw no one.

"That's far enough," the woman said.

Her voice came from the ruins of the corral. When I looked that way I saw a wizened little figure in a white blouse and long brown skirt step out from behind our hitched horses. She had white hair and brown skin—and a shotgun, pointed at us.

There was movement off to our left, and another, equally shriveled and wrinkled figure stepped out around the corner of the house. It was an old man, brown-skinned like the woman, wearing work clothes and a droopy, frayed fedora and a red bandanna around his neck. He was aiming a carbine at us.

I took a quick look around, half-expecting a geezer in a wheelchair to roll out from behind the nearest cactus with a Winchester. But no one else emerged.

I lowered my right hand and pointed first at the old woman, then the old man.

"'All of us'?" I said.

"We're enough," the woman said. "Get that hand back up."

"Yes'm."

I did as she said.

She narrowed her eyes and took in my suit and loosened tie. "You're dressed fancy for a gunman."

"Well, there's a mighty good reason for that. I'm not one."

The old man snorted.

"Who are you then?" the woman demanded.

I gave her my most charming smile. Which really is quite charming, I assure you. Dentists should put it up over their doors to give folks something to aspire to.

The woman tightened her grip on her shotgun.

"I'm delighted you asked," I told her. "I'm Otto Amlingmeyer —'Big Red' to my friends, which I hope will soon include you two —and this is my brother Gustav—known far and wide as 'Old Red.'"

I peeked over at my brother in a "Should I go on?" way.

He nodded.

"We work for the A.A. Western Detective Agency out of Ogden, Utah," I continued. "We're here making inquiries related to the demise of Mr. R.T. Mead."

"Inquiries for who?" the woman snapped.

"That's confidential, ma'am," Old Red said. "But it ain't Clay Aintree, if that's what you was thinkin'."

Apparently it was. And apparently she believed my brother.

"Well...all right, then," the old woman said.

She lowered her shotgun.

The old man followed suit.

Old Red and I brought down our hands.

"And you would be?" I asked the man.

He just jerked his stubble-covered chin at the woman. Apparently she did all the talking for the both of them.

"He's Gabriel Martinez. My husband," she said. "We live on the other side of this valley. Have for thirty years."

She noticed the way my brother was eyeing the bandanna around her husband's neck, and she nodded.

"Long enough for Gabriel to have his throat half-cut by a band of Apaches once," she said. "You should see what they did to his scalp."

I looked over at the old man again, and he gave me a toothless grin and tipped his fedora—but didn't lift it quite high enough for me to see underneath. Which was fine by me.

"So...what are you looking for?" Mrs. Martinez asked us. "The same thing Aintree's *matones* were?"

Old Red—in classic Old Red style—answered with questions of his own.

"You know for a fact the men who roughed up Mead work for Aintree? You see it happen?"

"No, we didn't see it happen," the old woman said. "But we may as well have. Saw the Munro brothers watching this place, then saw 'em riding away after, and everybody knows who they work for."

"Well…not everybody," I said.

Mrs. Martinez glared at me. "The Bar A, of course! Aintree!"

"I figured," I said. "But we don't like to make assumptions."

"You tell the sheriff you saw these Munros out here around the time Mead died?" Old Red asked.

Gabriel spat into the dirt. His wife looked like she wanted to do likewise.

"Yes, we told the sheriff we saw them," she said. "And the foreman at the Bar A said the Munros were with him branding calves at the time. So guess who the sheriff chose to believe?"

Mrs. Martinez focused on me.

"Not us," she explained. "So you don't have to assume."

"Gracias," I said.

"How well did you know Mead?" Old Red asked.

Gabriel spit again. For a man who couldn't speak, he was pretty good at making himself understood.

"Not at all. Not personally," said Mrs. Martinez. "But we knew him by reputation, of course. Everybody around here remembers what he did. At first none of us could believe he had the gall to come back. But then when he bought this place, it started to make sense."

"He thought he had a meal ticket here," Old Red said.

Mrs. Martinez nodded. "But I guess he pushed too hard. Wanted too much. So his meal ticket got canceled."

"And there's no way at all someone else coulda done the canceling?"

The old woman shot Old Red a glare even more fierce than the one she'd given me.

"I don't doubt what you say about those Munro brothers, ma'am," he added quickly. "I'm sure they was here. But you said folks remember what Mead did, too. Murder a man. There's been no talk about someone comin' out here for revenge?"

"No, there's been no talk like that. The killing's been done with for years now. No one wants to start it up again. Not any of us small-timers, anyway." Mrs. Martinez narrowed her eyes to wrinkled slits and re-tightened her grip on her shotgun. "You sure you two don't work for Aintree?"

"Yes'm. We're sure," I said. "Like I said, though, we don't like to make assumptions. Asking whether someone else mighta come after Mead…that just had to be asked."

"Just like this does," Old Red said. "We've covered Mead's enemies, but how about his friends? He got any around here? People he might confide in? Turn to for help? Maybe someone who'd hold on to things for him while he was off doin' his time?"

The Martinezes didn't look entirely convinced we weren't lying about not working for Aintree. I had the feeling we wouldn't get more out of them other than more glares and maybe some buckshot. But after a silent, seething moment, the old woman answered.

"There's his old lawyer. Charles Cornelius. He fought like the devil to save Mead's neck…though God knows he shouldn't have. Mead might go see him at his office in town. He wouldn't dare come by his house. And there's Billy Ray Feist. He saved Mead's life, too, in his own way. Testified at the trial. For the defense. He was a Bar A hand back then, but he got kicked by a horse a few years ago and was never the same after that. He lives in back of the Ringtail Saloon now. Cleans the place at night, picks up odd jobs around town during the day. Go talk to one of them."

"Why wouldn't Mead—?" Old Red began.

"*Go talk to them*," Mrs. Martinez cut in.

She raised her shotgun again. She knew now how much we appreciated absolute clarity, so she was making it absolutely clear.

"Go talk to them" was not a suggestion. It was a command.

Her husband gave the same command in the same way: by pointing his rifle at us again.

We'd worn out our welcome. In fact, we'd never been welcome at all—just momentarily tolerated. And the moment was over.

I reached up and tugged on the brim of my Stetson.

"Señora, Señor...*buenos dias*."

"*Vete, cabrones!*" the old man croaked.

I was touched. He could speak after all—though just barely to judge by his strangled whisper of a voice—and he'd favored us with what were probably his only words of the day.

Go away, assholes!

We went.

"A little embarrassing getting chased off by somebody's great-grandparents," I said to Old Red as we rode away. "What do you think? When I write this up for *Smythe's Frontier Detective* should I make 'em fifty years younger? And all men? Ten of 'em?"

"I was done lookin' there anyway," my brother grumbled. "And who says you'll write this case up at all? We ain't found shit yet."

"Good point. If the list wasn't hidden at Mead's place, it's worse than a needle in a haystack now. It's a needle in Arizona Territory. A needle in all God's creation. It could be anywhere...if it even still exists."

Old Red glowered at me.

"Sorry," I said. "Didn't mean to be discouraging. I'm sure we'll find it."

I let our mounts carry on a little further out of the valley.

"If the Munro brothers don't kill us first," I added.

Old Red's only reply was another glower topped off with an eye roll.

He didn't want to talk about the Munro brothers, but that didn't mean he wasn't thinking about them. He led us on another slow zigzag back to town, dipping into arroyos and weaving around knolls and boulders, eyes ever on the horizon looking for silhouettes or the glint of sun on rifled metal.

It's hard to keep yourself out of sight when riding into a little burg like Kingman, though. My relief at reaching the town limits unshot lasted less than a minute, in fact. We'd swung around to come in from the southwest rather than the northwest corner we'd left from, but before we could even ask anyone the way to the Ringtail Saloon there was the cowboy who'd been watching us earlier. He was leaning against an awning post again—this one in front of an undertaker's—a fresh cigarette hanging from his mouth so limply it looked like the ash was going to drop down onto the button-up front of his blue bib shirt. Seeing him more up close now I could make out his thin, sharp features and icy-blue eyes and the gunman's thigh strap on his fancy embroidered holster.

He gave us the same kind of long, obvious looking-over we were giving him, and as we were about to draw even he stared me dead in the eye and smiled. It was a lopsided grin, the left corner of his mouth sliding up into his gaunt cheek and taking the cigarette with it.

"Nice suit," he said to me.

"Thank you," I replied. "Want the name of my tailor?"

"Nah. I figure a real man don't need a suit like that till he's ready to head in here."

He put out a thumb and wiggled it at the storefront behind him. The one for the undertaker's.

"Napier & Sons of Ogden, Utah. That's where I got my suit," I said. "You might need one sooner than you think, friend."

The cowboy kept on grinning as we passed him by.

"No need to poke the bear," Old Red said under his breath.

"Oh, what's he gonna do? Shoot me in the back in broad daylight with a dozen townsmen around to see?"

A shot rang out, and I went stiff in my saddle.

Holy shit! I thought. *He shot me in the back in broad daylight with a dozen townsmen around to see!*

Of course, I've never been shot in the back before (though it's probably been a temptation to plenty of people...my brother included). But I can guess what it feels like, assuming you're still alive afterwards to feel *anything*. It would hurt. A lot. Yet I felt nothing.

Our horses whinnied and skittered, and once I got mine under control, I wheeled her around to look back the way we'd come.

The cowboy was standing in the middle of the street with his gun in his hand. It wasn't pointed at me, though. He had his smoking Colt aimed up over the buildings to his right.

I glanced that way, saw nothing but sky, and—after giving my heart another moment to stop pounding—looked the cowboy in the eye again.

"You got a reason for shooting clouds?" I asked him.

The cowboy's grin went even more lopsided. If he wasn't careful, his cigarette was going to end up in his nose.

"Yeah. There's one up there I don't like." He gave his gun a little swirl. "That one. Looks like a man I used to know. Smart-ass snooping son of a bitch who stuck himself in other people's business."

I looked up at the sky again and carefully considered what might be my final words on this earth.

"Really?" I said. "I think it looks like a bunny."

"All right, enough nonsense," Old Red said to me. "Let's just keep movin'."

Yet when we turned our horses around—me with much reluctance, seeing as it gave the cowboy a clear shot at our backs again —we soon found our way blocked. The few townsfolk who'd been on the street had quickly scattered into doorways and alleys, but two new figures appeared, each rushing around a different corner to take up position before us. I blinked at them as I reined up, thinking I'd been so rattled by the gunfire I was seeing double.

Standing in the street were two more cowboys, younger ones, each with the same square, freckled face and sandy hair and big, cockeyed smiles.

They were both left-handed, too. I could tell that from the identical Peacemakers each wore on his left hip. The Peacemakers they each had a hand on.

The cowboy behind us hadn't been shooting at clouds, of

course. He was summoning these brothers. *His* brothers, I assumed from their slanted, sneering grins. They must've been watching for us along different streets, and now that we were back it was time for a family reunion—with our little Amlingmeyer clan in the crossfire.

"Just for the record," Old Red said loudly, "my brother and I are holding our reins and don't intend to move our hands anywhere else. Isn't that right, Otto?"

"Indeed it is," I replied just as loudly. "Furthermore, I would like it known that I have just become a pacifist."

We were speaking for the benefit of the men and women watching what was happening from their hiding places on either side of the street. And for our benefit, too—it being to our distinct advantage not to be shot.

We weren't going to give the cowboys—the Munro brothers, clearly—an excuse to kill us, and there were witnesses to prove it. Not that their witnessing would do me and Old Red much good if the Munros decided to kill us anyway.

"My goodness, boys," the Munro behind us said. "I do believe these gentlemen have the wrong idea about us."

I heard the jingling of spurs as he drew closer. That he still wore them even when walking around town told me something about him I could've already guessed: that he liked announcing to the world that he was a cowboy, that he enjoyed making noise, and that he didn't care what he scratched up and ruined as he went about his business.

"We don't want trouble with you," he said. "We're here to invite you to lunch."

"Oh?" I said. "Up some alley, I assume. Somewhere out of sight. You want us to get off our horses and follow you away from prying eyes and you'll show us where you left the picnic basket and lemonade?"

"No no no. You really don't understand." The cowboy chuckled. "We've been asked to escort you to La Brasserie Hervé to dine with our employer. Clay Aintree."

"You should go," one of his younger brothers told us. "The pommes frites is real good."

"Watch out, they don't try to serve ya snails, though," said the other.

The elder Munro strolled past me and Old Red to take up position between his brothers.

"Hervé's is right around the corner. We'll show you the way," he said. "And don't worry. It's not up any alley and the front's practically all glass. You'll be in plain sight the whole time."

I looked over at Old Red. He gave me a shrug.

If it was an ambush, at least it was a creative one.

"Clay Aintree, huh?" Old Red said to the Munros.

"Pomme frites, huh?" I said.

The middle Munro took a drag on his cigarette, flicked it away, and nodded.

"All right," my brother said. "Guess it's time for lunch."

He turned his mount to the side and headed for the nearest hitching post. I did the same.

A minute later, we were following one Munro up the sidewalk while the other two—the twins—trailed close behind. The towns-folk had figured out by then that the air wasn't going to fill up with lead (at least *probably* not) and started coming outside again. A man in a bloody butcher's apron stepped out of his shop just in time to block us, and when he saw what he'd done his eyes widened and he hopped back inside with a quick, "Sorry, Wes. Excuse me." He nodded at the twins as we passed and said, "Jack. Jock."

Me and Old Red he ignored.

I looked back at the young men behind us. "Which one of you's Jack and which one's Jock?"

"It's Wednesday, so I'm Jock," said the one who'd told me to watch out for snails. (I could tell it was him from his unbuttoned vest and white shirt.)

He was still grinning, yet somehow I got the feeling he wasn't joking.

Wes led us left at the corner, then there we were: before, as promised, a big plate-glass window with these words painted across it.

La Brasserie Hervé
Cuisine Française
Breakfast • Lunch • Dinner
Est. 1892

I was relieved to see the place was real and not some other perverse joke of the Munros.

Old Red didn't look pleased, though. He was squinting at the lettering with a frown on his face. I doubt if the McGuffey's primer he uses to work on his reading every day ever mentions Jack and Jill going to a "brasserie" for some "cuisine Française."

"Well, well...a French restaurant," I said for his benefit. "Kingman's really coming up in the world. A few years ago, people here were killing each other over beef, now they got 'brasseries' and sidewalks and a courthouse. Next thing you know, someone'll open a roller-skating rink."

"They already did," said Jack. Or maybe it was Jock. I wasn't looking back. "Didn't last two months."

He sounded pretty disappointed.

Wes opened the door to the restaurant—ignoring the little "CLOSED" sign hanging there—and stood back with his arm swept out, waiting for me and Old Red to go in. When we did, he followed us, closing the door behind him. Jack and Jock took up position outside, blocking the doorway. Just in case someone tried to bust in demanding pommes frites and snails, maybe. Or to keep someone—namely us—from busting out.

The place was about the size of your standard diner, but the walls were papered and the cloths on the dozen or so tables actually crisp white rather than dingy and stained (or nonexistent).

There was but one customer, seated alone at a round table in a

BLACK LIST, WHITE DEATH   29

nook at the back of the room. Undoubtedly the man who'd summoned us—Clay Aintree. He was wearing a black suit and a red puff tie with a diamond stickpin, yet you could tell from his weathered, bronzed face and hands that he was no banker or merchant. He might be in a booth with plush, button-tufted cushioning now, but he'd spent years working hard under the hot sun.

He looked up from a plate of something brown and black and smiled.

"You are in for a treat today!" he called out.

We took a step toward him.

From behind us, I heard the sound of metal sliding from leather, followed by the unmistakable *click* of a hammer being cocked.

"Whoa," I said.

Old Red and I jerked to a stop.

"Don't worry, fellas," Aintree said. "Just enforcing the dress code."

"Your guns. On that table to the right. Now," said Wes. "Slow."

I looked over at my brother. He gave me a nod and—moving slowly, as directed—moved his hand down to the Colt at his side. I reached under my suit coat for my Bulldog.

A moment later, the guns were side by side on the nearest table.

"You sure that's it?" Wes said. "Just one gun each?"

"I left my Howitzer in my other pants," I said.

"Some treat," Old Red said to Aintree.

He waved us over, still smiling.

"The treat comes next," he said. "Hervé!"

As Old Red and I started toward the booth again—our guns left behind on the table—a tall, balding man leaned out of a door at the back of the room. He had a black mustache and a put-upon expression and circles under his eyes so large and dark they made him look like a lugubrious raccoon.

"Your guests have arrived, Monsieur Aintree?" he asked. Needless to say (but I'll say it) he had a French accent.

"That's right, Hervé! *Commencer à sortir la bouffe!*"

Also probably needless to say (but I'll say it, too) Aintree did *not* have a French accent. But his French didn't sound half-bad.

"That means bring on the grub," he translated for us with a wink.

Hervé nodded and disappeared back into the kitchen.

"Hope you brought your appetites," Aintree said.

"I left mine out in the street," said Old Red. "When someone took to shootin' as we rode by."

Aintree gave Wes a mildly disapproving look. "That was you?"

"Just letting Jack and Jock know it was time for your luncheon," Wes said.

"Oh. Well, there you go. No harm done," Aintree said. He spread his hands out, indicating that one of us should sit to his left, the other to his right. There were already full place settings there—forks, spoons, knives, glasses, and saucers of various sizes, with a small slip of paper on the big plate in the center.

Old Red slid into the booth on one side, I on the other. Wes moved on to one of the empty tables nearby, pulled out a seat, and straddled it backwards, staring at us.

There was some kind of fancy bread on an extra plate before Aintree—a flat kind crisscrossed with anchovies and olives—and the rancher tore off a corner and popped it into his mouth.

"So," he said as he chewed, "who the hell are you?"

I looked across the table at my brother. He was beetling his brow at the little slip of paper on his plate. He glanced up at me long enough to give me another go-ahead nod.

As usual, he was leaving the introductions to me.

"We're Otto and Gustav Amlingmeyer of the A.A. Western Detective Agency. Perhaps you've read of us in *Smythe's Frontier Detective*…?"

I'm sorry to report, Mr. Smythe, that Aintree replied with a confused "No." But if you prefer, you can insert this:

"Of course—it's my favorite magazine! Why, I have a subscription. A dollar a year is a small price to pay for countless hours of reading enjoyment!"

Aintree shifted his attention to Old Red, who was still fixated on the paper on his plate.

"You look put off by the menu, Mr. Amlingmeyer," he said.

"Ain't put off. Just got no idea what a 'dejoiner a pricks-fixie' is."

I looked down at the identical paper on my plate and saw that Old Red had managed to sound out (silently and not entirely successfully) the top words there.

Déjeuner à Prix Fixe

Appetizer
Pissaladière

Amuse-Bouche
Canapés au Saumon Fumé

Plat Principal
Coq au Vin

"Fixed-price lunch," Aintree explained. "With appetizer, *amuse-bouche*—that's a sort of one-bite extra appetizer—and main course. Not that y'all have to worry about that fixed price. That's on me. Turns out sometimes there is such a thing as a free lunch!"

"No, there ain't," my brother said.

The friendly smile Aintree had been wearing vanished.

"You're right, you're right," he said, nodding. "There is a price to pay for your lunch. But not necessarily a high one for you... depending. All you gotta do first is—"

The door to the kitchen burst open, and Hervé hustled out with a plate in each hand. He headed to our table and slid one before me, one before Old Red. Atop each was the same flatbread with olives and anchovies Aintree had been gnawing on.

"*Voilà*," Hervé said.

He stepped back, clasped his hands, and watched us expectantly. It felt like he was waiting for us to applaud.

"Looks…uh…interesting," Old Red said.

I tore off a corner of the bread as Aintree had and took a bite. "Delicious," I said.

It was true, too, though like my brother I'd left my appetite out on the street.

Hervé smiled.

"*Bon appetit*," he said, and he gave us a little bow before sweeping off.

I tore off another chunk of bread but only brought it halfway to my mouth. I was distracted by the stare I was getting from the man a few feet to my right—Wes watching me intently, his left arm resting on the top of his backward-facing chair, his right arm curled at his side to keep his Peacemaker pointed at us. He'd been all sneers and jeers outside, but around Aintree he'd gone ice cold.

"None for you?" I asked him, giving my bread a little waggle.

"I'm working," he said, expressionless.

"Us, too," said Old Red.

He hadn't touched his bread. He just looked over at Aintree and waited.

"You ain't gonna try the *pissaladière?*" Aintree said, looking disappointed.

Old Red just kept waiting.

I put down my piece of bread and waited with him.

"You're going to break Hervé's heart," Aintree said. "And mine."

We kept on waiting.

Aintree sighed. "Your loss. I hope you're not stubborn about every opportunity that comes your way."

"Such as?" my brother said.

Aintree's smile returned, and he tore off more of his *pissaladière*.

"The opportunity to work for me." He stuffed the bread in his mouth, then wiped his greasy fingers on a napkin. "I know what

Cornelius has you doing. Why not do it for someone who'll pay you twice as much?"

I tried to catch my brother's eye so I could give him a little waggle of the eyebrows—the kind that would say, "Play along. See what we can learn…then get us the hell out of here."

"That ain't how it works," Old Red told Aintree instead.

Aintree laughed. "You mean people don't switch sides if it suits them? Don't follow their own interests?" He shook his head and looked back and forth between my brother and me. "I was hoping you'd be men of the world."

"Like R.T. Mead?" Old Red said.

Aintree froze, and out of the corner of my eye, I saw Wes sit up straight in his chair.

"I suppose he was pretty worldly," my brother went on. "Killing someone for money, then trying to blackmail the man who paid him to do it." He waved a hand at the swanky restaurant around us. "This where you talked to him when he came back from Yuma? Agreed to his price…then set them after him?"

He jerked his head to the side at Wes, and beyond him, Jack and Jock still playing sentry out front.

Aintree picked up his last ragged corner of *pissaladière*, slowly slid it over his plate, sopping up the oil there, then put it in his mouth and started chewing.

"You know who works right over there?" he said.

He pointed at the window. It looked out on the town square, with the courthouse in the middle and Cornelius's office on the other side.

"The county sheriff," Aintree said. "Close personal friend. Known him twenty years. So if Wes and I say this conversation never happened and you say it did, do you know who he'll believe?"

"I can figure who he'd *say* he believes," Old Red said.

Aintree shrugged, then wiped his hands on his napkin again. "Same difference, practically speaking. Which means I can be honest with you."

He dropped his napkin on his plate and steepled his fingers.

"Yes. I met with Mead right here. Just like this. I buy the place out for lunch all the time, and I did it that day, too. And I heard Mead out and made arrangements to meet his terms. Then, a little later, he sent a message letting me know the purchase price I thought we'd agreed to was merely an installment. A down payment on a lease, you might say. No right of ownership. He changed the terms. So I did, too. Or tried to. I sent the Munro boys out to renegotiate, and...well...the conversation grew intense. Too much so. Entirely by accident, you understand. That unfortunate outcome was not our intention."

Wes slowly shook his head with mock gravity.

"Unfortunate outcome," he said mournfully. "Not our intention."

Aintree shot the gunman a disapproving frown. He wasn't helping his boss make his case.

"Look," Aintree said to us, "things used to be rough around here. A man had to fight for every inch of land and every dollar—and fight even harder to keep 'em. So I fought. And despite a few stabs in the back and *unfortunate outcomes*, I won. And now I don't want to fight anymore. Not in the old way. Not if I can help it. I want to eat Hervé's *canapés au saumon fumé* and enjoy a little peace."

Aintree chuckled grimly and nodded down at the untouched *pissaladière* on our plates.

"I poo-pooed this French stuff, too, at first. Came in here just to laugh at it. And then I found I loved it. Me—a man who spent his first five years in Mohave County surviving on boiled beans and frybread cuz he couldn't afford to slaughter one of his own cows. And called every mouthful a feast! And now look at me."

"What are we supposed to see?" Old Red said.

I wanted to kick him under the table. He wasn't just poking the bear, he was spitting in its eye and insulting its mother.

Aintree's expression hardened.

"You should be seeing," he grated out, "a reasonable man making you a lucrative offer."

"And if we don't accept it?" Old Red said.

"But promise to think it over and get back to you?" I added, unable to restrain myself any longer while my brother steered us step by step toward death's door.

"Oh, you'll give me your answer now. Before the *canapés* come," Aintree said. "And if it's not the answer I want to hear, what you're going to see next is the back exit and a quick…"

Aintree didn't tell us what would be so quick (though I had my guesses).

Something outside had caught his eye, and when he turned his head to look out the window, his expression grew even harder. Before he'd been stone, now he was cold steel.

Old Red and Wes and I all turned to look, too. The scene we saw hardly seemed worthy of the grim contempt Aintree was aiming at it.

A well-dressed, stern-looking woman was having words with Jack and Jock. They stood shoulder to shoulder before her, blocking her way into the restaurant.

At first, I thought we were just looking at a lady who really, really wanted some *canapés* herself and didn't appreciate a couple ruffians keeping her from them. But then she reached out, shoved Jack and Jock aside, and threw open the door, and as she came marching toward us, I recognized her.

It was the woman in the portrait in Cornelius's office. Mrs. Cornelius, I could only assume. (I doubt a lawyer would hang a picture of his neighbor's wife on his office wall. People would ask questions.)

"Lady, stop!" said Jack.

"Mr. Aintree, she won't listen!" said Jock.

They stepped in after her but stopped just inside the door.

The woman kept coming.

Hervé stuck his head out from the kitchen, popped his eyes, and instantly disappeared again.

Mrs. Cornelius was passing the table Wes had left our guns on by then. She gave it a quick glance as she swept past it. Then she locked eyes on me.

"You're the men from the detective agency?" she said. "Working for Charles Burton Cornelius?"

"That's right, ma'am," I said.

Wes got up from his chair but didn't move to stop the woman as she drew nearer.

"Mr. Aintree…?" he said.

Aintree didn't look at him, didn't answer. He just kept watching the lady with a mixture of scorn and wariness, as if he half-expected her to snatch up a plate and whip it at his face.

"What are you doing speaking to this man?" she asked me.

She didn't look at Aintree, but the way she sneered "this man" made it clear what she thought of him—that he was less man than roach.

"Mr. Aintree invited us to join him for lunch, and we didn't feel free to decline."

I pointed at the Colt still in Wes's hand.

Mrs. Cornelius scowled first at it, then at Aintree.

"Still a bully surrounded by bullies," she said.

"Don't you *dare* judge me," Aintree snarled back.

She stopped before the booth, and for a second, it looked like she really might pick up a plate and smash it over Aintree's head. But then she looked at me instead.

"I assure you," she said, "you *are* free to decline invitations from this man. All of them—whatever else he's offering you beyond a fancy meal." She looked over at Old Red. "Shall we go?"

"Mr. Aintree…?" Wes said again.

This time Aintree gave his head a quick little shake. His gaze flicked for just a second beyond the woman, out the window again.

Wes threw a look over his shoulder.

The little scene in front of the restaurant hadn't gone unnoticed. Here and there around the town square were men and women who'd turned to peer curiously at *La Brasserie Hervé*.

People were watching. Which meant Mrs. Cornelius was right. If Old Red and I wanted to leave—and I sure as hell knew I did— now was the time.

I started scooching out of the booth.

"Sorry we're gonna miss the can of peas, Aintree," said Old Red as he did the same, "but we got business elsewhere."

"*Canapés,*" Aintree muttered. "*Au saumon fumé.*"

He said nothing more as Mrs. Cornelius led us out. We paused only to collect and reholster our guns, then carried on quickly past a stunned-looking Jack and Jock, through the door to freedom.

The instant we were outside, the lady slowed her pace to a leisurely, respectable stroll—the kind that would show folks there was nothing to see here any longer. My brother and I matched her amble and took up position on either side of her, studiously ignoring, as she was, the onlookers still staring around the square.

"Thank you, Mrs. Cornelius," I said. "You got us out of quite a fix."

My assumption about her name seemed to be correct: She didn't contradict me. She merely nodded placidly, first to me, then to a squat gent in a black suit who tipped his top hat as he passed.

For a woman who'd just faced down three armed men, she was incredibly calm. More calm than me, I don't mind admitting. My nerves were still all ajangle, yet she looked as cool as cream straight from the icebox.

"That was mighty dangerous, what you just did," said Old Red.

"Not really, I think," the lady replied without looking over at him. "Aintree wouldn't have dared do anything in town with so many witnesses around. He prefers that sort of thing to happen out in the country, far from wherever he happens to be. If he was threatening you with his thugs, that was all bluff...for the moment. I assume he was pressuring you to come work for him?"

"That's it exactly," I said. "But how is it you even know who we are? And that we needed help?"

Mrs. Cornelius nodded again, this time to a woman of about the same age—somewhere in the vicinity of forty—stepping from a milliner's shop. Mrs. Cornelius carried on past her without answering my questions, apparently wanting a little distance between us and the other lady first. So in the meantime I made a quick but hopefully casual-looking scan of the square.

Our audience had broken up. No one was staring our way anymore.

"I came to have lunch with my husband," Mrs. Cornelius said. "We often eat together in his office. Today Charles had some important work he needed to finish first. But he did tell me about your arrival before I left to take a walk around the square. The way he described you…you are a distinctive pair."

"Thank you," I said—though, of course, it wasn't exactly a compliment.

We'd come to a corner now, and Mrs. Cornelius led us across the street, then turned right to keep us on the square.

"I usually avoid *La Brasserie Hervé* during the day," she went on as we walked. "Because *he* is so often there. But today…knowing you'd that come to Kingman…that justice might finally be done…I decided not to go out of my way to avoid him. I would look him in the eye without fear. Except when I went by the restaurant, I saw you in there with him. And I just couldn't help myself. I had to do something."

Old Red was sticking to the lady's right, positioning himself between her and whatever filth might be splashed up from the street, as a gentleman should (though of course you wouldn't think he was a gentleman to look at him). I noticed him lean forward a bit to peer curiously but shyly at the woman's face.

"If you don't mind my sayin', ma'am, it seems a little… personal between you and Aintree," he said.

I was watching the woman's face, too. And I saw surprise there.

"You mean no one's mentioned it yet?" she said. "How this matter *is* of great personal interest to me?"

"No, ma'am," I said.

"Ahh…"

Mrs. Cornelius's look of surprise faded quickly, replaced by what seemed to be her usual expression: the serene somberness whoever'd painted her portrait had captured so well.

"The man R.T. Mead killed for Clay Aintree and the Cattlemen's Association," she said, "was my husband."

It took a couple seconds for that to sink in. It didn't seem to make any sense at first, as Charles Burton Cornelius III, Esquire, seemed very much alive when we'd talked to him that morning. When I grasped what the lady was really saying I nearly stopped in shock.

Old Red almost did, too, falling behind for a moment as he did a little stunned stutter-step.

"But now you're...?" he said. "You...? Later on, you...? You married...?"

My bashful brother often finds it hard to speak to women. But now, with an awkward question to ask, he was getting so tongue-tied his tongue was going to end up looped into a hackamore hitch.

It didn't matter. Mrs. Cornelius knew exactly what he was asking.

"Yes," she said. "I married the man who defended my husband's killer. You have to understand: Charles had no idea what Aintree and his friends were planning. And once he did know it all, thanks to his work on behalf of Mead, he quit and tried to make amends for it. He's been fighting to help the small ranchers ever since. And he did everything in his power to make amends to me, too. And eventually, when I could look past my heartache and bitterness, I saw the good man that he is. And... well...with time..."

"You found yourselves compatible," I said.

Mrs. Cornelius looked over and gave me a small, prim smile of gratitude for offering the right words. "Exactly."

"So your first husband...?" Old Red said. "He was a...? You know...? A...?"

He was still twisting himself in knots to avoid offending the lady.

"He was suspected of illegal activity?" I said to her.

There are times my big mouth really does come in handy.

"No," Mrs. Cornelius said. "He was no thief. No 'rustler.' He was just another man struggling to turn a profit raising cattle. Succeeding a little more than some. And that was enough to make him a threat.

At first Aintree merely harassed Eli—that was my husband—through the law. Nuisance suits over property lines and water rights and easements. But then, when the Cattlemen's Association brought in Mead, he decided on a more drastic solution. A permanent one."

"Ah," Old Red said. "I see."

He rubbed his fingers over his mustache and started to get that faraway look that comes over him when he's lost in thought. But then he shook it off and literally looked far away—at the sidewalks and streets all around the town square. It wasn't hard to see what he was searching for. I quickly saw it, too.

Back and to the right were Jack and Jock Munro, following our path around the courthouse. Ahead and to the left was Wes Munro, circling around the square on the opposite side to meet us head-on. In the middle was us—and Cornelius's office, which we'd just reached.

"We'll leave you here, ma'am. With your husband," I said. "You really shouldn't involve yourself any further."

"Just two more questions," said Old Red.

Mrs. Cornelius had become a little flushed as she told us about the feud that had led to her first husband's death. But now she faced my brother with her usual placid solemnity back in place.

"Yes?"

"You know the way to the Ringtail Saloon?" Old Red asked.

Mrs. Cornelius lifted an eyebrow. I assume the Ringtail Saloon—where Mr. and Mrs. Martinez told us we could find Mead's old compadre Billy Ray Feist—was the sort of place a lady like her never spoke of and pretended not to see.

"It's on Beale, between Third and Fourth Streets," she said. "Across from Thompson's Grill. Two blocks directly south of here."

"Perfect. Thank you, ma'am," my brother said. "Question two…"

He walked around Mrs. Cornelius and me to the law office's front door. He opened it and held out a hand in a "ladies first" way.

"This place got a back exit?" he said.

Mrs. Cornelius gave him a nod and headed inside. "I'll show you."

We moved quickly through the book-lined waiting room and past the (again closed) door to the inner office. There was another door at the far end of the room, and Mrs. Cornelius led us through it. It opened onto a storeroom with cleaning supplies and a little cot (for when Mr. Cornelius needed a quick nap between clients and court dates, I assumed) and a stack of even more law journals. There was another door directly facing the first, on the opposite side of the room, and when Mrs. Cornelius opened it, we found ourselves looking out onto an empty lot and, beside it, a little red schoolhouse.

"Thank you, ma'am," my brother said.

He gave the brim of his Boss of the Plains a quick tug then took off across the lot at a pace that was just ever-so-slightly shy of a sprint.

I took the time to actually tip my hat to the lady.

"Yes. Thank you," I said. "And don't go rescuing any more detectives, if you please. It makes it look like we're not up to the job."

The slimmest wisp of a smile appeared on Mrs. Cornelius's grave face.

"Good luck without me," she said.

I heard her close the door behind me as I dashed off after Old Red. He was still ahead of me when he passed the schoolhouse, and he angled off to the right, headed for the nearest street corner.

As I drew even with the school, the front door opened and kids began pouring out, hollering and singing and whapping each other in the back of the head. Those in front stopped cold to take in the strange sight of a big, handsome man in a suit and Stetson seemingly running for his life past their schoolyard.

"If some cowboys come looking for me, don't tell 'em where I went!" I called to them. "I'm on a secret mission!"

It was even kind of true. But that didn't make it the right thing to say.

Half the kids cheered, the other half blew raspberries, and a gaggle of four peeled off from the rest and took off after me.

"Can we come too?" a skinny, pigtailed girl of nine or ten asked as the long legs under her calico skirt brought her even with me.

"No, you can't come too. How secret would that be? Go back to school."

"It's okay," said a younger boy with buck teeth and a cowlick as he huffed and puffed to catch up. "It's recess."

Old Red was only a few feet ahead of me by then. He looked back and scowled.

I gave him an apologetic shrug.

"Are you with the Secret Service?" another boy asked as he came up on my left.

"Oh, come on—look at the runty one's clothes," said yet another on my right. "They must be stock detectives."

My brother threw back another scowl—this time at the boy who'd called him "runty."

Fortunately, the schoolmarm had finally stepped outside to see what all the fuss was about.

"Margaret! Johnny! Ramon! Benjamin!" she hollered. "Get back here at once!"

Our escort dropped away with a collective "Awwww."

"Remember!" I called back to them as Old Red and I hurried off. "Whatever you do, don't tell those cowboys we're going to the train station!"

"The train station!" several kids gasped.

"That's not the way to the train station," the skinny girl said.

I had to hope she was the kind of kid people tend to ignore.

I finally caught up to Old Red, and he looked over at me and opened his mouth.

I held up a hand. "You don't need to say it. I know."

So he just rolled his eyes and left his "Idjit!" unsaid.

We hustled on across another empty lot, then swung left when we hit the next street.

Mrs. Cornelius's directions were spot on. There it was about halfway up the block, across from a shabby diner and a saddlery and an empty corral: a whitewashed building with the words "Ringtail Saloon" written across the high false front in slanted cursive script. Just in case a prospective customer couldn't read—a distinct possibility if your clientele tended toward cowboys, as my brother once demonstrated—an actual ringed tail had been nailed over the front door.

Old Red slowed to a walk and angled us to the right—away from the tail, toward the back of the saloon.

"How much money you got on ya?" he said.

"About forty bucks. Why?"

"'Cuz it ain't gonna be hard for the Munro brothers to figure out who we'd want to talk to next…even if they do end up at the train station."

My brother gave me another eye roll to show how likely he thought that was.

Before I could point out that this only half answered my "Why?" (and did it rudely), Old Red held out a hand expectantly.

I reached inside my coat and pulled out a leather billfold wallet—a Christmas gift from Col. Crowe, of all people, who'd informed me that if I wanted to keep it filled I'd do as he said. I pulled out all the greenbacks and handed them over.

My brother stuffed the bills into a pants pocket. (He'd received a wallet from the colonel, too—with the same advice—but I hadn't seen it since Christmas Day.) We threw a look back at the street corner we'd rounded a moment before, saw no sign of the Munros, and headed around the side of the saloon.

The back door was open. Why was soon clear.

A groan came from the rickety outhouse about thirty yards from the back of the building. My brother headed toward it.

Isn't the detective business fun?

Old Red motioned for me to move away from him a step, and as he neared the outhouse, he swung out to come at it from the right. He didn't want either of us standing directly in front of the door. Whoever was inside moaning—and he was still at it—might not like us interrupting his privacy. Might, in fact, dislike it enough to shoot us through the pinewood.

"Hey…fella…," my brother said. "You all right in there?"

The moaning stopped.

"Who is that?" a man said.

"Nobody in particular. Just wanted to make sure nobody done nothin' to ya."

"Oh. Well. No, I ain't all right. And yeah, I've had things done to me."

Old Red and I looked at each other from opposite sides of the outhouse.

Had the Munros paid a call on Billy Ray Feist before collecting us for lunch?

"First a damn bronc shatters my damn knee so I can barely goddamn walk anymore," the man in the outhouse went on. "Then I end up swamping in a damn saloon that serves 'whiskey' that ain't much better than turpentine and tobacco spit."

"Yet you keep right on drinkin' it," my brother said.

"Well, dammit, didn't you hear the first part?" the man snapped back. "I think I've earned the damn right to get a damn drunk on however I goddamn can."

It was Feist, all right. How many crippled ex-cowboys could there be living behind the Ringtail Saloon?

Well…a lot actually, this being the West. But I had a feeling there weren't three more loitering around nearby.

Old Red pulled out one of the bills I'd handed him a moment before.

"I could help you get yourself a higher grade of whiskey," he said.

He reached around to slide the bill through the crescent moon in the outhouse door. He let it go, and it dropped into the darkness on the other side.

"What the hell—?" Feist said.

There was the sound of rustling clothes and creaking wood

inside the outhouse as he picked up the bill and held it up to the light.

"You better not be proposing nothing indecent," he growled.

"*What?*"

My brother shot me a shocked look.

I spread my hands and shrugged.

Who knows what offers a man who lives behind a saloon might get? It turns out we didn't—and we didn't want to know.

"I'm here to ask you about R.T. Mead," Old Red said.

"Oh."

There was a moment of silence, then Feist chuckled dourly. The little laugh must've fired up his headache or stomachache or whatever was ailing him (likely both), because it quickly turned into another groan.

"Well, a damn dollar ain't gonna get me to tell you a damn thing," he said. "I wouldn't use that to wipe my…hmm."

Old Red had pushed another bill into the moon. A five this time. He held it half in, half out of the hole, and gave it a little waggle.

Feist shifted again, and the bill was yanked away.

"What do you wanna know?"

"Whatever you got to tell," my brother said. "Begin at the beginning. How you met Mead, what you did with him, how you helped him at his trial, whether you ever seen him after he came back from Yuma. The whole thing."

"The whole thing? Feeling like I do?"

There was a *rap-rap* on the outhouse door, followed by silence again.

On the other side of the crescent moon, it became clear as the silence stretched on, an outstretched hand was waiting.

Old Red sighed and peeled off another five and pushed it into the hole.

It was snatched away.

"Hmm. You did say *the whole thing*, didn't you?" Feist said.

There was another *rap-rap*, after which the silence returned.

Old Red peeled off a twenty.

I scowled and pointed at the bills still left in his hand. He had more ones and fives to choose from, yet he was going to shove more than half of what I had into an outhouse?

My brother gestured back at the street beyond the saloon.

There was no telling when the Munros might show up. Now wasn't the time to haggle.

Old Red poked the twenty into the moon.

It disappeared.

"I was a top hand at the Bar A when R.T. Mead came to the county," Feist said, settling back onto his seat inside. "The foreman knew I was willing to do any work needed doing. *Any* work. I do hate thieves. So he asked me to be Mead's guide, you might say. Show him what's where. Who's who. It was obvious what he was there for, and that was fine by me…until he said it was time for him to get to work, and the first call he had to make was on Eli Beetner. Now Beetner, he was a well-liked fella. Not one of the nesters and rustlers, but friendly with 'em. And not one of the big cattlemen, but generally friendly with them, too. Except for Aintree. Who was my boss and a man in the know. So I figured he knew something I didn't…and I did my job."

Feist went silent again, but only for a moment. He coughed, then groaned.

"You got anything to drink on ya?" he said. "All this talking's got me parched."

"I already gave ya enough cash to buy yourself whatever you wanna drink," Old Red replied. "Once you're done."

Feist started muttering something to himself—I couldn't quite tell what, and I wasn't inclined to lean in closer to the moon in the door to try to make it out. I assumed it had to do with my brother and how he was a damn this or a goddamn that. After a moment of it, Feist cleared his throat and carried on with his story.

"So I helped Mead with Beetner. He had a tip on where he might find him one day—riding back to his place from a meeting with the justice of the peace or something like that, I don't remember what exactly—and he needed me to make sure he had his sights on the right man. I didn't pull any trigger. And I figured

Beetner was thieving or helping those who were. Remember that. I was just a hand doing as he was told and protecting the—"

"You can skip all that. I ain't here to pass judgment," Old Red said. "I hear Mead got Beetner's name off a list he was given. You ever see it?"

"Yeah, I seen it. Not close enough to read, mind you. Mead checked it later. After he'd...you know. After he was done with Beetner. Wanted to ask me about the next man on the list. So he pulled it out and told me the name then put it away again in his pocket."

"What'd it look like?"

"Whaddaya think it looked like? A piece of paper. It wasn't on a damn scroll or stone tablets or something."

"All right, all right. And who *was* next on the list?"

"Andy Hutton. And I'll tell ya—*that* was a name that didn't surprise me. There was nothing ol' Andy wouldn't steal. He'd take the candy from a baby, then dump the kid from its crib and take that, too. I think he considered it immoral to actually pay for something. He'd showed up in Mohave County with maybe fifty head he borrowed from some Mexicans, most likely, and miracle of miracles, there were two hundred wearing his brand a year later. Bred like rabbits, those cows of his. Or so he'd say if ya asked about it. Say with a grin and wink. Brazen, that's what he was. Ain't nobody the cattlemen hated more."

Old Red furrowed his brow and cocked his head, his gaze going fuzzy as it will when wheels turn. I couldn't see how any of this brought us any closer to the list, but he seemed to think it did.

"But you and Mead never got around to this Hutton fella?" he said.

"Nah. Beetner getting killed kicked up too much fuss. If we'd started with Hutton most of the county woulda cheered. But Beetner—that didn't sit well. The sheriff had to actually take it serious. And people knew what Mead was—and whose payroll he was on—so it didn't take long for him to get pulled in and sized up for a rope."

"Which *you* saved him from—?"

Feist cleared his throat, then coughed, then farted, then groaned.

Any sound he could make seemed preferable to what he was going to say next.

"Yeah. I saved him," he said. "Testified that he stopped Beetner on the road outta town. Talked to him. Accused him of buying stolen stock. And Beetner didn't like it…and went for his gun. And that's when Mead shot him. Self-defense."

"But that ain't how it happened."

"Ain't my damn fault what a damn jury's gonna believe!"

I reached out and gave my brother a prod on the shoulder. When he looked over at me, I tapped my left palm as if pointing to a pocket watch there.

We ain't got all day with the Munros on our trail, I was saying. *Where's this getting us?*

"Is there somebody else out there?" Feist said.

It was actually quite the achievement for me that he hadn't noticed before that. I hadn't gone so long without speaking since I'd said my first "Mama" in diapers.

"It's actually my money that got you talking," I said. "So please—don't stop on my account."

"Well, who the hell are you, anyway?"

"The fellas who just gave you thirty bucks to answer questions," said Old Red.

"Thirty-one bucks," I corrected.

Old Red plowed on.

"And I ain't done with the asking yet. Now—did you and Mead talk after he came back from Yuma?"

"Just once," Feist grumbled.

"Yeah? And?"

"And there's not much to say, dammit. It's not like we was pals. He didn't seek me out for a reunion party. He just happened to come into the Ringtail, so we ended up talking."

"About—?"

"About not much! He said he knew he owed me and he'd pay off the debt one day. And I figured that was horseshit and more or less told him so. And I guess he'd got religion in prison, cuz he said, 'Put your faith in the good book. I did.' And he laughed and finished his drink, and I never saw him again. The damn bastard."

It was as if Old Red was struck by lightning. He went stiff and popped his eyes wide and took a startled step back from the outhouse.

"He said what now?"

"'Put your faith in the good book. I did,'" Feist repeated slowly and loudly as if shouting into an old geezer's ear. "He even had a Bible with him. I think he'd just got off the train from Yuma, and that was the only thing he owned. Then a few days later, it was going around how he'd bought himself a spread, yet I never got squat…"

"*Dammit,*" Old Red spat. He looked over at me. "I am a fool!"

Before I could ask him why or if he expected me to disagree with him (which would depend on his answer to the first part), a chorus of high-pitched voices rose up from the north.

"The train station!" some were shouting.

"That way!" yelled others.

"Don't tell them!" and "Shut up!" screamed yet more.

Recess at the little red schoolhouse had just gotten even more exciting—thanks to a visit from the Munro brothers, I could only assume.

It was my turn to spit out a "*Dammit.*" I meant to follow it up with "What do we do now?" but Old Red wasn't going to answer me. He was already showing me.

My brother was running away.

"What's going on?" Feist asked. "What's all that hollering about? Huh? Answer me!"

I didn't, though. I was too busy running away, too.

The last thing I heard Feist say was, "Well, that's just rude!"

Old Red and I had come down toward the Ringtail on Third Street, but now my brother was heading northwest toward Fourth. We were doubling back the way we'd come but doing it one block over.

Like the streets we'd run along a few minutes before, Fourth was pocked with empty lots and big spaces between the buildings. So as we swung north, I was able to look left and get glimpses of the schoolhouse.

The kids were still clustered up outside, half of them staring straight south, half to the southwest. I didn't spot any looking east —at us—but there was no telling how long that would last.

Old Red and I kept running.

"There a fire, or you two practicing for the hundred-yard dash?" asked a man sweeping the sidewalk in front of a barbershop.

Local comedian. I didn't answer him either. I had questions of my own. Like where were we going?

I asked it when Old Red finally slowed from a sprint to a quick-stepping strut.

"Might have to go all the way back to Mead's place unless I can get my brain to working," my brother panted. "What was it? Lamar V. Something the Fourth, Santa Rosa, California, December 1882? Or was it November?"

"What are you talking about?"

"The last name on the Births page, of course. In Mead's Bible."

"Oh. Of course. Silly of me to even ask."

We'd made it back to the courthouse square by then, and Old Red turned us left.

"Well?" he snapped.

"The baby's name? Lord, I don't remember." I racked my brain for a few steps. "Except he wasn't born in Santa Rosa, I do remember that."

Old Red scowled—though not so much at me, for once. He was more mad at himself.

"You're right. But it was something like that," he said. "Some-thing Spanish-like."

"Los Angeles?" I suggested. "Santa Cruz? El Cerrito?"

"Shut up! The more wrong words you throw at me, the less I can think of the right ones!"

"Fine. I won't help."

Old Red took to muttering to himself as we carried on along the square.

"Lawrence V. Weller the Fourth...? Lewis V. Geller the Fourth...? Leroy V. Zeller the Fourth...?"

"Why," I finally had to ask, though I knew the risk I was taking, "are we suddenly so interested in a baby born in 1882?"

"We're not!" Old Red exploded. "Jesus! You see, but ya don't *observe!*"

This last was a quote from his hero, Sherlock Holmes, of course. One originally directed at Dr. Watson and now thrown in my face every other day.

"What I *observe*," I said, staring hard at my brother, "is a crabby little crank without the sense to...hey."

I'd have to save that comeback for another day. Old Red wasn't listening. He'd suddenly veered left again—toward and quickly through a door.

We'd returned to the law office of our employer, Charles Burton Cornelius III.

"I thought you said we had to go back to Mead's place?" I asked as I followed my brother inside and closed the door behind us.

"Only if I can't remember..." Old Red mumbled.

He made a beeline for the nearest bookshelf and stuck his big nose close to one of the fat casebooks lined up there.

"Hello?" Cornelius called out. "Who's there?"

The door to the inner office opened, and Cornelius stepped out. Beyond him I could see Mrs. Cornelius sitting in front of his desk, which was covered with plates and cups and a picnic basket.

We'd interrupted lunch.

"Please excuse us, sir...ma'am," I said. "We just popped in to..."

I looked over at my brother, who was still squinting at one of the book spines.

"Puh...ruh...," he said under his breath, slowly sounding out something he saw there.

What *had* we popped in to do?

"'1876,'" Old Red read out.

He stepped back and started scanning the other books, leaning first left, then right, then hunching over.

"Tell me, Mr. Cornelius," he said without looking back. "Was R.T. Mead ever in here *after* he was arrested but *before* he went to Yuma?"

"Yes. Several times. The Cattlemen's Association put up bail for him, so he was free for a while before his trial. There was such an outcry from the community, though, his bail was eventually revoked."

"Ahh…" Old Red said. He reached out and tapped one of the law books with a pointed finger. "1882."

"Have you taken an interest in case law, Mr. Amlingmeyer?" Mrs. Cornelius said.

She rose from her seat and headed toward her husband in the doorway. Directly behind her, gazing down on her from above, was herself—the portrait of her hung from the office wall.

"I suppose you could say that, ma'am. One case in particular," Old Red said. He looked over at me. "Paso Robles. That was the town. P.R. For…"

He bent down and slid a book off the bottom shelf, then straightened up and pointed the spine at me.

I stepped closer and read out the words there. The first one would've been tricky for my brother, containing as it did the same letter pronounced two different ways, so he was leaving it to me.

"'Pacific Reporter. 1882. Volume 4. California, Colorado, Kansas, Montana—'"

"Yeah, yeah. Etc. etc.," Old Red said.

He opened the book and started flipping through the pages.

"That last name in Mead's Bible wasn't a name," he said. "It was a—"

"A court case!" I said. "Not Logan V. Keller or whatever. Logan versus Keller. In volume 4 from 1882."

See? I can observe eventually. You just have to lead me by the nose to whatever it is I'm supposed to see.

"That's how I figure it," Old Red said, still flipping. "Mead would've spent time right here, just like we did this morning, waitin' to see Cornelius. And he'd know these here books are mostly for show. Years could go by with no one lookin' at one in particular. So with his bail revoked and him goin' back to jail and maybe to Yuma after that, he'd wanna stash the list somewhere safe...cuz it was the thing keepin' him alive. And if he got lucky, and he knew exactly where to find it again, he could come back and...oh, hell."

Old Red had finally run out of patience with flipping pages.

He turned the book over and started shaking it.

"You can't mean it," Cornelius said. "You think Mead actually left the list—?"

A folded piece of paper slipped from the lawbook and fell to the floor.

"Hel-lo," my brother said to it.

He handed me the book, then crouched down and picked up the paper.

"Right here in your office, Charles," Mrs. Cornelius marveled. "Mere feet away the whole time."

Cornelius grunted out a little laugh and shook his head in disbelief.

"Astounding," he said. He took a step toward Old Red and held out a hand, the palm up. "Thank you. Your services are worth every penny."

"Yeah, well..." my brother said, standing up straight again. "We'll see about that."

He didn't hand over the paper. He unfolded it instead.

"That's not necessary!" Cornelius blurted out, taking another step toward us.

Old Red looked down at the paper.

"Just like I thought," he sighed.

"Now just a second, Amlingmeyer..." Cornelius said, taking another step forward—a wobbly one on weak knees.

Old Red turned his back to him to keep the paper out of his reach. Then he offered it to me.

I tucked the heavy lawbook I was holding under one arm, then took the paper and looked it over.

I saw what I expected to see: a list of names in black ink.

"Look at the first one," Old Red said.

I knew what he meant straight off. Even someone who could barely read, like my brother, would notice it.

The name at the top of the list—Eli Beetner—was scrawled out in different handwriting than the ones beneath it.

"It struck me as odd when I heard it this morning," Old Red said. "Eleven names on a death list. Not ten, not a dozen. Eleven. And when I heard that the first man on that list wasn't the most hated and shameless rustler in the county—that man was second —that struck me as mighty odd, too. Instead the Cattlemen's Association was gonna pay R.T. Mead to assassinate a respectable rancher...albeit one Aintree had been harassin'? Through you, Mr. Cornelius. Which meant you knew when he'd be comin' and goin' from town for court dates. And you could pass that on to Mead along with the list you got from Aintree...which was now longer by one name."

The more my brother spoke, the whiter Cornelius's face went. By the time Old Red was through, the man looked like a marble bust of himself.

"You can't be serious," his wife said. "Are you really accusing my husband of—"

"Killing your husband," my brother said, turning to face her. "Yes. I am. He wanted Eli Beetner out of the way, and he grabbed a chance to get it done. And he knew Aintree could never say boo about it, because then he'd be admittin' publicly that there was a death list, and he knew who was on it and who wasn't."

Old Red shifted his gaze to Cornelius.

"That's why you fought so hard to keep Mead from gettin' hung," he said. "He must've figured out what you'd done from the hullabaloo over Beetner. And if he got sent to the gallows, he'd have no reason to hold back the truth. So you did everything you could to get him off. When he came back from Yuma, I'm sure he squeezed you for money, too. You said he came to see you, and

I'm sure it wasn't to reminisce over the good ol' days. Then once you got lucky and he up and died, you had to make sure nobody else ever saw that list…and your handwriting at the top of it."

"Look…if this is a negotiating ploy…" Cornelius said, his voice so quiet it was barely above a warbly whisper, "it worked. What do you want? Five thousand? I could get it for you today."

Up until then, his wife had remained as stiff, silent and somber as her portrait. But now she turned and walked slowly back into the inner office.

"That ain't how the Double-A Western Detective Agency does things," Old Red told Cornelius. He headed for the front door. "Come on, Brother. "

I handed Cornelius the casebook—careful to keep the paper in my other hand, beyond his reach—and followed Old Red.

"Ten thousand," Cornelius said. "Fifteen!"

A sound from the other room—the opening of a desk drawer —startled Cornelius into silence. When I glanced back, I saw that he'd jerked up straight and widened his eyes.

"Eleanor?" he said, and he dropped the lawbook and spun around and rushed off after his wife.

"You don't suppose…?" I said to my brother, who'd stopped to look back, too.

"Ain't every day you find out your second husband had your first murdered," he said grimly.

"No!" Cornelius cried out, panicked. "Don't!"

"Well, shit," Old Red growled, and the two of us started rushing toward the door to the inner office.

We'd only taken two steps when we skidded to a stop again.

Mrs. Cornelius had appeared in the doorway. With a gun. Pointed at *us*.

"Oh," Old Red and I both said at the same time. We weren't really saying the same thing, though.

My "Oh" meant "Oh…I thought she was gonna kill Cornelius."

Old Red's "Oh" meant "Oh…maybe the whole thing was her idea. Her interrupting Aintree's talk with us makes a lot more sense if she was in on it all along. She'd know what was really at stake if that list got out, so she had to keep us on her side. But Aintree would suspect she's a fraud—he knew her first husband was never supposed to be on the list—which is why he looked at her with the contempt he did when she showed up playing the outraged widow. Why, it's so obvious in hindsight I'm kickin' myself."

(My brother can squeeze a lot into an "Oh.")

"So you and Cornelius was carryin' on before Beetner was even dead?" he said.

Apparently, Mrs. Cornelius didn't know how these things are supposed to work. Instead of explaining everything, she just started shooting.

The first shot went high into the top shelf of law books behind us.

The lady adjusted her aim and fired again, and this time the shot went low—but not low enough.

This one went into my brother.

He cried out and crumpled.

I had less than a second to decide what to do before Mrs. Cornelius got off another shot.

Do I throw myself between her and Old Red? That'd just get me shot, too.

Do I dig my Bulldog from its shoulder holster and shoot her first? I didn't have time.

Do I just stand there running through my options until I get a bullet in the brain? That was the way things were going.

So I acted. Foolishly, maybe, but I had to do *something* fast.

I scooped up the lawbook Cornelius had tossed aside and went charging toward the doorway. When Mrs. Cornelius saw me coming, she tried to get her pistol—a little rubber-handled, nickel-plated twenty-two of the sort Arizona lawyers keep their desks, I guess—aimed at my chest. I swatted the gun out of her hand with one swing of the lawbook, then backhanded the book the other way right into her face.

There was a crunch as her nose broke, and the woman flew

back into the doorjamb, knocked her head hard against the oak, and pitched forward to the floor.

"Hey," said Cornelius from a couple steps away. He'd been coming over to stop his wife, I think, but I wasn't in the mood to take chances (and what's more, I didn't like him).

I lifted the lawbook up with both hands and brought it crashing down over his head.

Cornelius grunted out an "Oof," stumbled away on even wobblier knees than before, then collapsed to the office floor. Lucky for him he was rich and it was carpeted, so at least he had a soft landing.

I quickly traded the casebook for the gun on the floor, then spun around and hurried back to my brother. He was sitting up, clutching the boot on his right foot, which was a huge relief. Dead men don't do such things.

"You think they're all there?" he groaned.

"Are what all there?"

"My toes, dammit!"

I looked more closely at the boot. There was a little hole right where the piggy who had roast beef would usually reside.

"Aw, hell," I said.

Blood began dripping from the bottom of the boot, and Old Red grimaced and lifted his foot higher so we could see underneath.

There was a little hole there, too. The bullet had passed clean through. The only question was whether it had smashed a toe or two on its way. It had definitely hit something other than leather.

I heard shouting voices outside now—"Were those gunshots?" someone was saying—and the front door came swinging open. I looked up expecting to see concerned citizens crowding in to find out what was going on.

Instead I was looking at Wes Munro. He was gazing down at something to my left that put a big, gleeful smile on his face.

It was the slip of paper I'd dropped when the fuss kicked up, the side with the list on it turned up toward the ceiling.

When Munro noticed me watching him, he jerked his hand toward his gun belt.

Fortunately, my hand already had a gun in it.

"Don't," I said, whipping the business end toward him.

He froze, except for his face. The grin there quickly melted away.

"Brother," I said, "I'm sorry, but we still got work to do if you're up for it."

Wincing, Old Red let go of his foot and spun on his butt to face Munro.

"All right. We can count my toes later," he grated out. He held out a hand. "I'll watch him. You get that list to the sheriff."

"Right."

I gave my brother the twenty-two, then picked the paper up off the floor.

"It don't matter what you do with that," said Munro. Concerned citizens *were* beginning to come up behind him now, and he lowered his voice so just Old Red and I could hear. "The sheriff's not gonna do squat to make trouble for Clay Aintree or Charles Cornelius either one."

"Oh, I don't think even Aintree and Cornelius believe that, or they wouldn't have wanted this so bad," I said, giving the paper a wave before tucking it away safely inside my coat. "But just in case, my brother and I have an ace in the hole none of you even know about."

I decided not to tell him what that ace was, though. I thought it would be more fun to make him and the others wait for it to get played.

"You will note," I said to Old Red, "that Wes is here on his own." I turned back to Munro. "Jack and Jock looking for us at the train station?"

"Yeah," Munro growled.

"See?" I said. "Talking to those schoolkids wasn't such a dumb thing to—"

"I'm sittin' here bleedin', for Christ's sake!" Old Red snapped. "Go!"

I couldn't blame him, of course. I just hadn't been able to resist pointing out one of the few things I'd done right on one of our most disastrous assignments yet. We'd be limping home (literally, in my brother's case) with no fee and plenty of expenses (train tickets, meals, rented horses, medical bills of a size yet to be determined, the big, stiff drink I intended to get the first second I could, etc.). Even when it came to reading— the crux of the whole thing, it turned out—my brother hadn't needed my help. I sometimes joke that I'm only around to carry things and keep Old Red from getting shot, and I'd messed up half the job.

"I won't be gone long," I said.

"You'd better not be," said Old Red.

Enough blood had dripped from his boot now to form a puddle the size of a saucer.

So I went—fast. Being there on the courthouse square already, the sheriff's office was less than a minute's dash away. The sheriff himself wasn't—it was lunchtime, after all—but I rushed through explanations to the deputy on duty there, handed over the list (after insisting on a signed receipt), then hurried back to my brother's side.

Munro was gone, having taken the opportunity to slip away as townsmen pushed past him into Cornelius's office. A now woozy-looking Old Red was still sitting in the same spot on the floor, the gun down and his boot and sock off.

All his toes were there. The space between the two of them was just ever-so-slightly bigger (and much bloodier).

"We have three doctors to choose from in Kingman," a plump businessman kneeling next to Old Red said proudly.

"Doc Gimble's a drunk," another man said.

"Doc Bartlett's a quick," whispered another.

"Who's the third?" my brother asked weakly.

"Doc Perez," the plump man said.

Old Red pointed at him.

"Him," my brother said.

Then he passed out.

"Good lord," another man said from the inner office. "Who broke Mrs. Cornelius's nose?"

I scooped up my brother—there being an advantage for once to him being as scrawny as a half-starved prairie chicken—and headed for the door as quick as I could.

"One side. One side. Coming through," I said. "And somebody tell me how to get to Doc Perez's."

Perez turned out to be a fine—if not inexpensive—man of medicine, and after stitching and bandaging Old Red's foot, he suggested we wait a bit before traveling lest the wound open again. So my brother stewed in our hotel room in between interviews with the sheriff, and I've made use of the time to work on the ace in the hole I mentioned to Munro.

This very story. If, as Munro predicted, the sheriff really does do squat with what we've told him and given him—the list that proves by the handwriting upon it who condemned who to die six years ago—that's something the good people of Mohave County deserve to know. And know it they will, thanks to *Smythe's Frontier Detective*.

See, Mr. Smythe? You can fight against crime in the West, too, all the way from your office in New York. For that I thank you.

I also thank you in advance for speedy and generous payment.

We need it.

Sincerely,
O.A. Amlingmeyer
The St. Nicholas Hotel
Kingman, Arizona Territory
March 22, 1894

EXPENSE REPORT: EL PASO

AMUSE-BOUCHE (INTERLUDE)

Diana Crowe
The A.A. Western Detective Agency
Chamber of Commerce Bldg., Rm. 303
Ogden, Utah

Dear Miss Crowe:

I hope that this letter finds you well. I know you face twin difficulties—what with me being absent and my brother being present—but you can take comfort from the fact that I shall be returning soon to dispel the gloom that has, I assume, settled over Ogden while I'm away. Joyous as this will no doubt prove to you and the community at large, I ask that no special fuss be made upon my homecoming. A parade and the key to the city should more than suffice.

Of course, I will excuse my brother from the festivities, as both his temperament and his current state of convalescence disincline him toward the making of merry. All the same, please convey to him my well-wishes (and feel free *not* to convey back the "Feh" they will surely elicit).

From Col. Crowe, too, I will expect no happy jigs or hosannas when I get back, though he'll have more to celebrate than most. Despite your father's lack of confidence in (or fondness for) yours truly, I can proudly report imminent success in the assignment he almost denied me. In fact, word of my ultimate triumph should have reached Ogden well before this letter via both telegram and newspaper account (not to mention folk tale and song, as I'll be surprised should my experiences not pass into the realm of legend quite quickly).

This missive, then, should be looked upon as a sort of addendum to the good news I trust you have already received. Some of its particulars you will find alarming, even horrific beyond the bounds of believability. But their veracity I vouch for with a hand upon the Bible. (I found one here in my hotel room. Really. I vouch for that, too.)

As you know, I was dispatched here to El Paso to take possession of a singular package on behalf of our detective agency. I would be doing so alone, my brother being unable to travel (because of the injury he recently sustained in Arizona); you being unavailable to travel (because of your nursemaiding of the aforementioned brother); and your father being unwilling to travel (because he's a fussy little tyrant busy). I shall always remember the stirring words with which you and my brother countered the colonel's concerns about my fitness for the task at hand.

"This calls for discretion," said he, "and this big oaf's about as discreet as a stampede through a revival meeting."

"That's a bit of an overstatement," said you. (Yes. "*A bit.*") "But all our other operatives are either on assignment or on the mend. Who else can we send?"

"Heck, boil it down, and he's just movin' a box from here to there," said Old Red. "Even he couldn't booger things up *too* bad."

Ahh, the faith you all put in me brings a tear to the eye...

though be it one of gladness or sadness, I cannot at this moment say. Either way, I cheerfully embraced this opportunity to prove my worth to the A.A. Western Detective Agency as something other than a bodyguard for my brother's big mystery-solving brain.

Though your father seems to believe me incapable of so much as boarding a train without much whooping and hollering and an accidental death or two, I managed to make my way to El Paso without starting any riots. There, as arranged, I crossed the border and met with the colonel's old amigo Major Madero.

The major, you might recall, had requested that we make our rendezvous at El Club de Mucha Magia in Ciudad Juárez. The Mucho Mojo Club the gringos called it when I asked for directions across the river in El Paso. A funny look they gave me, too, as if I'd asked the way to the nearest snake pit. Yet the "club" turned out to be nothing but a grubby little watering hole not twenty paces past the south bank of the Rio Grande. The only thing unusual about it was that the walls, rather than being covered American saloon-style with paintings of half-naked nymphs and Custer about to lose his scalp at the Little Bighorn, were so thoroughly plastered with pictures of the Virgin Mary you had to wonder how the cockroaches got in and out.

The major was waiting for me at a table near the door. He was dressed civilian-style, in a creamy white suit I would've soaked soppy with sweat had I been fool enough to wear it out under the midday Mexican sun. The major, however, looked cool as a cucumber.

(I'm not sure why folks assume cucumbers are habitually cool. It's not like you'd want to substitute them for ice in your lemonade on a broiling day. Still, the point being: The man looked comfortable and composed—though his words told a different story.)

"I hope I can trust you to be discreet," he said. "I do not wish to be publicly associated with this in any way."

He brushed the fingers of his left hand over the bulky leather grip resting at his feet.

"I understand," I said.

"If my role in this were known, certain people would be unhappy with me. *Very* unhappy," the major went on.

"I understand."

"You must take great care in the days ahead. I've done my best to keep this quiet, but Chihuahua is not a hospitable place for secrets. Every cactus and ocotillo has eyes."

"I understand."

"Trust no one. Rangers, soldiers, Pinkertons, bounty-hunting scum—all lust for the prize I give to you."

"I understand."

"Take nothing for granted. Treachery could await you at any—"

"Major," I cut in, "do you want your bribe or not?"

What can I say? "Discreet" really *isn't* my specialty.

"Yes," the major said.

"All right, then."

There was a grip by my side, too, and I slid it over to him.

He didn't reach down for it.

"Tell me, Mr. Amlingmeyer," he said. "Do you believe in the devil?"

"I hear he's in the details, but other than that, I don't give much credence to earthly sightings."

Major Madero smiled—though not, I could tell, at my supposed wit. The joke was a private one all his own.

"Perhaps you will change your mind about that," he said. "A deal was made with *el Diablo*, the peasants say. What I give you rightfully belongs to him."

"I've heard those stories."

The major patted the big handbag he'd brought with him. "Then you know better than to open what's in here."

At that I had to laugh.

"Sir," I said. "You and Colonel Crowe go back a ways, so I know you'll understand this. I have my instructions, and they include confirming that I indeed have what I was sent for. So if the choice is between looking Satan himself in the eye and disobeying a direct order from C. Kermit Crowe...well, let's just say it's not Old Scratch's boot I'm worried about keeping out of my backside."

"I see," the major said, and he shrugged in a resigned, "At least I tried" sort of way. Then he picked up the grip I'd pushed over to him and got to his feet. "Vaya con dios, Mr. Amlingmeyer."

And off he went. Quick.

I picked up the bag he'd left me and, not finding myself consumed by hellfire, tipped my hat to the nearest St. Mary.

"Thank you, ma'am," I said.

The grip was a lot heavier than the one I'd brought south—as was to be expected, of course. Still, I couldn't just go by the weight. Like I'd told the major, I had my instructions. This was no gift horse: We'd paid Major Madero a thousand dollars for it from the Double-A's not exactly abundant funds. It was time to look it in the mouth. And the eye.

Now, that was easy enough in the instructing. "Once you have it, take it somewhere private, take it out and look at it," the colonel had said. "I won't have you carrying a pickled cabbage all the way to Austin."

Yet how would this taking-out-and-looking actually work? This, I believe, the colonel had not thought through. Which is why I took the liberty of switching to a deluxe suite once I'd recrossed the Rio Grande and checked into the Vendome Hotel. You'd wired ahead to reserve me a room, yes, but this amounted to little more than a broom closet a man of my size would have to sleep in standing up. And comfort wasn't even the crux of the matter. I needed a fireplace—because I was going to need tongs. Big ones.

Once safely ensconced in my more capacious new digs, I opened the grip Major Madero had given me. Inside, cushioned all around with straw, was a small wooden cask. This I removed and placed upon a table. As I carried it, I could feel the back-and-forth sloshing of liquid within, and something thumped dully against the sides. Whether it was the something I'd been sent to fetch remained to be seen, however.

One end of the cask wasn't nailed down but had been instead

sealed round with wax. After a good ten minutes whittling at this with my pocketknife, I was able to pry the top off like I was opening a can of airtight tomatoes. The stench that plumed out into the room was overpowering—an unholy brew of alcohol and rot—and I staggered back coughing and retching. After a moment, though, I was able to collect myself, and I picked up the tongs and walked back to the table.

I know I need not protect your ladylike sensibilities, Miss Crowe, as you've seen and done things in your detectiving that would set most men to swooning. Still, I would be remiss if I did not pause for a quick caveat.

From here, things get pretty damned disgusting.

Using the tongs, I fished from the murky fluid in the cask a man's head. I placed it on a pillow I'd put upon the table, then stepped back to inspect it.

The face was bloated and mottled, the black tongue protruding from between distended lips, the eyes squeezed shut. Yet the long dark hair and thick mustache and big, beak-like nose were all just as I'd seen them in the newspapers.

I was looking at Maximo the bandito—or the topmost ten inches of him, anyway. On the other side of the border, he was, to some, a hero. On our side, he was a murderer of the worst sort. Robbing and killing people is bad enough, but when you blow up trains to do it? Well, then you've made an enemy of the Southern Pacific Railroad, and God have mercy on your soul. The man had a five-thousand-dollar bounty on his head. And now I had the head.

All that remained was to plop Maximo back in his brine, reseal the cask, and proceed to Austin, where I would claim both bounty and bragging rights for the A.A. Western Detective Agency. What could go wrong so long as I remained discrete?

I brought the tongs in toward the head again—at which point the eyes popped open wide, and I very indiscreetly screamed.

I dropped the tongs and jumped back a mile or two. When you've been around death as much as I, looking at a decapitated head shouldn't be especially unnerving. But it's another thing entirely when the head in question is suddenly looking at *you*.

Of course, as you know, the flesh can get up to all kinds of tricks even after the spirit has left it. Parts go stiff, limp, contort, swell, shrivel, open, close. So the head was just reacting to the air or the change in position or some such, I figured. As I bent down to pick up the tongs again, though, I noticed something unsettling.

Maximo's eyes followed me.

I stood and stepped to the right.

The eyes stayed with me.

I took a few steps to the left.

Again—the eyes followed.

"Sweet Jesus," I whispered.

Maximo's mouth started moving, too. No sound came out, but it sure looked like he was trying to say something.

It was then that I remembered the stories I'd read about Maximo—the ones the major had alluded to. I'm sure you saw them yourself.

According to the papers, the man was half-Mexican, half-Mescalero and all evil. He'd sold his soul to Satan for a bundle of dynamite, the Mexicans said. He was a shape-shifting shaman who couldn't be killed by mortal man, said the Indians.

Of course, I'd put as much stock in all this as I do your average campfire spook story. Yet I couldn't dismiss what I was seeing with my own eyes.

If you or my brother had been there, doubtless you would have commenced to detect, throwing yourselves to the floor hunting for hidden wires or mirrors or who knows what-all. I opted for a more direct approach.

"Are you…alive?" I asked the head.

It glared at me as if displeased by such a stupid question.

"If you can understand me, blink."

Maximo shut his eyes, then promptly opened them again.

I nearly fainted.

Maximo blinked two more times. His lips were still moving without making a sound.

"I'm sorry," I said, "but if you're tryin' to talk, it ain't no use. I hate to break it to you, but you're a tad short on lung power. And lungs."

Maximo took to looking at something off to my right, and he waggled his thick eyebrows until I was looking thataway, too.

He was staring at the fireplace.

"You're cold?" I said. "You need me to stoke up a fire?"

Maximo glowered at me again. I could tell from the movement of his lips that he was saying the same thing over and over. Two syllables—a hard, lip-smacking sound and a mouth-rounding O with what looked like a "lll" in between.

"P...p...pillow?" I guessed. "You want me to put your pillow in the fireplace?"

From the expression on his face, it was plain Maximo would've smacked me upside the head had he hands to do so. As it was, he had no choice but to keep repeating the same silent word while still wiggling his bushy brows at the hearth.

"B...b...bellows!" I cried. "That's it, ain't it?"

Maximo blinked, then grinned.

A shiver ran through me from head to toe. Maximo's smile was more unnerving than his frown.

I walked over and picked up the bellows propped beside the fireplace. There was no need for further brow-furrowing to get across the gist. I knew what Maximo had in mind. It was about the most grotesque, indecent thing a human mind could possibly imagine.

And it worked.

"Thank you," Maximo wheezed once I got some air moving through him. I'm sure it wasn't comfortable having the bellows' nozzle stuck up his throat the way it was, but he seemed remarkably content even if he did look like the world's most monstrous candy apple.

"How is it you ain't dead?" I said.

I gave the bellows another pump so the head could answer. The "breath" that puffed out of his mouth was what you might expect from a man who's been feasting on week-old horse meat and gargling with kerosene.

"I am unhappy," Maximo said.

"Fair enough. If I were in your shoes, I wouldn't be too tickled neither. You wouldn't hear me grousin' about it, though."

Maximo's mouth started moving, so I squeezed more air through him. I missed the first few words, but I could guess what he'd said.

"...struck a bargain with me. He would have me in hell when I was through on this earth, but..."

Maximo's voice faded off into a raspy sigh, and I had to work the bellows hard to hear him again. I felt like I was playing Satan's own concertina.

"...could choose the time of my own departure. I thought that meant I would live forever, but now I find it more curse than..."

Breath left him again.

"Are you sayin' you won't die till you decide to?" I asked.

Maximo just blinked his eyes, for which I was thankful.

"Well, amigo," I said, "I hate to break it to you, but it probably is time you moseyed along. You went and got yourself shot by the rurales half a week back. If a couple of 'em hadn't known about the bounty the Southern Pacific's got on you, you'd be looking at dirt right now."

Maximo gave me a glare to let me know he was dead, not dumb. He knew what had happened to him.

"Point is, the rest of your body's been bug-feed half a week," I said. "Even if you could find it, that ain't anything you'd wanna hitch yourself to again."

"I agree," said Maximo (with more help from the bellows). "I am willing to accept my fate. But not yet. Not like this. A condemned man is sometimes granted a last request, yes? Well, then—"

"I'm sorry, but could you speed it up? My arms are getting tired."

Maximo scowled at me again.

"Champagne," he growled.

"Champagne?"

"Champagne." His eyes darted toward the cask he'd been jarred up in. "They filled that with the only alcohol they had on hand. Tequila. I hate tequila."

"And you like champagne?"

"I've never had it." I got the feeling Maximo would have shrugged if he could. "But if one must end one's days in such a fashion, why not do it with style?"

"You want me to dump out the tequila and replace it with champagne?"

Maximo blinked a yes.

"You know that'd take at least five or six bottles, don't you?"

Maximo blinked again.

"You sure you wouldn't prefer Dr Pepper?"

Maximo did *not* blink.

"Look," I said, "I feel for you. I do. But champagne's pricey stuff and the folks I work with gave me just enough spending money to get home without starving. So it isn't a matter of not wanting to help. It's that I...what are you doing?"

Maximo had sucked his upper lip into his mouth and was vigorously gnawing away at it. I gave him a few puffs of bellows-breath so he could explain himself.

"I am biting off my mustache and the lip that goes with it. After that, I believe I will chew through my cheeks."

"Why in God's name would you do that?"

"Because if I do enough damage, I will be unrecognizable—and you will not be able to collect your reward." Maximo bugged his eyes at me. "With a little effort, I think I can get these to pop out. The last thing I'll do, of course, is bite off my tongue. Or should I swallow it?"

"Alright, alright—it's a deal!"

Maximo grinned, triumphant. I'd been outmaneuvered by a head.

"Don't go anywhere," I told him as I went out the door a minute later. I'd slid him off the bellows so he was on his pillow upside down. It was a bit of a low blow, perhaps, but what can I say? I'm a sore loser.

Soon, I was at the front desk arranging the extension of our agency's credit to cover service from the hotel restaurant—which is in possession of quite the selection of fine wines, luckily enough. Presently, I was told, someone would be up with six bottles of chilled Billecart-Salmon Brut Réserve. I didn't really care if it was chilled, of course, so long as it was bubbly and golden and just all-around champagney enough to satisfy Maximo.

"Good news!" I said as I let myself back into the room. "The hotel EEP!"

Bad news. My prisoner had escaped. Both Maximo and the cask were gone.

As I stood there frozen in the doorway, wondering how a head could box itself up and make its getaway, I noticed a noxious odor in the hall. Tequila and decay. Some of Maximo's *au jus* had spilled upon the carpet lining the corridor.

I applied a little brain power to that and found it made sense. Surely Maximo hadn't walked himself out of the room, and whoever *did* take him had done so in a stinky, dinky, tequila-filled barrel with a loosened lid. No surprise that some liquid had slopped out onto the floor.

I'd only been gone a few minutes and hadn't passed anyone carrying a suspiciously familiar cask as I came back up the stairs. Which suggested the thief was close by—as did the fact that he'd known when opportunity had presented itself. It couldn't be coincidence that he'd broken in at precisely the right moment. He'd been keeping an eye on my room.

Conclusion: *His* room was but steps away. And I knew how to find it.

I got down on my hands and knees and sniffed my way up the hall. The smell led me to the very next room. When I took a big whiff at the bottom of the door, the scent of tequila was so strong I may as well have been sticking my nose in a shot glass.

I stood, drew my Webley Bulldog from its shoulder holster, and aimed a heel at the doorknob. The first kick didn't do the trick, so I tried another. Unfortunately, instead of busting out the lock, my foot crashed straight through the door itself.

"What the——?" I heard a man cry on the other side.

"You know what I'm here for," I said as I tried to wriggle my foot back through the splintered wood. "I suggest you give it up without any fuss."

A door creaked open up the hall, and a pop-eyed old lady leaned out to peer at me.

"Uhhh...house detective, ma'am," I said. "I'm sorry for the fuss, but certain guests will insist on trying to make off with the towels."

The woman ducked back into her room and slammed the door. I got the feeling she had some towels to unpack.

I had my foot free by now, and with another shove, I was able to bust into the room before me. I had my Bulldog at the ready, as I figured I'd be facing a rival detective or bounty hunter, and such gents aren't known for their sportsmanship when losing out on a reward.

What I wasn't expecting was a couple cowering in bed with the sheets pulled up to their naked shoulders.

"There's no need for that!" cried the male half of the duo. He was a fiftyish fellow with a prodigious gut that bulged against the linens below his broad, quivering face. "I was going to pay! I swear! But not till afterward!"

On the bedside table to his left, I saw, was an opened bottle and two glasses half-filled with tequila.

It was nice to know my nose was in good working order.

Not so nice to know: I was in the wrong room.

"I don't know who you are," the woman snapped, "but Marshal Cunningham's already had his cut for the month and he's not going to take kindly to dumb bastards horning in. So I suggest you get your ass outta here fast."

She was a little, wiry thing with a wildness in her eyes that would've done a rabid badger proud.

I acted accordingly.

"I beg you to forgive the intrusion, miss," I said to the gal as I backed out.

"Carry on," I told her customer.

Of course, carrying on wouldn't be so easy now that the man had a foot-sized hole in his door. But that was his problem. I had my own—like having no idea where Maximo was. Fortunately, there promptly arrived a clue so clear-cut and unequivocal even I couldn't follow it wrong.

A man screamed. And it wasn't a "There's a spider on my sleeve!" scream either. It was a big, loud, long "That head ain't dead!" scream, and it was coming from the room right across the hall.

I moved to the door, took careful aim, started to bring up a foot—and then, on a whim, reached out and tried the knob. It wasn't locked.

I stepped into the room and closed the door behind me.

The fellow who'd been doing the caterwauling didn't even look at me. He was backed against the wall, staring in horror at the head that lay on the floor before him.

"It's...it's..."

"Mine," I said.

The man tore his gaze away from Maximo. If the revolver in my hand bothered him, there was no way to know it. His eyes couldn't have gone any wider or his face more pale. He sure didn't look like a lawman or bounty hunter. In my experience, such men don't go for bow ties and white seersucker suits. This gent didn't have any tan to him either. Or much grit.

He'd already thrown up once, and from the way he shivered and clutched his stomach, it looked like he was headed for round two.

"You don't have anything to worry about from ol' Maximo there," I told him. "Me, on the other hand—I oughta concern you. So talk before I show you why. Who are you and why'd you make off with my little friend?"

The man took a shuddering breath that puffed up his chest,

and he produced a hanky with which he proceeded to wipe his face.

"I'm Francis Lenahan."

He said it like it meant something. As if he'd announced "I'm Tom Edison" or "I'm Grover Cleveland" or "I'm St. Peter—didn't you notice the halo?"

"Of The New York World," he added when I didn't immediately fall to my knees.

"Congratulations. I'm sure your mother's very proud. But I don't see what that has to do with anything."

Lenahan had regained his composure enough to look indignant.

"I've been writing about Maximo for months. Hell, I *made* Maximo." He glanced down at the floor and went green again. "In the press, anyway. So when one of my friends in the rurales told me Maximo had been killed and some gringo detectives had finagled a way to nab the reward for themselves—a reward that wouldn't have been worth a plugged nickel if not for me—well…"

"You decided to claim the reward for yourself."

"Not for myself!" Lenahan protested. "For The World!"

"Right."

I heard heavy steps in the hallway, and there was a knock and the murmuring of voices.

The management had arrived, I assumed. And if the law should follow suit…well, discreet it would not be.

It was time to smooth things over, quiet things down, and get a story straight.

I holstered my Bulldog.

"I'm not authorized to cut anyone in on the bounty, Mr. Lenahan," I said. "But I can offer you one hell of an exclusive."

"You'd let me come with you to Austin?"

"Sure, if you wanna come. But that isn't what I'm thinking of." I pointed at Maximo. "How'd you like an interview?"

"It talks?"

"With a little help."

"My god. So he really did make a deal with the devil."

"I reckon so...though you'd have to ask him for the particulars."

Lenahan gulped and swiped his hanky across his forehead.

"All right," he said. "It's a deal."

"Excellent."

Maximo's cask was on a table nearby, and I bent down, took his head by a lock of tequila-slick hair, and walked him toward it.

Maximo started chewing at his mustache again.

"Oh, don't be like that," I said. "The champagne's on its way to my room. Just one more quick ride down the hall, and you'll be done with tequila forever."

Maximo was pouting as I lowered him back into the cask, but at least he wasn't trying to eat his own face anymore.

The champagne did indeed arrive soon after. And so it is that, through the miracle of the telegraph lines, the front page of today's New York World will feature The Last Will and Testament of Maximo the Bandito (as dictated to Francis Lenahan). The first train to Austin leaves in less than an hour, and I fully expect to make it to the governor's office well before word of the article trickles back to whatever rivals might complicate the journey. So by the end of this very special day, I will have secured for the A.A. Western Detective Agency both a heap of free publicity and five thousand dollars.

Minus expenses. As I mentioned when the notion first arose, I find your father's new policy requiring itemized reports for all outlays and incidentals a bit insulting. Still—I am endeavoring here to comply, in my way. I leave it to you to present my report to the colonel in whatever fashion might best smooth the way for payment. By which I mean you should feel free to lie through your teeth. There are times it's called for, I've found.

Here's the tally, as tabulated by the Vendome Hotel (which will be forwarding its own invoice independently):

- $20 for one night's stay in the hotel's "Grand Parisian Suite" (I needed extra room, remember?)

- $17 for the repair of one door
- $90 for replacing approximately forty feet of hotel carpeting (soaked, alas, with particularly pungent tequila/preservative)
- $175 for seven bottles of Billecart-Salmon Brut Réserve

Yes, *seven* bottles of champagne. Six was enough to refill Maximo's keg when it was time for him to close his eyes forever and take his final dunk. But we had to toast the man's memory with something, didn't we?

Your humble (and ever-truthful) servant,
O.A. Amlingmeyer
The Vendome Hotel
El Paso, Texas
April 1, 1894

WHITE DEATH

MAIN COURSE (NOVELLA #2)

Day 1: Buckets of Blood

Afternoon

It took the new clerk and the new patient a day and a half to reach the sanatorium from Ogden. The rails only took them as far as Idaho Springs, thirty-six miles east of Denver. The last twenty miles they had to cover in a surrey sent down the mountain to fetch them. The driver—a wiry Irish groundskeeper in a pea coat, scarf, and fingerless gloves—let the clerk sit up front beside him. The patient was put in back by himself.

Though the driver was friendly enough to both men, he didn't shake the patient's hand.

The driver also didn't ask the patient any questions. He knew the destination and could see how loosely the little, limping man's sheepskin coat hung on his bony build, as if he'd recently lost a quarter of his weight. That told the story. The beginning, anyway.

And probably the end, too. It was a familiar story to the driver, who'd taken a lot of patients up to Echo Lake.

He'd taken far fewer back down again.

So the first hour on the thin, winding road up-up-up was passed chatting with the clerk. They talked about the weather (cold, gray), admired the scenery (undulating, rocky, increasingly tree-laden), noted game (mule deer, bighorn sheep, a lonely-looking moose) and traded jokes (some funny, most not). But the closer they got to their destination, the quieter the driver grew. The clerk tried to draw him out with questions about the sanatorium, but the responses became shorter and shorter until they were only nods, grunts or shrugs. No more jokes, no more smiles. As if the driver was steeling himself for something unpleasant. Or someplace.

Later—after the conversation had finally faded away entirely and the only sound was the steady clopping of the horse's hooves —the patient sat up straight and stared off to the right. The driver and the clerk looked that way, too.

About thirty yards beyond the road, a thin mist puffed out from behind one of the trees in the thick spruce and pine forest. A cloud of breath in the frigid mountain air. A shape stepped out into it, gaunt and dark. A feminine figure in a black mackintosh, the face a gray blur.

The woman raised a long, bony arm in greeting, and the men in the surrey all did the same.

"One of the patients," said the driver. "They're big believers in fresh air up here. Long walks for everybody, every day." He glanced over his shoulder. "That'll be you soon."

The man behind him said nothing.

A minute later, they saw the first buildings: quaint little one-room cottages with porches and chimney pipes and whitewashed sides. A little further on was something larger and starker—a windowless structure with all the character and charm of a cardboard box. Just beyond that was a similarly bare and bleak-looking barn.

Then the main building came into view. Its center was a

brown, steeple-roofed chalet, while stretching off to either side were long, one-story extensions. It looked like a gigantic owl swooping down on its prey, wings outstretched, window-eyes wide.

A forty-ish woman in a blue dress covered by a white apron—a nurse—came out the front door to meet them. Which isn't to say *welcome* them. That would have required a smile. Her expression was neutral, cool, businesslike as she took in the passengers: the one in front big and barrel-chested and nattily attired, the one in back scrawny and jug-eared.

"Mr. Pycroft," the woman said to the clerk.

"Mr. Melas," she said to the patient.

She'd never seen either man before, yet she'd known at a glance which was which.

"I am Miss Rosenkoetter, the head nurse," she went on. "Mr. Melas—I assume you're capable of bringing your things in unassisted?"

"Certainly," Melas said.

"Good. The orderlies are occupied, and we have no porters here. Please go inside, both of you."

"Yes'm," said Melas.

"Ma'am," said Pycroft, tugging on the brim of his tweed cap.

The nurse turned to the driver as the men collected their carpetbags and began to climb down.

"Mail's in the back, ma'am," he said. "And I've got that ink and paper we've been waiting for. I can bring it in once I've got Hippocrates put away."

He pronounced the horse's name "Hippo-Crates."

"Fine," Nurse Rosenkoetter said. "That will be all, McCandless."

"Yes, ma'am. Thank you, ma'am. Good day, ma'am."

The driver gave the men a farewell "Fellas," snapped the reins, and steered his quick-trotting horse in a circle that sent them around the side of the big building. Both he and Hippo-Crates seemed eager to get to the barn—and away from the nurse.

Pycroft and Melas followed Nurse Rosenkoetter through the front door, across a broad lobby, and into an office. A booklet and a small metal bucket were sitting atop a desk there, and the nurse picked them up and handed them to Melas.

"For you," she said. "I'll let Dr. Swann know you're here. He's asked to see both of you together when you arrive."

Her expression didn't change, but something about her tone— going from impersonal to curt—suggested This Wasn't Usual.

She went through another door at the back of the room, leaving the men to stare in confusion at the little bucket.

"How nice," said Pycroft. "You get your own spittoon."

"Feh," said Melas.

The booklet, on the other hand, was self-explanatory. Melas sounded out the words slowly.

"E-cho…Echo…Lllake…Tuber…Tuberculosis…Sanato-rium…Patent…Rule…Book."

"Patient," said Pycroft—a.k.a. Otto Amlingmeyer, a.k.a. "Big Red," a.k.a. me.

"I figured," grumbled Melas—a.k.a. Gustav Amlingmeyer, a.k.a. "Old Red," a.k.a. That Grouchy Little SOB I Put Up with Somehow, a.k.a. my brother.

We were on our first incognito assignment for the A.A. Western Detective Agency. So far, I considered our false identities a great success. We fooled *you*, didn't we? (Or did we?)

Nurse Rosenkoetter returned.

"Dr. Swann will see you now," she said from the doorway.

She stepped aside to let us pass, then closed the door firmly behind us. It didn't *clang* like the metal of a cell door slammed shut, but there was something about it that seemed to suggest inescapable captivity. Or maybe just an irritated lady.

"She always so warm and inviting?" I asked the puffy, rumpled, bearded man awaiting us—Dr. Herman Swann, the sanatorium's chief physician and superintendent.

"Yes, actually," he said. "That is about as warm and inviting as our Nurse Rosenkoetter gets. Fortunately, what she lacks in personality, she makes up in efficiency."

He was seated behind a desk, slightly slumped in his chair so that his round belly was angled upward. He drummed his thick fingers on his bulging vest as he looked us up and down. He didn't rise to shake our hands or offer us the seats opposite his desk.

Warm and inviting didn't seem to describe him either.

"You sure she wasn't mad?" Old Red asked. "Maybe got the idea there's something she ain't bein' told?"

Swann shrugged. "Could be. After all—there *is* something she isn't being told."

He gave us a significant look and drummed his fingers again.

"Usually you wouldn't see a new patient and a new employee together, would you?" my brother said. "Not when they first show up."

Swann nodded slowly. "No, I suppose not."

"Then that was a mistake. A dumb one."

Swann sat up straight in his chair, suddenly scowling at us. He didn't look capable of throwing us out on our ears—he was altogether too soft and gray to get *my* bulk up off the floor, that was for sure—but he didn't look averse to trying.

"What my brother means to say," I said, "is that you've got to treat us exactly as you would if we really were a new patient and a new clerk. We've gone to a lot of trouble to establish these new identities." I jerked my head at Old Red. "Heck, he even took a bath."

"Feh," my brother muttered.

"But what's done is done," I went on. "I'm sure you can think of some reason to have seen Mr. Pycroft and Mr. Melas together, should anyone ask. Let's just carry on. Anything new we need to know? We haven't heard from the trustees in a few days, and I don't know how up-to-date they are anyhow."

Swann had been starting to relax, but my mention of the sanatorium's Board of Trustees put the frown back on his face. It had been the board's idea for us to spend time at the place disguised as a staff member and a patient. They'd told Swann about it—there was no way it'd work without his help—but that didn't mean he had to like it. And he obviously didn't.

"No," he said. "Everything's been normal since we buried Wroblewski."

"*Buried* Wroblewski?" Old Red said. "You didn't ship him to his folks?"

"Do you know how much shipping a body to Chicago would cost?" Swann asked. He said "Chicago" the way some people say "cockroach"—with a lip-curling look of disgust. "Our charity patients know if they pass away at Echo Lake, they will remain at Echo Lake. None have complained so far."

"Well, I'm sure they don't when it comes time for the burying," I said.

Swann turned the lip-curling look of disgust on me.

"All the board said was that this Wroblewski 'fell' and 'bumped his head,'" Old Red said. "What else can you tell us about his death?"

Swann shrugged. "You have the gist of it. We believe in the healing power of clear, cold air, physical stimulation and mental tranquility. So the patients are encouraged to exert themselves—within reason—out of doors each day. Long, solitary perambulations are particularly healthful, in my opinion, and Wroblewski was engaged in one along the slopes near the lake when apparently he swooned and struck his head on a rock. In his weakened state, that was enough to kill him."

"So no one saw it happen?" my brother asked.

"I suspect if someone saw it, you wouldn't be here," Swann replied.

Old Red gave that a grunt and a nod.

"Who found him?" he said.

"A patient. Miss Johansen."

"Her and him have any special connection?"

Old Red wasn't so uncouth as to waggle his eyebrows, but he did lift them.

Swann furrowed his.

"I'm sure I wouldn't know," the doctor said.

My brother beetled his bushy brows in irritation, but he let the matter drop.

"How about the other charity case that ended up dead?" he said. "All we was told was 'unusual circumstances.'"

"It wasn't as unusual as certain people like to think." Swann stared off into the corner, shaking his head at the memory. "What it was was messy."

Old Red opened his mouth to snap something at the man. Not wanting to get kicked out of the place five minutes after we'd arrived, I jumped in quick.

"Details would be most helpful, Dr. Swann."

Swann turned his gaze my way and heaved a sigh.

"His name was Palomares. From Cleveland." The doctor's lips curled just enough to let us know he regarded Cleveland about as highly (which is to say lowly) as Chicago. "He seemed to be doing well, but then a month ago he collapsed entirely. Went practically comatose. We moved him to the infirmary, and at some time in the night, he regained consciousness. The crushing disappointment of the relapse was too much for him, apparently. When the night nurse was out checking the wards, he got up, found a scalpel, and opened his radial arteries. By the time the nurse returned he was drained as dry as an upturned bottle. Hardly a drop left in him." Swann sighed again. "All on the floor."

"You don't call that unusual?" Old Red said.

"No. I don't," Swann snapped. "Suicide happens here. How could it not? Tuberculosis is considered a death sentence. The people who come to Echo Lake are clinging to their last hope. We can help most of them. The ones we can't…some choose to go before their crumbling lungs fill with fluid and they drown in their own bloody juices. You'll hear it soon enough. The desperate hacking and gasping that comes before the death rattle. It will make slicing your wrists seem easy."

My brother and I glanced at each other.

And you wanted to be a detective…my look said.

Well, it ain't always this *grim*, said his.

When Old Red spoke next, his tone was gentler.

"Was there a coroner's inquest? For either man?"

"Not anything formal, no. Just some paperwork. We're a tuberculosis sanatorium in the mountains twenty miles from the nearest town. If we say we had a death here, it's no mystery. The coroner understands that." Swann gave us a glower. "The board should, too."

"They're worried that someone has a grudge against your charity cases," I said. "Two deaths like this in one month—they felt it worth lookin' into. If everything's peachy, we'll be outta your hair in a week with our agency's fee the only harm."

Swann snorted. I couldn't tell if he was scoffing at someone bothering to murder men dying of tuberculosis or the notion that a TB sanatorium could be "peachy."

"*Does* anyone have a grudge against the charity cases?" Old Red asked.

"Well, of course! You've got respectable families paying two hundred dollars a month to send their loved ones here, and then those loved ones have to share a ward with Irish and Italians from the tenements? Polacks and Jews? How would *you* feel?"

That relit the fire in Old Red's eyes. I could see he was tempted to tell Swann exactly how he felt. About him.

"Anyone in particular upset about that?" I said quickly. "So upset they'd do something about it?"

"Certainly not. Most of our patients can barely keep themselves alive, let alone go around killing off the others."

"What about the staff then?" I asked.

"Preposterous. They are professionals, one and all. Healers and caregivers. Which isn't to say *they* don't have enemies…the kind who might stir up trouble for them with rumors and lies purely because of the diligence with which they pursue their work."

My brother and I sat staring at the man a moment, waiting for him to say more—and hopefully something specific. But he just glared back until it was obvious we'd gotten all we were going to get on either the deaths or these supposed rumors and lies.

Time to move on—and move in.

"All right, then," I said. "From here, we should proceed as if Gustav is indeed your new patient Mr. Melas and I your new clerk Mr. Pycroft. What would you do and where would we go?"

"Well, first I would examine 'Mr. Melas.'" Swann lifted his

hands toward Old Red and fiddled his fingers in the air. "Examine examine. You're fine. Then I would tell you to report to Nurse Rosenkoetter to be taken to a cottage. All new patients are quarantined for forty-eight hours upon arrival. After that, assuming you don't develop anything too nasty, you'll join the other patients in the men's ward. Since you're a charity case, you'll be seen to from there on by my assistant, Dr. Holly. As for you, 'Mr. Pycroft,' I would let you know that your desk is in the outer office and you should begin familiarizing yourself with our filing methods. Now. Nurse Rosenkoetter can show you to your room when she's done with 'Mr. Melas.' Interview concluded."

He shooed us away.

I held up a finger.

"Speaking of the files, we thought perhaps Mr. Pycroft, in acquainting himself with them, might want to visit with the patients to double-check their information. As an excuse for me to get the lay of the land, y'see. That all right by you?"

"No. But do it if that will take you a step closer to leaving. Just try to be discreet, if you can."

I gave Swann a tight smile. "Good thing I've been practicing."

Old Red rolled his eyes at that. My practice so far has *not* made perfect.

"Just one more thing," he said to Swann.

"*Yes?*" Swann hissed through gritted teeth.

My brother waggled the little silver bucket the nurse had given him. "What the hell is this?"

"As you surely know," Swann replied, his tone suggesting doubt that Old Red actually knew anything at all, "consumptives are prone to racking coughs that produce copious amounts of mucus and blood infused with the tuberculosis bacillus. We require our patients to direct all such sputum into their personal expectoration receptacle."

"Oh," I said. "You mean you give everybody their very own blood bucket. How very thoughtful."

"It beats sliding around on disease-ridden phlegm all day,"

Swann said. He grabbed a file off his desk and flipped it open. "Now if you will excuse me…"

He pointed his eyes at the file, but it was obvious he wasn't reading anything. He was just waiting for us to leave. So we did.

We found Nurse Rosenkoetter at one of the desks in the other office across the hall. As we approached, she hopped to her feet like a soldier snapping to attention.

"I'll show you to your cottage," she said to my brother.

Me she gave a piercing stare of the "Don't you have work to do?" variety.

"I promised Mr. Melas I'd see him settled in," I said. "We got to be real chums on the journey here."

I beamed at Old Red.

With some (barely) concealed effort, he forced himself to smile back.

"Fine. Follow me," the nurse said, striding briskly toward the door.

Of course, I had no problem keeping up as she swept through the lobby, but Old Red was bobbing up and down on a right foot, still stiff and sore from the bullet that had passed through it a couple weeks before. The nurse glanced back and noted his gimpiness…and didn't still slow in the slightest.

She led us out the front door again, then around the building, to the left. There the cottages and other outbuildings—maybe a dozen in all—were spread across a gently sloping hill. At the bottom of the incline was Echo Lake, its edges iced silver-gray, the middle still a dark blue that spoke to cold but unfrozen depths. Scattered around it here and there were bundled, slow-moving figures—patients out for their daily "perambulations."

"You will be quarantined for two nights, Mr. Melas," Nurse Rosenkoetter said. She hadn't put on a coat before stepping outside, I noted, and the frigid air didn't seem to affect her at all. Maybe because she was pure ice inside to begin with. "You should use your time alone to rest and study the patient rulebook. Have you brought any other reading material with you?"

"Just a magazine or two," Old Red said.

Or eleven or twelve actually. He'd packed a pile of *Harper's* and *McClure's*—the last run of Sherlock Holmes stories leading up to "The Adventure of the Final Problem." Buried beneath the magazines was the reading textbook he'd been slowly working through, *McGuffey's Eclectic Primer*, the latter there to help him decipher the former.

"No fiction, I hope. No novels," Nurse Rosenkoetter said.

"Nope. No fiction. All factual. All educational."

"Good. Novels aren't allowed. Over-stimulating to the brain."

"Patients ain't supposed to think?" my brother said.

He threw me a little glance I could read easy as *McGuffey's*.

You shoulda been the patient. If they ain't supposed to think, you're perfect for it.

I clapped Old Red on the back.

"You're peaked, Mr. Melas. Scrawny and sickly and weak. All that energy you'd put into thinking and talking you need to steer toward healing now. Only then will you build your vigor and grow as full of strength and energy as a man like me."

I gave Old Red another smile.

This time he didn't smile back.

We'd reached one of the little cabins by then, and Nurse Rosenkoetter pulled a set of keys from her pocket as we stepped up onto the porch.

"You should sleep in that if you can," she said, nodding at a chaise longue to the left of the door. A pillow and a thin-looking blanket rested on the foot of it. "Stifling indoor air isn't good for a man in your condition."

"And stayin' out all night freezin' is?" Old Red said.

Nurse Rosenkoetter had started to open the door, but she stopped with the key half-turned in the lock.

"Dr. Swann and Dr. Holly believe so," she said without looking back. "Where is *your* medical doctorate from, Mr. Melas?"

"Ain't got one," my brother said.

"Then I should hope you'd listen to those who do. Your life depends upon it."

The nurse finished opening the door but stepped back without going inside. The room beyond her looked small and sparse. A bed, a chair, a coal box, a small stove, and four walls—that was it.

"An orderly will bring you dinner at seven, and the night nurse will check on you at eleven," Nurse Rosenkoetter told Old Red. "You'll see the privy if you step around the corner and look toward the main building. If you need assistance, come in the front door." She swung her arctic gaze over to me. "Visitors are not allowed."

I gave my brother a tip of the hat.

"Guess I'll be seeing you later, Mr. Melas. Make the most of your rest time, hm?"

"Yeah...sure," Old Red grumbled.

We'd known about the quarantine—that my brother would be stuck on his duff for two days while all the detecting was left to me —but there'd been no way around it. He could no better pass for a doctor's clerk than I could for a shriveled-up consumptive.

He shuffled inside and closed the door behind him.

Nurse Rosenkoetter marched past me, obviously assuming I'd scurry along after her like a duckling hustling to keep up with momma. Old Red likes to make the same assumption about me. He's usually right—and the nurse was, too.

"Once I've got my things put away, I'll need to chat with each of the patients," I said as I caught up to her. "Dr. Swann wants me to make sure everyone's file is up-to-date. Sounds like the last fella who had my job wasn't all that efficient."

More than that, he was "incompetent and unmindful of important protocols." At least that's what Swann had told the board after firing the man a couple weeks before. Perhaps saying more would have been indiscreet. Or maybe more like inconvenient...?

"The afternoon exercise period concludes at five," Nurse Rosenkoetter said. "Followed by bed rest until six-thirty, followed by preparation for dinner until seven, followed by dinner until seven-forty-five. After that, patients have free time in the parlors and activity rooms until nine. You may have your 'chats' then."

"Doesn't leave me a lot of time for it."

The nurse shot a stern look over at me. (And up at me, me being over six feet and her barely reaching a slight five. Despite her small, seemingly cool exterior she gave me the impression of a Jack in the Box: a little package from which something bigger and perhaps alarming might burst if you turned her crank too many times.)

"Then you will have to be *efficient*," she said.

"Well...I'll do my best."

She didn't give me the chance to draw more out of her. The second we were back inside, she started playing tour guide.

"Men's cloakroom, offices, infirmary," she said, pointing to the left. She swung her finger to the right. "Women's cloakroom, kitchen, dining room."

The finger swung back to the left, this time to jab at a long, narrow, shadowy hallway.

"Men's ward."

The finger went right again toward an identical hallway opposite the first.

"Women's ward."

There was a flight of stairs at the end of the lobby, and as we approached, she pointed around one side of it then the other.

"Privy, linen closet, orderlies' quarters. Privy, more linens, cooks' and servants' quarters."

We started up the steps.

"Stairs," I said, pointing down.

She glared at me.

I decided not to point up and say "Ceiling."

When we reached the second floor, I saw that it was a wide square of doorways all facing the open-air stairwell in the center. Nurse Rosenkoetter started with the door directly before us and slowly turned in a circle to point at them all.

"Closet, Dr. Holly's rooms, my room, nurses, nurses, Dr. Swann's rooms, guest room, guest room, privy, bath, clerk's room, closet."

She was back to where she'd started.

I pointed at the second-to-last door she'd named.

"*My* room?"

Rather than answer, the nurse pulled out her key ring again and walked over to the door.

"Will I get one of those?" I said, nodding down at the keys as she slid one into the lock.

"That's up to Dr. Swann."

"Be a little awkward, me not being able to lock and unlock my own door."

"*That's up to Dr. Swann.*"

"Alright, fine. I like to tell the folks I work with 'My door is always open.' I guess this time it'll be literal."

Nurse Rosenkoetter pushed the door open, revealing the room beyond. And I call it a "room" though there was nothing roomy about it. I would've thought she'd mixed up "clerk's room" and "closet" if not for the narrow bunk pushed up against one wall. I could *maybe* squeeze all of my bulky self onto it if I bent my knees, bowed my head, and gave up eating for a week or two. Beside it was a tiny, rickety-looking table and, atop that, a candle. That was it for furnishings. There was no window, and the walls were bare plaster with a row of pegs poking out for me to hang my clothes on.

No wonder the previous clerk had been "inefficient." They made the poor man sleep in a shoebox.

"Cozy," I said.

"Now that you and Mr. Melas are settled, I can return to my regular duties," said the nurse. "If you need anything, ask one of the orderlies."

The way she spun on her heel and tromped off down the stairs gave me the impression she thought we'd never speak again...and that it would suit her just fine. I didn't disappoint her by asking where the orderlies might be. Looking for them would give me an excuse to poke around.

I stepped into my boudoir, closed the door, and tossed my carpetbag onto the cot. The bag seemed to take up half the bed. As I took off my cap, coat, and gloves, I heard footsteps and voices down in the lobby. Lots of voices, lots of footsteps. And lots and lots and *lots* of coughing.

The patients were coming back in from their outdoor exercise. Next, Nurse Rosenkoetter had said, would be time for bed rest.

Time for *me* to get to work.

I could still hear hustle-bustle as I headed down the stairs, and nearing the lobby I saw two groups milling around by the cloak rooms: a couple dozen women on my left, a couple dozen men on my right. Standing a little apart from them were two young women dressed like Nurse Rosenkoetter and two men in crisp white uniforms.

The orderlies had been found, no poking around required. As I neared the bottom of the stairs, they and the nurses and most of the patients turned to gaze at me curiously. I even fancied that the looks from some of the female patients could be labeled "intrigued," the ladies for the most part appearing pale yet not so frail as to lose all appreciation for a strapping example of manhood. Two of the women caught my eye in return, as they seemed to be in the range of my own age—one blonde and wan and twentyish, the other red-haired and less ashen-skinned and perhaps twenty-five. They were on opposite sides of the gaggle of female patients, so I had to pick one to steer myself toward.

I headed for the blonde. Not out of a natural fondness for blondes, mind you. I am open to all colors of the rainbow when it comes to fair young ladies and their hair. But I needed to speak to "Miss Johansen," the patient who'd found Wroblewski's body, and the name had a Scandinavian ring to it that seemed to fit the pale young lady with the golden locks. I was working up an excuse for approaching her when someone else approached me first.

"The new clerk?" a tall, broad-shouldered man said, intercepting me with arm outstretched.

He was bundled up for the outdoors like the patients, yet two things told me he wasn't one of them: the healthy glow on his handsome, square-jawed face and the lack of a blood bucket in his hand.

Observant, huh? I'm no Sherlock Holmes or even a Gustav "Old Red" Amlingmeyer, but I have my moments.

"That's right. Albert Pycroft," I said. "And you'd be Dr. Swann's assistant Dr. Holly…?"

The man winced almost imperceptibly—except of course I perceived it—as we shook hands. I got the feeling it was the "Dr. Swann's assistant" that had done it. If so, I could sympathize. Playing assistant to my crotchety brother was bad enough. Doing it for a crotchety doctor in a gussied-up leper colony might be even worse.

"Getting settled?" Holly said with a little nod at the stairs behind me.

"Done. Wasn't much settling to do," I said. "Or much room to do it in."

Holly gave that a good-natured chuckle. "Turner used to complain about that, too. Said the only reason he didn't feel like a sardine in a can was because he couldn't have any company."

"Turner was the clerk before me?"

Again, Holly winced—the "Damn…look what I went and stepped in" kind this time.

"Yes, well, pleasant ride up the mountain?" he said quickly.

Turner seemed to be a sore subject.

I made a note to bring it up again first chance I got.

"Lovely, yes," I said. "Came up with a Mr. Melas. New charity patient. I hear you'll be getting acquainted with him soon."

"Indeed." Holly's eyes darted this way and that, and when he went on it was in a hushed voice. "I don't use the c-word around the guests, Mr. Pycroft. They all know who the charity cases are, but pointing it out…it can despoil the healthful harmony we work so hard to nurture."

"Noted," I whispered back. "No c-word around the patients."

"I avoid that one, too, actually," Holly said. "'Patients.' I prefer to say Echo Lake has *guests*…because guests are expected to leave after a pleasant visit. Patients, on the other hand…who can say? You understand?"

I nodded gravely. "Gotcha. No c-word around the p-words."

Holly gave me an uncertain smile. "Yes. Well. Good. And where are you joining us from, Mr. Pycroft?"

I was all set for that inevitable question. My wily colleague in the A.A. Western Detective Agency, Diana Crowe, had helped me prepare a thorough history for my alter ego. A plausible one, too, she'd insisted. No misspent youth taming tigers for Barnum & Bailey for Albert Pycroft...darn it. No, he was to be a fuddy-duddy—former secretary to a hospital administrator in Lincoln, Nebraska. Hobbies and interests: trainspotting, stamp collecting, and watching paint dry. It was going to be a challenge to convince people that I'm dull, but I understood the importance of suppressing my natural ebullience in the interest of discouraging curiosity.

"Nebraska," I said.

That was as far as I got. A sudden explosion of moist, rasping coughs cut me off.

One of the "guests" nearby—a thirty-ish woman with dark, curly hair—was hunched over, hacking into a handkerchief. The redhead was with her, and she put a comforting hand to the woman's shoulder as the white fabric of her hankie turned crimson.

I had to fight the urge to take a big step backwards. Maybe even take a couple dozen that would scoot me right out the door.

Our clients, the Board of Trustees, had assured us there was no danger of infection so long as we didn't go slathering ourselves in someone's "sputum." (A fancy term I learned from Webster's, for the mucusy phlegm hawked up from the lungs. Let it be your Word of the Day. If you manage to work it into casual conversation, let me know and I'll send you a nickel.) Despite the reassurances, it was hard to stay still and composed when someone was retching out her insides ten yards away.

The still I managed. The composed perhaps not.

The coughing woman glanced over at me, pain and embarrassment contorting her features. She raised up a little bucket—identical to the one my brother had been issued—and dropped her soaked hankie into it, revealing lips and chin smeared with blood.

"Are you all right, Leah?" the redhead asked her.

The woman nodded.

"I think so," she said tremulously.

But the words themselves seemed to break something inside her. Her eyes popped, and she lowered her head over her bucket and began hacking so hard it was a wonder her lungs didn't pop out of her mouth.

In fact, something *was* soon coming out. I could hear the little chunks splatter and flecks of blood ricocheted up to dot the woman's face.

I stopped resisting the urge to step back. I stepped.

Holly started forward.

"Excuse me," he said to me.

He hurried to the woman's side and steered her and her friend off toward his office. Despite his coming to help, I noticed the redhead give him a resentful glare as he guided them away. One of the nurses went with them while the orderlies stood around eyeing the floor warily, as if on the hunt for a rat that had dared mingle with the patients.

One of the orderlies pointed down.

The coughing woman had left a thin ribbon of red behind her. The specks were tiny—little bigger than ruby pinpricks in the floor. Yet given what it was—blood possibly straight from the woman's diseased lungs—one touch of it for an orderly or nurse or me could bring slow, painful death.

"We need Sophie out here with a mop," the pointing orderly said.

Meanwhile the remaining nurse had begun shooing everyone —including the blonde I'd been heading for when Dr. Holly inter- cepted me—off to the men's and women's wards on opposite sides of the building. I fancied the young lady gave me a long, lingering look as she went, but then again, I'm prone to fancying such things, so who knows? The orderlies left, too—off to find Sophie and her mop, I assumed.

Within seconds, the lobby was empty and quiet. I'd quickly gone from the center of a crowd to being utterly alone. The only evidence anyone had been there with me a moment before was the faintly glistening trail of fresh blood leading off to the infirmary.

Evening

From what Nurse Rosenkoetter had told me, the patients (and that's how I still thought of them despite Holly's "guest" talk) would now change from their winter clothes into whatever someone wears for pre-dinner bed rest. So this wasn't the time for me to mix amongst them asking a lot of questions. I had the feeling they wouldn't be in the chattiest mood anyway, given what we'd just witnessed in the lobby. That didn't mean I couldn't acquaint myself with them, though.

I headed to the clerk's desk outside Dr. Swann's office and began going through the files.

There were plenty to go through. Most were in a row of stacked drawers of the fancy new sort business-types call "filing cabinets." Others were tucked away in the desk. I know a bit about clerking, having spent time at it for a Kansas granary before hitting the cow trails with my brother. So I could see right off that despite his supposed inefficiency, Turner, my predecessor, had an orderly mind and tidy habits. The paperwork was neat, the files well-organized and clearly labeled.

There was a drawer marked "Bills/Receipts." One marked "Personnel." One marked "Applications/Waiting." One marked "Discharged." One marked, rather mysteriously, "Medical Records (1) A-K" above another marked "Medical Records (1) L-Z" above another marked "Medical Records (2) A-Z." (Why the one? Why the two?) And one marked, even more mysteriously, "D—"

I started with "D——" How could I not? Maybe it stood for "Dirty Pictures."

It didn't. It was just more medical records—files with applications and intake forms and pages of scrawled notes signed either "Swann" or "Holly." (At least I assumed they were signed either "Swann" or "Holly." The signatures were so squished and sloppy they looked more like "Swaaa" and "Homu.")

It took me a while to spot what these particular patients had in common: a notation, signed by one doctor or the other, indicating a date and an hour beside the letters "TOD." After which there were no more notes.

These folks hadn't all been whisked away from Echo Lake by some enigmatic stranger named "Tod"—though I'm sure that's what they would've preferred.

TOD was "Time of Death."

There must have been four dozen files in that drawer. Meaning, given what Swann had said about not moving dead charity patients down the mountain and back to this hometown or the other, there must have been a *lot* of bodies thereabouts. I hadn't spotted a graveyard on our way up, but surely that was by design. The sight of all those crosses would hardly make for a warm welcome to Echo Lake.

I flipped through to the Ps, then the Ws, but each time failed to find what should have been there. There was no Palomares, no Wroblewski.

The files for the two recently deceased charity cases weren't there.

I closed the drawer and went back to "Medical Records (1) L-Z," thinking perhaps the dead men's paperwork simply hadn't been moved to the proper place. Turner had been fired around the time Wroblewski died. Maybe he'd gotten behind on his filing.

Palomares and Wroblewski weren't in "Medical Records (1) L-Z," either. Nor were they to be found in "Medical Records (2) A-Z."

What I did find was an explanation for the (1) and the (2). As I flipped through the first drawer, I saw Lanes and Millers and

Newtons and Olivers and Parkers. As I flipped through the second, I saw Lanzatellas and McCarthys and Nuzzolis and O'Haras and Pacanowskis, mostly from your Clevelands and Chicagos and Pittsburghs.

The paying and charity patients lived mixed in together in the wards. Their filing, on the other hand, was strictly segregated.

Pleased with my detective work (though unsure it meant a damned thing), I moved up to "Medical Records (1) A-K." There was another file I wanted to find—the one for the only (living) patient Old Red and I knew by name. "Miss Johansen."

I hadn't seen her in the charity file. But there she was—"Johansen, Ingrid"—among the Jacksons and Johnsons. I gave her paperwork a skim, then pulled out a few files around it.

I'd begin my review of patient paperwork with a quick inter-view with one Ingrid Johansen. Maybe she'd even turn out to be the blonde I'd spotted. And if our conversation strayed to tragic recent events (and what she'd seen of them)…well, folks would just have to forgive a lowly clerk for being curious.

Heavy footfalls told me I'd soon have company, and I closed the drawer and turned to face Dr. Swann's office with the files under my arm and a prim, professional smile on my face.

When the door swung open, Swann froze a moment, evidently surprised to find me doing exactly what he'd suggested an hour before.

"Oh. Well," he said. "Time for dinner."

He turned and lumbered off toward the lobby. I followed him with the files, thinking they'd give me an excuse to eat with Miss Johansen. But when I stepped into the dining hall, I found the patients already there—and already divvied up with men at one long table and women at another. Dr. Holly, Nurse Rosenkoetter, and a handful of nurses and orderlies were seated at a smaller table—evidently where staff took their meals together.

When Holly saw me taking this all in, he raised a hand and smiled.

When Nurse Rosenkoetter saw me, she just went back to picking at something on her plate with such dour distaste one could only assume she'd been served a heaping helping of sawdust.

The fare—laid out on another table along the wall—turned out to be *slightly* more appetizing than that, though it emphasized heartiness over flavor. Swann picked up a plate and began loading it up with boiled chicken and boiled potatoes and cheese the color of dirty socks. Beyond this cornucopia of blandness were pitchers filled with milk and—providing the one literal bright spot— orange juice.

As I took up a plate for myself, one of the male patients scooched back his chair and walked over to join me. He was a tall, thin fellow with a long oval face and a remarkably small, pinched mouth.

"Welcome to Echo Lake," he said. "You're the new clerk…?"

"That's right. Albert Pycroft."

"Harold Phillips," the man said.

"Pleased to make your acquaintance, Mr. Phillips."

"Likewise, Mr. Pycroft. Some of my fellow guests and I were hoping you'd join us for your first meal here."

He jerked his chin over his bony shoulder, and when I looked past him, I saw an empty chair beside his, at the far end of the men's table. The patients seated near it were watching us with an amused, expectant air.

I was being dared. Did Albert Pycroft have the fortitude—in a ranch-hand bunkhouse, it would've been "the cojones"—to eat his dinner with a bunch of lungers?

The folks at the staff table were watching us, as well, I noticed. So were the lady patients. So were the rest of the men. Hell, if the place had mice, I could only assume they were staring at me, too. Everyone was watching me.

I gave Phillips a smile.

"How kind of you. Just let me fill up my plate here, and I'll be right over." I nodded down at the food table. "Recommend anything?"

"Salt and pepper—and lots of it. But you'll have to smuggle in your own, I'm afraid. Dr. Swann thinks it excites the blood too much for the rest of us."

"Ah, well…can't have excited blood, can we?"

Phillips shrugged in a noncommittal way, clearly unconvinced that keeping his blood nice and calm would make a bit of difference.

"Would you like me to hold those for you, Mr. Pycroft?" He gestured at the file folders still tucked under my left arm. "They look rather precarious there while you're trying to serve yourself."

"Oh. Yes. Thank you." I put my plate back down so I could hand over the files. "I wasn't sure what to expect here in the dining hall, so I came prepared to get a little work done."

"I see," Phillips said. He held his free hand out toward the table behind me. "Please…don't let me keep you from your food any longer."

As he turned and headed back toward the empty chairs, he gave the men seated near them a nod. One of them—a white-haired man with a face so pale and gaunt it looked like Death himself had traded his black cowl for a worsted suit—grinned back at him.

Dr. Swann, meanwhile, appeared far from pleased. In fact, he looked so mad I half-expected him to whip his plate at me like a discus. Some folks don't need salt and pepper to get their blood excited, I guess. All they need is me.

I turned back to the food trays and helped myself to a soppy chicken breast and a potato that crumbled into mushy shards when I speared it with a fork. It wouldn't be the fanciest meal I ever had, but then again I've eaten campfire-roasted Gila monster when times were bad enough on the trail. (Those scaly SOBs are actually rather tasty, provided you don't eat the parts that'll kill you.) I'd survive some over-enthusiastic boiling.

As I headed toward Phillips and the seat beside him, however, I saw something that took away what little appetite I had: Phillips and his friend the skeleton had opened a couple of the folders I'd handed over and were poring over the confidential files inside.

"I told them not to," said a young man across the table from

Phillips beside Death. He was slender and sallow, like most everyone around him, with a wispy little blonde mustache that seemed to be his signal that he wasn't the gawky schoolboy he resembled.

I glanced past him to see if Dr. Swann or Dr. Holly or Nurse Rosenkoetter had noticed what Phillips and his other friend were up to. Though Swann was still fuming he wasn't hurling his big bulk over his chicken and potatoes to come snatch the files away. And Holly and Nurse Rosenkoetter were merely watching me curiously and coldly, respectively, so they didn't seem to realize the size of my mistake either.

I was a fool, but so far as they knew, not one Phillips had managed to take full advantage of yet.

"Good thing there's nothing in those files but invoices for milk deliveries," I said for the benefit of the other male patients a little further up the table. "Otherwise you could've put me in quite a pickle...am I right?"

I sat down and stared hard at Phillips.

He smirked back at me a moment, then closed the folder before him and slid it my way.

"We certainly wouldn't want to do that, would we, Foster?" he said.

"Of course not," said Death—a.k.a. "Foster," apparently. "What kind of welcome to Echo Lake would that be?"

"A mighty bad one," I said.

Foster grunted out a chuckle. He was a middle-aged gent in what was probably a well-tailored suit before the consumption consumed every ounce of fat on him. His white hair, I noticed now, wasn't just short but patchy, with naked scalp showing like scraps of fish belly slapped here and there across his head. He gave me a skeletal leer before closing his folder and pushing it over to me.

I gathered and stacked the folders, then picked up a fork.

"I already feel like I'm getting to know you fellows—to my chagrin—but perhaps some introductions would be in order...?" I said.

Phillips held a hand out toward Foster.

"Mr. William Foster of Philadelphia," he said. He swung the hand over to the younger fellow with the gossamer mustache. "And Leslie Breckinridge of Hartford, Connecticut."

Phillips didn't bother with any of the men to his left, though most were watching us curiously. Apparently he, Foster, and Breckinridge were their own little clique.

"Albert Pycroft, most recently of Lincoln, Nebraska," I said. I took a bite of potato. It had all the zesty tang of a baked dishrag. "So what's next on your agenda? Short-sheeting my bed or slipping a toad down the back of my shirt?"

"Both excellent ideas!" Phillips said. He stroked his jutting jaw. "Decisions, decisions…"

The man wasn't making a great impression on me. He was the first tuberculosis patient I'd gotten acquainted with, and already I was rooting for the tuberculosis.

Foster chuckled again.

"Sorry to have taken advantage, Pycroft," he said, not looking sorry in the slightest. "You must understand—most of the time, we're monstrously bored here. There's usually nothing to do but eat flavorless food and go for tedious walks and stare at the same dull walls and vapid faces. You simply offered an opportunity to break the tedium."

"Well, that's all right then," I said. "I'm just pleased endangering my employment could bring you such enjoyment. If I'd known you were so starved for entertainment, I would've brought along some flies you could pull the wings off. Or perhaps you don't need 'em since you've got clerks to torture."

"Oh, there's no need for *us* to torture clerks," Phillips said. "They do that quite capably themselves."

Foster went for an outright laugh this time. Breckinridge looked like he wanted to join in but couldn't quite bring himself to do it.

"I can see what *I've* done that might qualify as self-torture," I said to Phillips. "Here I am sitting next to you. But if you want me to understand how that applies to any other clerks, you'll have to speak a little plainer."

Phillips and Foster looked at each other with amusement. Needling me really was just a diverting pastime for these two, and any slights slung in reply were simply part of the fun.

Phillips turned back to me with his little puckered prune of a mouth twisted into a self-satisfied sneer.

"If those 'invoices' you loaned us were as thorough as they could be, you'd find the answer there," he said. "A special notation in Miss Johansen's file under the heading 'Romances, Doomed.'"

"'Lovers, Star-Crossed,'" Foster added.

"'Taste, Bad,'" Breckinridge muttered.

Phillips laughed and jerked his head at the young man across the table from me.

"Breckinridge wishes *he* were a notation in Miss Johansen's file," he said.

"He isn't?" said Foster. "Under 'Suitors, Spurned'?"

"Shut up," Breckinridge said, looking like he wanted to sink under the table and die. Given his all-around pallor, he seemed entirely capable of it.

"Is that why there was an opening for a clerk?" I said. "Turner couldn't keep his mind on his files?"

Phillips shrugged. "Something like that. The exact details were never shared with us lowly, unimportant patients."

"'Guests,'" Foster corrected with a smile.

"Inmates," Breckinridge said.

I tried a bite of chicken.

"Uh oh—cooks messed up with this one," I said as I chewed. "Accidentally left some taste in it."

I leaned forward toward Breckinridge.

"Would you mind pointing out this Miss Johansen?" I said. "I'm double-checking everyone's information, you see."

"Miss Johansen?" Phillips said loudly. He sat up straight and scanned the female patients seated between us and the staff table. "That's her."

He pointed with a little jab of his fork.

The lady in question stared back at us from halfway down the women's table. Her face was already familiar: She was indeed the blonde I'd started toward in the lobby. My instinct for which young ladies to approach has failed me on many an occasion, so it was nice to see that this once it had been correct, even if foiled by circumstances.

Miss Johansen didn't seem thrilled to be the object of Phillips's attention, but she did at least attempt a smile for me.

I nodded and smiled back.

"I understand the poor woman had quite a shock recently," I said.

"Oh...you mean finding that dead Polack in the woods?" said Phillips.

Breckinridge winced, and a few of the men further down the table looked up from their grub to glare.

"Is that why you wanted to speak with her first?" Foster asked me. He waggled his alabaster eyebrows. "Or did you pick her out for her age?"

"I chose those files at random," I said.

"Sure, you did," said Phillips.

He gave Foster and Breckinridge a big wink.

I cleared my throat and cut off a crumbly piece of potato I had no desire to eat.

"So what else do you do around here for fun other than gossip and try to get clerks fired?" I said.

Phillips sighed and rolled his eyes but otherwise didn't protest the ungraceful change of subject.

"We take long walks," he said. "We write letters to our loved ones...if any still love *us*. We observe the deterioration and death of those around us. We deteriorate and die ourselves. It's a regular Coney Island."

"There are also arts and crafts," Foster told me with mock seriousness. "I've become rather partial to pottery."

"Foster is making an urn for himself," said Phillips. "It's touchingly optimistic, actually. You know—seeing as we don't have a crematorium here."

Foster shrugged. "I'm hoping they'll fire me in the kiln when I go."

"Cheerful company you keep," I said to Breckinridge.

He was trying to look amused and not entirely succeeding.

"Nothing they say isn't true," he said. "Well…except perhaps for the part about the kiln. They know Dr. Swann and Nurse Rosenkoetter wouldn't stand for that. The grounds need fertilizing. We'll all be enriching the soil by and by."

"Not here, I won't. My spot's already picked out in the family plot," said Phillips. He leaned toward me and dropped his voice to a whisper. "The graveyard here is altogether too democratic if you know what I mean. There's no telling who you'd end up rubbing elbow bones with for all eternity."

"They say Dr. Holly even wants Echo Lake to start admitting *Blacks*," Foster added.

He and Phillips looked at each other and shivered.

It no longer seemed mysterious to me that one of the patient deaths we were looking into involved a man slitting his wrists with a scalpel. If one had been handy, I'd have been tempted to follow suit just to escape my present company.

"So…any of you fellows follow baseball?" I said.

I was giving up on investigating. My goal now was to eat as much as my suddenly nonexistent appetite would allow before escaping to try again with someone else.

Foster *was* a baseball fan—it turned out he loved it almost as much as lugubrious sarcasm—and despite the obviousness of my ploy, he took the bait. He bored the others with talk of the Phillies' chances in the upcoming season while I polished off my potato and most of my chicken breast. It was easy to do, actually, as the food was so soggy it didn't require chewing. I could've sucked up my dinner with a straw.

"Thank you, gentlemen," I said when I'd stowed away enough to get me through until breakfast. "It's been…something."

"Our pleasure," said Foster.

"Well, I wouldn't go that far," said Phillips—though clearly my discomfort had indeed brought him plenty of pleasure indeed.

"Nice to meet you," Breckinridge mumbled. He looked ashamed of the impression they'd made. Perhaps I'd try again with him later, away from bad influences.

I scooped up the files and my plate and made my escape.

There was a small side table near the door to the kitchen upon which folks had been piling their dirty dishes, so I headed that way. I took care not to let my gaze stray to the staff table, but I imagined I could feel both the heat of Swann's stare and the icy disdain of Nurse Rosenkoetter's. As I put down my plate, I heard movement behind me, and I turned, half-expecting to find either the doctor or the nurse stepping up to lecture me about dining amongst the patients.

Instead I found myself face-to-face with one of those patients. The very one I'd been hoping to speak to, in fact.

"Excuse me," said Miss Johansen.

She had her own plate in her dainty hands. Apparently, the young lady had finished her meal at precisely the same moment as me. Quite a fortuitous coincidence. Or not.

I stepped out of her way.

"Excuse *me*," I said.

She gave me a smile, then moved past to put her plate atop mine.

"If I may inquire," I said as she turned around again, "would you happen to be Miss Ingrid Johansen of Evanston, Illinois?"

"Why, yes. I am. Why do you ask?"

She batted her eyes. And lovely eyes they were—the powder blue of a Kansas summer sky. Her skin was as white as the clouds you might see in such a sky, as well. She was such a wispy-pale thing it seemed you could see right through if you stared hard enough.

I explained that I was the new clerk and was making a review of the files and had by complete happenstance, pulled hers as one of the first to double-check. Would she mind confirming her particulars for me?

"Not at all," she said. "I'd be happy to assist you in any way I can."

She seemed on the verge of another eye-bat, but two more patients—a couple older ladies who excused themselves with looks of self-satisfied amusement on their sallow faces—stepped up with their own dirty dishes to deposit. I got the feeling folks had been making bets as to when Miss Johansen and I would strike up a conversation, and if so these two looked to have played the odds just right.

"I was just about to go to the women's parlor to do some reading," Miss Johansen said to me. "Perhaps we could have our conversation there?"

"A splendid idea. Shall we?"

I held a hand out toward the door. Under normal circumstances, I might have offered the young lady my arm. Purely out of politeness, you understand. But I figured such familiarity, even offered with the proper decorousness, would be more than Dr. Swann and Nurse Rosenkoetter could tolerate.

It also would have brought me in contact with the peculiar jewelry dangling from Miss Johansen's bony wrist. Her bucket. Currently clean, so far as one could tell with the naked eye, yet I hardly wanted to put that to the test. It had been unpleasant enough contending with the bunkhouse lice I picked up from time to time in my cowhand days. Tuberculosis would make a head full of nits seem like an ice cream social.

As we made our way toward the lobby, I flipped open Miss Johansen's file and pulled out a pencil. I didn't shout out "Look, everybody—I'm just going about boring ol' clerking business exactly as you'd expect! Nothin' to see here!" but I may as well have.

Before we even made it to the parlor, Miss Johansen had confirmed her home address, her parents' names, her marital status ("available"), and her age (twenty-one—though I also got a coquettish reminder that a gentleman isn't supposed to ask). In the parlor—a large, carpeted room in the lady's wing with high windows looking out upon the road down the mountain—we settled into side-by-side armchairs and moved quickly through her medical history. (Quickly both because I lacked the expertise to decipher most of the scribbled notes and it was so apparent that the lady's enthusiasm for chitchat was wasting away every second we talked TB)

"One final question," I said. "I see a notation here that you recently had an upsetting experience. The details are hazy, however. I hate to make you speak of anything unpleasant, but would you mind providing a few particulars?"

Miss Johansen looked down at the file in surprise. "That's in there?"

It wasn't actually. But how was she to know that when the chicken scratch on the paperwork was five feet away and, for her, upside down?

"Dr. Swann was concerned about the impact it might have upon you," I said. "You know the staff here does all they can to keep things…tranquil. I don't know what happened, but it sounds anything but."

The young lady turned away to stare out the nearest window. Dusk was giving way to night outside, and the distant peaks had faded to a line of jagged black cutting across a purple-gray horizon. Of the road and the trees one could see nothing already. Before, the sanitorium had seemed like an out-of-place dollop of civilization in the midst of the wilderness. Soon, when the last trace of light had died, it would seem like a lonely dollop of *something* in the midst of utter *nothing*.

I would say Miss Johansen heaved a sigh, but the heaving of anything seemed beyond her. She took in a deep breath that turned wheezy, hacked out a little embarrassed cough, then slowly, carefully exhaled lest the coughing grow worse and her bucket be needed.

"One of the male guests died in the woods," she said softly. "I found him. That's all."

"I'm sorry. I'm sure that was most upsetting. Was he a friend?"

Miss Johansen shot me a sidelong, irritated frown, then quickly smoothed her features into something more appropriately placid and sad.

"I barely knew him," she said. "Mr. Wroblewski was in his

thirties, I believe. Some sort of factory worker. If you're curious about him, perhaps you could ask Mrs. Kowalska or Mrs. Goldman."

She nodded at two older ladies—the same ones from the dining room—who'd settled in to read by the fireplace nearby. One looked up from her Bible and smiled. The other stayed hidden behind her *Ladies' Home Journal*.

"It's you I'm curious about," I said.

Miss Johansen smiled.

"And your experience that day," I went on.

Miss Johansen frowned.

"You were out taking the air alone when it happened?"

"Yes," the young lady said curtly. "I was walking. Near the north end of the lake. It was the warmest day we'd had in weeks, and all the other patients were having a baseball game. Well, except for Mr. Wroblewski."

"A baseball game?"

It seemed like the kind of hogwash Foster and Phillips would have tried out on me. But there was no sign Miss Johansen was joking. In fact, she couldn't have looked less amused.

"Mr. Foster's family sent him gloves and bats and balls for Christmas," she said. "Most of us found the idea ludicrous, of course—people of such delicate health roughhousing in the dirt. But Dr. Swann liked the idea. Said it might help us rebuild our vigor…provided we didn't become over-excited. He needn't have worried, in my opinion. There are few things less exciting than an afternoon of baseball. At any rate, the first day it felt even vaguely spring-like, the men organized a game. The women organized a picnic and watched."

"And you and Wroblewski organized long walks alone by the lake."

Miss Johansen shrugged. "I guess he wasn't a sports enthusiast. I'm certainly not. I prefer solitude and the splendors of nature."

The woman behind the *Ladies' Home Journal* let out a little cough. Or maybe it was more of a snort.

"Anyway," Miss Johansen said, "I heard a splash in the lake, and when I turned that way, I saw Mr. Wroblewski tumbling down into the rocks by the eastern shore. I started toward him, but I could tell from how he stopped…the way he lay sprawled there on his back…the limpness…blank, staring eyes up pointed up at the sun…"

The young lady sniffled and put her fingers to her forehead.

I did the gentlemanly thing and offered her a handkerchief. The generous thing, too, for I certainly didn't want that hankie back after she took it, no matter how demurely she pressed it to her nose. The tuberculosis bug wouldn't be stopped by "demure."

"Thank you," Miss Johansen said. "It *is* upsetting to recall."

"Thank *you*. I appreciate your going through it again for me."

I made a show of adding more notes to her file, even though all I was scribbling was, literally, *Scribble scribble scribble*.

"I must admit it's been more draining than I anticipated," Miss Johansen said. "I think I should turn in early. Perhaps we could carry on our conversation tomorrow. When I have more energy."

She threw a little sidelong glance at the ladies pretending to be absorbed in their reading nearby.

And when we have more privacy, she was adding.

"Of course," I said. "I just have a few more details to double-check. Purely administrative matters. Nothing upsetting, I promise."

"Fine. Until tomorrow then."

We both rose, and I gave her a "Good night" before she headed toward the door. As she left, I noticed that the redhead who'd caught my eye earlier had joined us in the parlor. She was seated on the other side of the room bent over a jigsaw puzzle, but I caught her peeping up at me for a second. She and Miss Johansen ignored each other.

"So you're curious about Wroblewski, hmm?" someone said.

I turned to find that the woman behind the *Ladies' Home Journal* had finally lowered it.

"Just making sure the records are thorough, Mrs….?"

"I am Goldman," the woman said. She jerked her head at the lady with the Bible. "She is Kowalska."

I gave both women a smile and a nod.

"Pleased to meet you. I'm Albert—"

"Yes, yes. Albert Pycroft, the new clerk," Mrs. Goldman cut in. "Do you want to know what *really* happened to Wroblewski? *Not* a friendly man—such a grouch, even when he was practically well enough to go home—but he didn't deserve what happened to him."

"Oh, Bitsy," Mrs. Kowalska groaned, rolling her eyes.

Mrs. Goldman didn't stop.

"'Fainted and hit his head'—that's what you'll see in *his* records," she said. "But I don't believe it for a second."

"Really?"

I sat back down and got my pencil ready for more scribbling.

Mrs. Goldman leaned a little closer. (Though not *too* close, thankfully. It would've been rude for me to lean away from her, but I wasn't going to let her breathe in my face, even if she was about to whisper the name of a murderer. Her eyes still flashed with the spark of life and vitality, but the face around them was drawn and pale.)

"Dr. Swann doesn't want anyone to know," she said. "I've seen them, though. They watch us in the woods. They sneak in close at night. Even come inside sometimes. To steal things. And now they've *killed.*"

"'They'?" I said.

Mrs. Goldman nodded gravely.

Mrs. Kowalska sighed in a way that made me think her friend was about to lean in even closer and say, "The Leprechauns."

"The Indians," Mrs. Goldman said instead.

"Indians?"

Mrs. Goldman gave me another nod.

Mrs. Kowalska shook her head.

"What kind of Indians?" I said.

"What kind? How should I know what kind?" said Mrs. Goldman. "I'm from the Bronx."

"They're the skulking-around-in-the-dark-and-only-Bitsy-can-see-them kind," said Mrs. Kowalska.

"Ah," I said. "I know the tribe well."

I did, too. They tended to be spotted by jumpy pilgrims from the east who imagined Sitting Bull and Crazy Horse were alive and well and eyeing their scalps.

"Let me tell you something, Mr. Pycroft," Mrs. Goldman said. "Write it down in my file if you want."

She held up her left hand, the thumb and forefinger an inch apart.

"You see that?" she said. "That's my bladder."

"Oh, Bitsy!" Mrs. Kowalska said.

"A thimble!" Mrs. Goldman went on. "So I'm up every night two, three times. How can people sleep with all the coughing and gasping around here, anyway? When we may as well be lying in the same bed, the way they pack us in together? I can't. Sleep? What's that? So who's going to see the Indians come out at night? Who's going to hear them? Me."

"Or the night nurses," said Mrs. Kowalska. "Only they *don't* see."

Mrs. Goldman waved that away as if it were a pesky fly.

"They have work to do," she said. She slapped the magazine resting on her lap. "Or they're reading *Ladies' Home Journal*."

Mrs. Kowalska shook her head again, then leaned in toward me as Mrs. Goldman had. She was as withered and white as her friend—so gaunt one couldn't even call her death warmed over. Both women looked like death served cold.

"Plenty of people besides Indians like to sneak around at night," she said.

She gave me a knowing look. Which was a bit frustrating since she was doing all the knowing.

I said what one does when one hopes the knowing can get spread around a little more liberally.

"Oh?"

"Well, for instance…" Mrs. Kowalska began.

It's also where she stopped.

A hard, quick *clack-clack-clack* on the floorboards grew steadily louder, and we all turned to find Nurse Rosenkoetter striding toward us. Toward *me*, her cold, steady stare soon made clear.

"Mr. Pycroft," she said. "If you please."

She stopped, back ramrod straight like a soldier on review, and nodded toward the doorway behind her.

Let's go, the gesture said.

"Thank you for the conversation, ladies," I said to Mrs. Goldman and Mrs. Kowalska as I stood. I gave the files in my hand a little jiggle. "We'll be talking more soon. I plan on double-checking all the guests' particulars."

"I'll be looking forward to it," said Mrs. Kowalska.

"Remember what I told you," whispered Mrs. Goldman. "Watch out. Don't get tomahawked."

"Thank you, ma'am," I whispered back. "I'll try."

When I turned to join Nurse Rosenkoetter, I caught the redhead looking at me again from her spot across the room. Our eyes locked now, and I gave her a friendly nod.

She just went back to her puzzle. So I went back to mine.

"There something I can do for you?" I asked Nurse Rosenkoetter.

I expected a lecture about stirring up the patients. Instead she spun on her heel and led me from the room in silence.

"It's Mr. Melas," she said, voice low, when we were out in the hallway. "He's gone."

Night

"What do you mean 'gone'?" I spluttered. Because that's what would've been expected. Surprise.

I wasn't shocked, though. Just irritated.

My brother couldn't leave the detecting to me, even for a few hours. Instead of trusting me to do the nosing around, he had to sneak out to stick *his* big nose in…and then get caught doing it.

"One of the orderlies brought him dinner, but he wasn't there," Nurse Rosenkoetter said. "Now I'll have to send all the orderlies out searching for him if he doesn't turn up soon. Did he say anything to you that might indicate where he might've gone?"

I nodded and snapped my fingers.

"You know what? He sure did. Said he couldn't wait to get a look at the lake. Big fishing enthusiast. Wondered if y'all might have trout. Of course, I told him that'd have to wait till his quarantine was over. But I betcha he decided a little early peek couldn't hurt. You know how anglers get. All twitchy if they don't have a pole in their hands and a fly in the water. Tell you what. I'll go see if I can't rustle up our Mr. Melas before you have to send the orderlies out into the cold. They've got their regular duties to attend to, and me, I'm just settling in. It'll probably take me all of five minutes to find the man without disturbing anyone else's routine. And don't you worry—I'll give him a good talking to about following the rules."

Nurse Rosenkoetter eyed me dubiously a moment. She'd marched us from the women's wing out into the lobby by then, and she stopped by the foot of the stairs and gave me a curt nod.

"Fine. See if you can find him on your own. As you say, we've already had enough disruptions to our routine today."

She put some extra ice in her expression to let me know I'd done most of the disrupting.

"I understand, ma'am," I said. I hurriedly turned to go. "I'll just run up and grab my coat and…"

I stopped with genuine reluctance and moved in closer instead. Anxious as I was to make my escape from the lady, there was a question to ask first.

"You know…Mrs. Goldman just told me something interesting. She claims there's Indians about. You think there's anything to that?"

Nurse Rosenkoetter scowled and gave the very idea a dismissive snort.

"Certainly not," she said. "I take it from your accent you're not from the east?"

I fought the urge to say, "Accent? What accent?" I've been working to sound less like the farmboy-turned-cowboy I used to be. I guess I need to work harder.

"That's right, ma'am. I'm from Nebraska."

"Well, you know how Easterners are. They don't understand the West. It's all cowboys and bandits and wild Indians to them. In reality, any Indians were cleared out of this region decades ago. There was a mining camp a mile or two east of here, but that's been abandoned for years, as well. That's why Echo Lake is the perfect location for an institution like ours. Isolation is critical, both to inhibit the spread of the disease and to give those afflicted with it the peace and tranquility necessary if there is to be any hope of recovery. Wild talk of skulking savages destroys that peace and tranquility, Mr. Pycroft. I hope you will not indulge it—or indulge in it—again."

I did my best to look appropriately chastened.

"I understand," I said. "I'll just go peel Mr. Melas away from the lake and get him tucked in again in his cabin. Please don't trouble yourself or the orderlies any further. Good night, ma'am."

I turned and hurried up the stairs. I didn't hear a "Good night" in reply as I went.

Up in my mousehole on the second floor, I passed by the coat and cap on their pegs and went first to the carpetbag on the little sliver of a cot. At the bottom, beneath the assorted clothes and toiletries and magazines, was my Webley Bulldog. I pulled it out, laid it on the bed next to the file folders I'd been carrying around, then slipped it into a pocket once I had my overcoat on.

Nurse Rosenkoetter may have scoffed at the idea of "skulking savages," but a man had been brained in the woods not a mile away. I didn't think an Indian had done it, but perhaps *someone* other than gravity had. Until I knew for sure, I wasn't going to do any skulking of my own without my Bulldog by my side.

It was one of those clear mountain nights the stars are so bright and bountiful it looks like you could reach up and scorch your fingertips on them. The moon was but a sliver, though—a slicing gash of light that shared little of its shine with the likes of me so far below. I was quickly kicking myself for not asking for a lantern before heading out into the darkness. I could make out the low outlines of the cottages just east of the main building, though, and I headed toward the one Old Red had been deposited in, moving slowly lest I stumble over stones or stray baseballs or another dead lunger.

"Mr. Melas?" I said. "Oh, Mr. Melas! You out here?"

No answer. And no light I could see in my brother's cabin. Which meant I had no idea where he was.

I looked toward the lake. Old Red was no angler, so I didn't really expect him to be down there scouting for spots to settle in with rod and reel. The water was a patchwork quilt, star-dappled black alternating with splotches of hazy gray where the spring thaw hadn't melted through the ice yet. If my brother was nearby looking for the place Wroblewski had died, he'd have little luck without a lantern of his own, and I saw no yellow glow moving along the shore or the slopes beyond.

"Damn it, Brother," I muttered, and I slipped a hand into the coat pocket that held my gun.

I'd started off annoyed. Now I was getting worried.

What if Old Red hadn't crept out to do some snooping? What if Echo Lake really did have its own resident killer, who'd spied new prey left alone for easy picking? What if that killer saw more new prey blundering through the dark looking for the fool brother who'd dragged them into detective work—and up a lonely mountain to their doom?

Indeed, I did have the skin-tingling feeling I was being watched. There were plenty of black corners someone could be peeping around, and not far off was forest that could hide a thousand eyes. A whole tribe of Mrs. Goldman's Indians, perhaps, eager to make up for years of laying low and keeping their war clubs clean.

"This'll make quite an exciting sequence when I write it up for *Smythe's Frontier Detective*," I murmured to myself.

Looking for silver linings, you see. It is my intention to die happy.

And then suddenly there it was. The sound of approaching footsteps. The ghostly ectoplasmic cloud of expelled breath from beyond the nearest cottage. An obsidian shape emerging from the gloom.

I tightened my grip on my gun.

The dark shape stopped.

"Oh. There you are," it said. "Your sneakin's gettin' better. Usually I can hear you a mile off."

I sighed.

It was Old Red, of course. He looked at the hand I had jammed into my pocket.

"You ain't about to shoot me, are you?"

"I don't know," I said. "I'm still thinking it over."

But I slipped my hand out and pointed at his cottage.

"Can we get inside? We got things to talk about, *Mr. Melas*, and I'd rather not freeze my ass off while we do it."

My brother grunted and limped off toward the door.

A few minutes later, after Old Red stoked up the smoldering fire in the little cabin's stove, I was settled in the room's only chair while he sat back on the one piece of furniture left to him—the narrow bed.

"One of the orderlies came out with supper while you were gallivanting around," I said. "Nurse Rosenkoetter was gonna send a search party out for you till I told her a cock-and-bull story about you being fired up to fish the lake."

My brother gave me a skeptical look.

"Hey, I thought it wasn't bad as cock-and-bull stories go," I said. "I had all of one second to come up with something, thanks to you. All you had to do was stay nestled up all comfy-cozy, but no. You had to go for a stroll."

"'My mind rebels at stagnation,'" Old Red said. "'Give me problems. Give me work!'"

He was quoting Sherlock Holmes, of course. I was in no mood for it.

"You had work: Stay here like the sickly man you're supposed to be…and half still are," I said. "If you were bored, you coulda just pulled out your *McGuffey's* and practiced your A-B-Cs."

My brother swiped a hand at me.

"Feh," he said.

Eloquent, ain't he?

"'My mind rebels at stagnation,'" I said with a sneer. "Well, 'Feh!' to that! That's just using The Man as an excuse. You don't think patience is part of The Method? You don't think Mr. Holmes knew how to bide his time?"

"I'm sure he did," Old Red snapped back. "But then he didn't have to worry about Doc Watson boogerin' everything up while he was bidin'."

"And you *do* have to worry about *me?*"

"Quite a mess you made in El Paso without me."

"So me and that newspaper fella ran up a little tab! The agency still cleared more than three thousand dollars, and we got us some good publicity."

"'Good publicity'? That bull? Now if I'd been there——"

"The agency would've cleared a wee bit more, and I would've had a lot less fun."

"Fun? *Fun?* Are we in this business for fun?"

"Yes, we are, actually. Your idea of fun. Prying and spying and stirring up trouble. And that's *so* much fun to you, you couldn't stay out of it for one damn day. No, you had to toss the plan out the window and get noticed creeping out to meddle. So let me ask you: Who did the boogerin' this time?"

Old Red clamped his mouth shut and glared at me. Then he sagged and looked away and let out a long breath.

It was a miracle.

I'd won the argument. For the moment.

"What were you looking for, anyway?" I asked.

"The place the second patient died. Tracks." My brother shrugged. "Whatever else I might find."

"So you were just taking shots in the dark, in other words. Cuz you were bored."

Old Red met my gaze again, the fire quickly rekindling in his eyes.

"I found what I was lookin' for," he said. "Too much of it, in fact."

"What does that mean?"

"It means I'm pretty sure I can tell where that fella tumbled down to the lakeshore. There's still skids in the mud and blood on the rocks all these days later. But it looks like half the lungers here have managed to haul their scrawny asses up to the ridge to see it for themselves. If there really is a killer, and *if* he left tracks, it's all under a hundred other footprints now."

"You didn't happen to notice any moccasins in among those prints, did you?"

"Moccasins? No." Old Red rolled his eyes. "Don't tell me someone's tryin' to blame the murder on Indians."

"Brother...someone is trying to blame the murder on Indians."

"I told you not to tell me. Well...as long as you got started, you may as well carry on and give me the details."

So I did. When I was done passing along what Mrs. Goldman had said—about seeing Indians sneaking around stealing things—my brother shook his head.

"Mighta been Utes or Cheyenne or Arapaho up here once upon a time, but not since you were in diapers. Hell—don't look like a soul's called this place home since Jehovah made it."

"Nurse Rosenkoetter mentioned a mining camp. Off to the east, she said. But yeah—apparently that's deserted, too. Until they started building the sanitorium seems like there was nobody up here but sheep and deer."

"And the occasional moose," Old Red reminded me.

"Yes. And the occasional moose. Not the strongest murder suspect." I rubbed my chin. "Who knows, though? I don't believe I've ever seen one angry. Maybe they're real bastards if you rile 'em up."

My brother eyed me dubiously.

"I *am* joking," I assured him.

"Thanks for lettin' me know. It's hard to tell sometimes," he said. "And by the way, I *have* seen an angry moose, and he was quite a handful. But even with all the trompin' around folks did on that ridge, it wouldn't have been enough to cover up moose tracks."

I nodded gravely. "So we're ruling out the moose. This is excellent progress we're making."

"You were the one who was supposed to be makin' all the progress. I was supposed to be sittin' here twiddlin' my thumbs till they fall off. So…you got anything for me other than 'Indians' we know ain't here?"

"Well, it just so happens I do."

I didn't have *much* more than nonexistent Indians, but I wasn't going to let on that I knew that.

I proceeded to tell my brother about the gloom and cruelty I'd seen in some of the male patients; their resentment of the charity cases; their unhappiness with Dr. Holly for suggesting Blacks be admitted among them; the missing files for the dead men, Palomares and Wroblewski; the unexpected baseball game the day of Wroblewski's death; the seeming flirtation (or more?) between Miss Johansen, the woman who found Wroblewski's body, and my predecessor Turner; and the noise the young lady heard that drew her attention to the lake around the time Wrob-lewski died.

It was that last that had Old Red bolting up straight on the bed.

"Noise? What kinda noise?"

"A splash."

"What kinda splash?"

"What do you mean what kinda splash?"

"I mean was it a 'ker-SPLOSH!' or a 'splish-splish-splish' or a 'SPLASH-splish-splish' or what?"

"Miss Johansen didn't say."

"And you didn't ask?"

"No. It just sorta glided by in the conversation. I didn't think to pull out a tub of water and make the lady recreate it."

My brother stamped his left foot down hard on the floor-boards. "Damn it! I knew you wouldn't ask the right questions!"

"'The right questions' being 'Was it a ker-SPLOSH or a splish-splish-splish?'"

"Yes! It makes all the difference!"

"Alright, then—if I'm so incompetent, you take over being Pycroft. I'll stay out here and be Melas and have me a nice little vacation while *you* do all the work."

"If only I could! I need clay to make bricks, and all you can bring me is crap! Col. Crowe should've sent me here with Diana or Burr. Hell, Capt. Zimmer would do a better job than you."

You'd think I'd be used to my brother's insults by now, but this one hit me like a slap.

Yes, I'd made missteps. Yes, I hadn't asked all the right questions. I was doing my best, though, and I didn't think that was half-bad. Yet here was Old Red telling me he had more faith in our little detective agency's other operatives...and even Captain Zimmer. Colonel Crowe's dog.

"Well, don't worry—you won't have to rely on your big, dumb brother much longer," I said, getting to my feet. "Just one more day sitting on your ass and you'll be free to come inside and ask about ker-SPLOSHes and splish-splish-splishes to your heart's content. Now I'm leaving before that crusty nurse sends a search party out looking for *me*."

"Fine! Go! And the next time you come around, do it with data!"

Old Red's magazines and books had been spread out on the foot of his bed, and he reached over, snatched up the December *McClure's*, and stuck his prodigious nose in it.

It was the issue with "The Final Problem"—the story that told the tale of Sherlock Holmes's death. Though he'd been working on his reading, my brother still wasn't far beyond "See John run. Run, John, run!" A Doc Watson story would take him days. Why he'd want to spend all those hours reliving the death of his hero was beyond me, especially with Death himself so at home thereabouts. If you wanted to feel gloomy, all you had to do was look around.

Me, I'd had enough gloom for one day. And enough of Gustav Amlingmeyer.

I stomped out without another word.

I might have been through with gloom, but I quickly discovered that it wasn't through with me. The wind had both picked up and cooled down, chilling me to the bone in seconds, and a wall of dark cloud had appeared to the west, swallowing the peaks and stars there—indeed the whole horizon.

The creepy-crawly feeling that I was being watched soon returned, as well. I looked this way and that as I hustled from Old Red's cottage, half-expecting to spot one of the supposedly nonexistent Indians staring back at me. The whole Sioux nation could've been out there gawking at me unseen for all I knew, so dark had it become.

I had a little light to navigate by as I neared the main building, thanks to the windows facing the lake. In one, I noticed—the window to the very parlor room I'd been in a while before—was the silhouette of a woman looking out at me. Whoever it was, she ducked away before I could make out her features. Yet even with whoever it was gone, the sense that eyes were upon me remained.

It was a relief to finally get back inside the sanitorium—but not as much of a relief as I'd have wished. The gas lamps were turned down low, bathing the lobby and halls in a drab, dull glow that hurt my eyes. Warmth, I found as I started to unbutton my coat only to button it right back up again, was no more abundant than light. Cold, fresh air was Dr. Swann's prescription for his patients, and I guess the staff had to put up with a regular dose, as well.

In other words, it was cold as hell in there.

From the low, distant murmurs from the men's and women's wings, I took it that things were winding down for the night. Nurse Rosenkoetter stepped from the infirmary as I headed for the stairs, looking like she expected explanations. I just gave her a wave and a "Found him and tucked him in!" without slowing down. I heard hacking, strangled coughs coming from behind her and thought of the woman with the dark curly hair—Leah Blum—who'd had an attack in the lobby earlier. If it was her, she sounded even worse off than before.

Nurse Rosenkoetter closed the door to the infirmary. It must have been a thick one—by design most likely—for the sound of coughing instantly stopped.

Back in my room, I hung up my cap (my coat would remain wrapped around me till I could slip under the covers), then turned to the tiny bed. I was curious to see how much of myself I could actually fit upon it. I froze before I could try.

Something was on the bed already. And not my carpetbag or the patient files I'd left there myself.

Nestled atop the dingy, thin pillow was a cardboard shoebox with a red ribbon wrapped around it. A folded piece of paper was tucked beneath the ribbon. Written on it were the words "For our new friend."

I slid the note out and opened it up.

> *Dear Albert—*
> *We look forward to getting to know you!*
> *—The Welcoming Committee*

I put the note on the bed and picked up the box. It had a little weight to it that filled me with hope. Just enough for some cookies or a nice slice of pie. I'd forced myself to eat enough boiled chicken and potatoes to get me through the night, but something with actual flavor would be a sweeter way to end a distasteful day.

I untied the ribbon and flipped up the lid.

Some of what was inside the box was quickly *outside* the box—racing up my arm on the left, scuttling over my wrist and dropping onto the bed on the right. I yelped and slapped at the one making a beeline for my left shoulder. In the process I let go of the box, and when it hit the sheets, more plump, glistening, brown shapes raced out.

The box had been filled with roaches. Big ones—longer and

fatter than a man's thumb. There might have been as many as a dozen. I wasn't going to pause to get an exact count as they scattered. I still had one scurrying up my upper arm with plans, it seemed, to take up residence in my ear. I gave him another slap that sent him soaring toward the door—minus several legs and sundry other parts, which he left as a parting gift on my palm.

"Crap! Shit!" I cried. "Gawdesus!"

I think the "Gawdesus!" was a combination of "Goddamn!" and "Jesus!" I was so filled with shock and disgust I couldn't even blaspheme properly.

I stood there a moment, panting, as my guests quickly made themselves at home in various corners and crannies.

What kind of sick bastard would do something like this? I thought.

But I already knew the answer.

A literally sick bastard. A dying bastard. A bored and cruel and doomed bastard.

Probably two of them, actually. Maybe three.

Just how far would such bastards go to amuse themselves before Death swung his scythe?

I waited for someone to burst in and inquire about my cry. Chastise me for my vulgarity. Ask me what the hell "Gawdesus!" means.

No one came. I heard no door opening nearby, no hurried footsteps on the stairs. Just the echoes of isolated coughs from the men's and women's wards and, far off, a low moan.

Or was that the wind? It was picking up even more outside. As I stood there listening for help that wasn't coming I could hear gusts beginning to whistle around the corners of the building.

Perhaps my shouts had been swallowed up by the noise. Or perhaps the staff at the Echo Lake Tuberculosis Sanitorium was so accustomed to gasps and shrieks that even "Crap! Shit! Gawdesus!" wouldn't raise an eyebrow.

As I caught my breath, I saw that one roach had refused to scatter with the rest. He'd taken up position atop the rotten potato that had given the box its deceptive heft. He stood there, antennae aquiver, as if daring me to try and swipe his dinner. A defiant little

King of the Hill. I almost had to admire him for that. He didn't even move as I slowly reached down and put the lid back on the box.

I walked King Roach and his potato throne out to the hall and left him on the floor by the door. Then I went back inside and started getting ready for bed. What else could I do?

I checked carefully under the pillow before resting my head upon it, of course. I pulled the bed out from the wall a bit, too, to make reaching me a teeny bit harder. But I knew, once my eyes were closed, there was nothing I could really do to keep away visitors—six-legged or two.

There was a lock on the door, but I had no key. So the door was a mere formality. My room was open to all.

It was going to be a long, long night.

I stared at the ceiling and listened to the wind and the occasional coughing of the "guests" and distant footsteps that always stayed distant…so long as I remained awake.

Day 2: The Storm

Morning

My little roommates never came back to visit me in the night. I think. Who can say, though? Maybe they played hide and seek in my hair in the few moments I managed to sleep.

Knowing I was sharing my room and perhaps even my bed with vermin wouldn't have been enough to keep me up most nights. I've slept soundly in ranch bunkhouses full of things so nasty they make a dozen roaches look like a litter of fuzzy puppies. But add in the whistling of the wind and the coughs from downstairs and that *very* unlocked door a few feet away, and sleep—the restful, deep, dead kind anyway—became impossible.

So I had to settle for the unrestful, shallow, half-awake kind.

Which gave me plenty of time to lie there thinking about where I was and what happened there and death, death, death.

Not exactly picture postcard material. "Come to Echo Lake and have mortality rubbed in your face!"

I don't claim any special mastery over the mysteries of life and death—my brother, of course, would tell you I have no mastery over any mysteries at all—but I do know there's a finality that I accept. We are here, and then we are not here. Hardly profound or comforting, but at least definitive. Given our very limited time with the "here" part, one might ask why Old Red and I have devoted ourselves to unearthing the particulars of strangers' violent "not here"—often bringing us closer to our own in the process. The answer being...

What *was* the answer? The closest I could come was "Well, Old Red's good at it, and what the hell else were we doing?" Not the most inspiring reasons to risk death again and again. And ours could be as close as a murderer haunting the halls and hills of the sanitorium. Or even closer—already inside me—if I'd breathed too deeply near the wrong coughing patient or wrapped my hand around a doorknob contaminated with drops of blood and sputum too small for sight yet brimming with doom.

"All right, enough of that, dammit," I finally said to myself, sitting up.

I had no idea what time it was—other than time to stop torturing myself and *do* something.

I got dressed and put on my shoes (after checking them for new residents) and left. The little box from the Welcoming Committee was still sitting in the hall outside my door, but I didn't check to see if the King of the Hill remained inside atop his potato. That would be a discovery for someone else, most likely. I felt a little bad about that, but in the moment I was in too much of a hurry to stop and deal with that box.

I needed sunlight. Fresh air. Trees. Life. *Now*.

I got the fresh air and trees when I stepped outside. It was fresh, *freezing* air, though, and the green of the trees had been smothered under a shroud an inch thick.

It had snowed in the night. And it was still coming down in fat, lazy flakes from a solid gray sky. There was enough light to tell me dawn had arrived, but it was diffuse and dull, giving the whole world the same deathly pallor as the sickly men and women deep in their last moments of sleep inside.

I headed east, toward the lake and the bluff upon which Wroblewski had died, looking for a sign of life to cheer me. The sight of a single frolicking squirrel would have been worth a pound of gold to me. A moose would have been priceless. For a herd of elk, I would've given my soul. Yet I saw nothing.

Until I did. "Life" didn't seem like quite the right word for it, though.

Just before I started passing the quarantine cottages, a glance to the left stopped me dead in my tracks. Past the little huts and the larger outbuildings beyond them, on a rise sloping up toward the north, stood a tall, thin figure, hooded and cloaked in black. Watching me.

I blinked, thinking I was dreaming. Or, sleep deprived, hallucinating. But it was real.

It wasn't watching me, though. Leastways not anymore, if it had been at all. It was moving slowly up the slope toward an outcropping of trees.

It turned right and disappeared into the forest.

I don't know about you, but every so often, I find myself living a metaphor. Maybe it's the kind of thing you notice when you're a writer. It's not always pleasant in the moment—often quite the opposite, in my experience. But it does add a bit of depth to your tale-telling, provided you live long enough to pick up your pencil again.

My metaphor that morning: I had seen the Angel of Death… and I followed him.

If Old Red had been there I'd have shared this cheery literary thought, if only to get the first "Feh" of the day out of him. As it was, all there was to hear were the crunch of my footsteps in the fluffy fresh snow and the creaks of the trees as they swayed in the strengthening wind.

I passed the cottages, then one of the outbuildings, then another—noticing as I did so the dull halo of a light in one of its frosted glass windows. Perhaps Death and I weren't the only ones up at that early hour.

The last of the outbuildings — the brown, gable-roofed barn where Hippo-Crates made his home—was tucked away behind the main building. Once past it, I could see that there was a trail into the woods just a little way up the snowy slope. That's where the black figure had gone. Tracks in the snow told me that.

I kept following. Why? You tell me. I'd been pondering such questions all night, and *I* didn't have an answer.

The trail wasn't long. Perhaps fifty curving yards at the most. After I'd been on it half a minute, I could see where it ended—and why it existed at all.

At its end was a clearing in the forest dotted with brown humps in six tidy rows. It was a place you'd need near at hand yet out of sight.

I was approaching the Echo Lake Tuberculosis Sanitorium's graveyard.

The black figure was already there. Seeing it up close, standing still before the grave markers, I realized it was a little smaller than I'd first reckoned. And familiar.

It was the woman in a black mackintosh we'd spotted from the surrey on our way to the sanitorium. She wore a dark shawl draped over her shoulders and head—what had appeared to be a hood from a distance—and when she turned to look back at me, I could see ringlets of ruby hair that framed her pale, pretty face.

She was the redhead I'd eyed and been eyed by the day before.

I reached up and touched the brim of my cap. (Greeting a lady or not, I wouldn't be doffing it in that cold.)

"Please pardon the intrusion, Miss. I...wanted to pay my respects here and didn't realize someone else was doing it already."

It was a weak lie, but she let me get away with it. She nodded, then turned away to face the graves again. The markers were identical wooden arcs about two feet high with names and dates carved into them.

JAKUB WROBLEWSKI, said the nearest. LUIS PALO-MARES said the one next to it.

The woman bowed her head and clasped her hands, saying a silent prayer. Then she turned toward me again. Her eyes were moist now with tears that would freeze upon her cheeks if spilled. She opened her mouth to speak, then clinched her lips tight and took a step toward the trail.

"I hope you won't go without allowing me to introduce myself," I said quickly. "I want to get to know all the guests. I may be a humble clerk, but I like to think I'm here to help."

The woman gazed at me a moment, clearly debating whether to respond or beat a hasty retreat. She'd have a good excuse for hurrying off: The wind seemed to be picking up by the second, and little swirls of blowing snow had started to dance around the graves like restless spirits.

"I know who you are," the woman said.

"I imagine you do." I dared a small smile. "I'm sure my arrival has been quite the sensation...if only because everyone up here is so starved for entertainment. But that means you have me at a disadvantage, Miss...?"

The woman went back to debating. She stared at me in silence so long I could actually see the tears in her eyes drying.

"MacGowan," she finally said.

"Ah. That explains it."

"Explains what?"

"Why you and I could be taken for cousins."

I did lift my cap now—just enough to show off my cherry-red Amlingmeyer hair.

Her left hand jerked up to the side of her face, fingertips brushing self-consciously against her crimson curls.

"In truth, though, I don't have a drop of Scot in me," I said breezily, trying to put her at ease. "None that my folks would own up to anyway. The Pycrofts are English on every branch and leaf of the family tree, to hear them tell it. They're awful snobs. Being so much as a Yorkshireman is practically a crime to them. Me, I think a wee drop of Scot's blood would do us some good. A proud, hale and hearty people, you Scots."

"Yes…well…I'm not feeling very hale or hearty now."

Miss MacGowan's brown eyes darted toward the trail. She was still thinking of making her escape.

"Purely temporary, I'm sure, given the no doubt excellent treatment you're receiving," I said. "Are you…under the care of Dr. Swann or Dr. Holly?"

That was my delicate way of asking if she was a charity patient. Or my attempt at asking with some delicacy. From the way Miss MacGowan frowned, you'd have thought I'd simply said, "You poor or what?"

"Dr. Swann," she said stiffly.

So—not poor.

My brother's not the only one who can deduct, despite what he'll tell you.

"Good, good. The head man himself," I said. "Only the best for you, then."

The young lady—she looked to be in her midtwenties—gave that a sour look, as if suspecting me of sarcasm for some reason.

"And where have you joined us from?" I asked.

"I'm from Biloxi, Mississippi."

"Oh my! All the way down there! I wouldn't have thought you were from so deep in Dixie."

Miss MacGowan just eyed me silently.

"Didn't notice an accent," I explained.

"Not all of us from 'Dixie' sound like hicks, if that's what you mean."

"Goodness, no! That is certainly *not* what I was thinking. It's simply that I—erroneously, I see—assumed that everyone from thataway speaks with that certain melodious drawl one associates with our Southern states. Your voice, being so melodious without it, gives no hint where you hail from. That's all I meant."

It was a wonder I wasn't huffing and puffing by the time I was done. It took a lot of digging to get out of that hole.

I switched to a safer subject.

"This weather must be an adjustment for you. Surely you don't get snow on the Gulf in April."

Miss MacGowan reached up to brush off a particularly large flake that had landed on her cheek. She frowned down at her fingertips, then up at the thick, gray clouds.

"We don't get snow on the Coast at all," she said.

"Well, you'll be seeing plenty of it over the next few days. Looks like Old Man Winter's got one more hurrah in him. A big one, too, judging by this wind."

Her frown deepened, and she glared up again at the clouds as if they spelled out insulting words meant just for her.

So much for safe subjects with Miss MacGowan of Biloxi, Mississippi.

"Do you really think so?" she said.

"Well, one can always be wrong about the weather. But unlike you, I grew up with real winters—and real blizzards. And if I were a betting man, I'd put my money on a squall. Quite the step backward for you all up here, I understand. I hear just a week or so ago it was warm enough for a game of baseball."

"So I've been told."

"Oh, so you missed it? You were out on one of the long walks in the woods Dr. Swann recommends?"

"Yes." Miss MacGowan wrapped her arms around herself. "Now if you'll excuse me, I'd like to go back inside. Southerners aren't accustomed to this kind of cold, remember, and I'd like to check on a friend in the infirmary."

"Of course. Miss Blum. I hope she's doing better today. Please don't let me detain you any longer."

She started to leave. So I detained her a little longer.

"Before you go, I'm just wondering one thing," I said. "I hope it's not too personal a question. It looked like you were visiting one of these two newer...additions to the grounds. Mr. Palomares there or Mr. Wroblewski. Was one of them a particular friend of yours?"

The young lady looked back at the graves with such unconcealable sadness and regret it was obvious her answer would be "Yes."

"No," she said instead. "I barely knew them. Good day."

The way she hurried off now made it plain there'd be no more detaining. I gave her a moment to hustle down the trail on her own lest it seem like I was chasing her.

"Well, long as I'm here," I said to the grave markers, "y'all got anything to tell me?"

The wind shushed through the trees. In the distance, a crow cawed.

Jakub Wroblewski and Luis Palomares said nothing. Their neighbors remained mum, too.

"That's what I thought," I said.

I turned and headed back into the forest.

When I reached the slope at the end of the trail, I headed down toward the outbuildings and cottages. If I'd had a sled with me I could've made the journey in style: What had been perhaps two inches of snow when I'd stepped outside was already well on its way to three. The only thing to slow me would've been the growing wind out of the west. Instead of drifting down gracefully, the big snowflakes were beginning to blow in at an angle. By the time I reached the door to Old Red's cabin, I was so covered in them it probably looked like a polar bear was coming to call.

My brother was sound asleep when I came stomping in, brushing the snow from myself, and he sat up with a start and greeted me with a warm "Shut that damn door!"

I did as he asked before heading to his little stove and stoking up the dying fire there. I said nothing for a moment, giving him time to wake up some more and remember that he owed me an apology for his words the night before.

I glanced back at him as he stretched and yawned and scratched his head. And did not apologize.

"Well?" I said.

"Well what?" said Old Red.

I stifled a sigh.

It's a good thing I have so much practice being patient and

forgiving. It's how I can put up with all the practice my brother gets in being ornery and rude.

"Well…look at you sleeping in past dawn," I said, giving him a shake of the head and a tsk-tsk. "This easy quarantine living is turning you soft."

Old Red glared at me, then ran his hands through his gravity-defying, pillow-mussed hair. "I was up late."

"Uh oh. Don't tell me the Welcoming Committee dropped in on you, too."

"What Welcomin' Committee?"

"I guess they let you be. Lucky you."

I moved over to the chair nearby, plopped down, and filled my brother in on the "present" I'd found waiting for me when I'd gone to bed.

"Reminds me of your first night at the Cross J four years ago," Old Red said when I was done.

I grimaced at the memory. "A tarantula in my boot. Quite a welcome to ranch life."

"Yeah, well…there's assholes in every bunkhouse."

"And every sanitorium. These particular ones I figure I met yesterday."

"Them fellas who guyed you at dinner—Phillips and Foster?"

"Yeah. Seems like their style. The shame of it is I don't think they're who we're after. Nasty sons of bitches, but there was that baseball game going on when Wroblewski died, and they must've been there."

"Why 'must've'?"

"The game was only happening at all 'cuz Foster's big on baseball. His family sent him bats and gloves and such, and apparently Dr. Swann actually thought a game was a good idea. I can't imagine Foster would let the other patients use his stuff while he was off doing something else—like cracking Wroblewski's skull. Seems to me if there was a game, he'd be in the thick of it."

"Or the game was just the distraction he was lookin' for. You should check on where he was at the time. 'Seems to me' and assumptions ain't data, y'know."

I unstifled my stifled sigh from earlier.

"Fine," I said. "I'll just bring it up in casual conversation... along with whether that noise in the lake Miss Johansen heard was a 'splish' or a 'ker-splosh.'"

"And find out who all was at the game and who wasn't. And where they was playin'. And if any of the baseball gear went missin'. And when that warm snap started and when it ended."

I drooped forward and buried my face in my hands.

"And here I thought having you out of the way for a few days would be a relief," I groaned. "Instead I got so many questions to remember I won't be able to recall what my own name is supposed to be."

"Ain't you got a question for *me?*" my brother said. He didn't sound sympathetic.

I looked up and shrugged. "Just the same one as always, I guess. Why do I let you get me into these situations?"

Old Red swiped a hand at me. "You know the answer to that: You ain't got nothin' better to do."

I went back to practicing my patience and forgiveness and did not tell him to go to hell.

"I'm talkin' about what was keepin' me up late last night," he went on.

"Oh. That. I just figured you was lying here pondering on the inescapable certainty of death, like me. This place does bring out the grim in a person."

"No, I was not lyin' here ponderin' on the inescapable certainty of death. I was up off my ass gettin' something done. Goin' through all these little huts out here, to be specific."

"What were you looking for?"

"I had no idea...till I found it."

Old Red slithered a hand under his blanket and pulled out a big, clear bottle. There was writing in the glass—words spelled out in different directions—and I leaned forward and squinted at it.

"'Gordon Dry Gin. London, England,'" I read out. "So that's what kept you up so late: You were getting soused."

"It was empty when I found it," Old Red growled.

"Riiiiiiight. Sure it was." I shook my head as if bitterly disappointed. "Shameful. Out here drinking on the job…and you
didn't even share."

"The point is," Old Red said, unamused (of course), "I found
this bottle and half a dozen like it beneath the floorboards under a
bed. So someone had been sneakin' out to that cabin to tipple."

"Very interesting. And probably completely meaningless. Like
I just said, this place is about as dismal as it gets. So somebody
decided they couldn't get through the days without some extra
nerve tonic—the dry kind from England, and lots of it. So what?"

"So I don't know. Might fit into things, might not. Finding out
is just part of the work."

"Yeah…the part I now have to do by myself while you're out
here hunting up garbage to puzzle over."

"If that's frustratin' to you, just imagine how I feel."

"Oh, I know how you feel. You made that plain enough with
all your bitchin' about me not…"

I stopped myself as—much to my surprise—a grin spread over
my face.

"What?" Old Red asked warily.

I pointed at the gin bottle. "Did you read the writing on that
all by yourself last night?"

My brother nodded. "Wasn't too hard. It was plain to see what
kinda bottles they was even without readin' the writin' on 'em."

"Yeah, but still—I'm pretty sure 'gin' ain't in *McGuffey's*. That's
all 'Jim and Jane like to skate.' No 'Gordon' or 'London, England'
in there either. You worked that all out on your own. Didn't
need…"

I felt my grin begin to melt.

"…any help from me," I'd been about to say.

"…a hint," I said instead.

"Like I said, the bottle itself was hint enough," Old Red said
gruffly, embarrassed by the pride that had shown on my face.
"And you're missin' the point, as usual."

"I guess I am…because I still don't see it."

"How about a neighborhood liquor store? You see *that*?"

"No, I don't see any…oh. Right."

It wasn't just that someone had been boozing it up in one of the cabins. How'd they have so much booze to begin with? It's not like they were handing out bottles in the dining hall. Dr. Swann wanted his patients drinking milk and orange juice, not Gordon's gin.

I still didn't see how it fit in with the deaths we were investigating, but it might be more clay for bricks, as Old Red liked to say (because Holmes had said it). One more thing to build with.

My brother shushed me. Which was a little annoying, as I wasn't saying anything at the time. I guess he just assumed *something* was bound to pop out of my mouth, and he didn't want to hear it.

He cocked his head and tapped his upraised ear.

I stayed shushed and listened. Then I heard it, too.

From the distance, cutting through the whistling of the wind around the sharp corners of the cottage, came the nickering of a horse.

Old Red snatched his shoes up from the floor. When he had them on, he grabbed his sheepskin coat—actually *my* sheepskin coat, borrowed to give the impression he'd recently lost a lot of weight—and hopped off the bed. We headed outside and turned to the east—the direction the noise had come from.

Snow was still falling in huge flakes, practically clumps now. Months before, at the Columbian Exposition in Chicago, I'd seen a Viennese novelty in one of the exhibition halls: a transparent globe of glass filled with water and white flakes and a wee little cathedral. Shake it, and you made your own little blizzard right in the palm of your hand. Looking out at Echo Lake now was like peering into one of those globes, freshly swirled. All you could see at first was a blur of white. Through it, eventually, I caught glimpses of even more white, though mottled here and there with blue and green and brown—the frozen lake and rocky, tree-studded incline beyond it, mostly covered now in powdery snow.

Then the nickering came again, turning into a whinny.

Following the sound, I spotted a faint dab of gray moving toward us from the edge of the forest at the south side of the lake.

"I'll be damned," I said.

I'd been expecting to see McCandless, the groundskeeper who'd driven us up in the surrey the day before, or some other surprise visitor riding in from Idaho Springs twenty miles down the mountain. But though this was indeed a surprise visitor—quite a surprise—she didn't come in riding and she wasn't from Idaho Springs.

It was a lone, dun mare, unbridled, unsaddled, riderless. She trotted straight toward us, nickering again and again as she approached.

She was happy to see us, and I soon saw why. Her neck looked long and thin, her withers pointed and bony instead of smoothly rounded. She hadn't been eating right for some time.

Just as she reached us, a male voice called out, "What is going on here?"

We looked back to find a bundled-up Dr. Swann and Nurse Rosenkoetter stomping through the snow toward us. We must have been noticed from the windows of the main building.

"Ask her," I said, pointing at the mare as she came to a stop before me and my brother. "I was just checking on Mr. Melas— making sure he was minding Nurse Rosenkoetter and staying put —when we heard her out here."

The mare shook her head and nickered again. Horse for "Well…where's the damn food?"

Old Red stepped up and stroked her scrawny neck. Her coat was such a pale shade of gray it was almost as white as the big snowflakes sticking to it.

"Where'd you come from, girl?" he said. He looked back at Swann and Nurse Rosenkoetter. "Ever seen her before?"

"I have no idea," said the doctor.

"No," said the nurse. "Do you think someone's out there in the snow? Injured, perhaps?"

"Look at the ribs on this poor creature, Nurse Rosenkoetter," said Swann. "It must've been wandering around for a week at least. If someone was riding it, they're miles away and well beyond our helping."

Old Red scowled at the doctor in a way I knew well. It was the glare he gave someone (usually me) who's overlooked the obvious. (Obvious to my brother, anyway.) Usually he'd follow this up with a Holmes quote—"You see but you do not observe" was a favorite —but he resisted the urge this time.

"Wherever she came from, it's probably your barn that brought her. She smelled Hippo-Crates back there and figured if you had one horse you wouldn't mind another." Old Red gave the mare a pat, then locked eyes on Swann. "You should have someone fetch your man McCandless. This little lady needs food and a good groomin'."

"Yes. All right."

It was obvious who the "someone" was Old Red meant to do the fetching. There weren't many candidates for the job.

Swann turned to her.

"Nurse, please tell McCandless to come collect this animal."

Nurse Rosenkoetter looked back and forth from her boss to my brother. She didn't look suspicious exactly—that would require her to have an expression on her face, which seemed to be a bad habit she studiously avoided. But it was clear she'd noticed something odd going on between Dr. Swann and Old Red.

"Yes, Doctor," she said.

She gave my brother one more long look before spinning around and striding off.

"She suspects you're not just another patient," Swann said to Old Red when she was out of earshot. "You're not doing a very good job of blending in." He frowned over at me. "Either of you."

"Hard to blend in when there's half-starved horses coming at us out of nowhere," I said. "What do you think, Brother? This one here for a dose of Dr. Swann's cure? She's skinny enough to be a lunger."

"Don't use that word," Swann snapped.

"I'm sorry," I said. "She's skinny enough to be a...do you prefer 'patient' or 'guest'?"

Swann rolled his eyes. "'Patient' is fine. No need for euphemisms with me."

"We're wastin' time," Old Red said. "I got questions to ask before Nurse Rosenkoetter gets back with McCandless."

Swann swatted away the snow collecting on the front of his belly-bulged coat. "Well, get to it then. If I'd known I'd be out here listening to you two jibber-jabber all morning I'd have put on a hat and gloves."

"Did you come out to watch that baseball game a week or so ago?" Old Red asked.

Swann moved on to brushing snow from his shoulders with irritated flicks of the wrist. "What you mean is 'Where were you when Wroblewski went off the cliff?' Well, I was in my office. Doing paperwork. That's most of my job, you know."

"Funny you should fire the man who's supposed to help you with it," Old Red said. "Why'd you do that?"

The doctor froze mid-flick.

"There were...indiscretions," he said slowly.

"With a female patient?"

"Yes...that was part of it. Though I don't believe there was anything...truly seamy. Nothing *physical*, if you follow me. That would've been suicide."

"I've known men who'd be willing to take their chances with that," I said. "'Hell of a way to go,' they'd say."

Swann glared at me. "Then you've known some truly despicable and stupid men."

I shrugged. "I've lived an interesting life."

The horse snorted impatiently, wondering why we were just standing there instead of bringing her a nice full nosebag.

Old Red reached down and rubbed her chest.

"If the lady was part of why he was fired," he said to the doctor, "what was the other part?"

"Keys for the sanitorium. Turner had a full set of duplicates, and he 'lost' them. I think he might have given them to one of the patients."

"The young lady he was chummy with?" I said. "Miss Johansen?"

Swann coughed out a bitter little laugh. "And here I was thinking you two were completely incompetent. You did manage to learn *something*, didn't you? Yes—I'm thinking of Miss Johansen. Turner was smitten. A lovestruck fool. Everyone could see it. The way he fawned over her. The way she encouraged it. Used it. It was embarrassing. I was thinking of dismissing him even before his keys 'disappeared.'"

The doctor narrowed his eyes and cocked his head.

"Will this be in your report to the board?"

"Depends on if it matters," Old Red said. "I guess we'll see."

"So on you'll go," said Swann, "dragging out every piece of dirty laundry you can find in the vague hope that it somehow 'matters'?"

"Exactly!" I said. "Why, you could be a detective yourself, Doc. You picked right up on how it works."

"You got any more dirty laundry you want to tell us about?" Old Red added. "Sure would save time."

Swann's round face was already pink from the cold, but now his cheeks flushed red. There was something he wanted to tell us all right: where we could stick our questions. But he didn't want that in the report to the board either.

"I'm not aware of anything else that could possibly be relevant," he said instead.

A door opened and closed in the distance behind us, and we glanced back to find Nurse Rosenkoetter returning with a very surprised-looking McCandless, a bridle in his hands. The horse whinnied impatiently as they approached.

"And I would remind you, *Mr. Melas*," Swann said loudly, "that you're supposed to be in quarantine—"

"Oh, surely we can forget that now that I've been seen out talkin' to—"

"—*and to quarantine, you shall return*," the doctor went on. He turned toward me. "And you, *Mr. Pycroft*, will sit at the staff table for breakfast this morning. No more mingling with the patients at meals."

"I understand," I said. "But I'll need to mingle with them every other chance I get if I'm gonna get our questions..."

I stopped bothering to talk. Swann wasn't listening. He'd swiveled back to Old Red to flap his hands at him as if shooing a stubborn goat out of the cabbage patch.

My brother—stubborn goat that he is—stood his ground.

"Just tell me one more thing," he said. He pointed straight up. "This here snowstorm. How common is it for up here this time of year?"

Swann furrowed his brow. He obviously hadn't been expecting the "one more thing" to be a question about the weather.

"We can get heavy snows practically into May," he said. "The patients from back east are sometimes caught by surprise by it, but not those of us who've been here a while. Now if you would—"

He gave Old Red another shoo-shoo hand-flap.

When my brother didn't immediately shoo, I gave him a hand-flap, too.

"Nurse Rosenkoetter and McCandless can see this," I said under my breath. "You don't go, it's gonna look mighty peculiar."

Old Red stared hard at me, stroked the horse's neck one last time, and trudged off.

"See ya tomorrow, Mr. Melas!" I called after him. "You listen to the doctor and stay put now, you hear?"

Old Red ignored me. Which was fine, as I'd spoken as much for Nurse Rosenkoetter's benefit as his.

"How about you, McCandless?" I said as she and the groundskeeper drew near. "Ever seen this gal before?"

I nodded at the horse.

"I don't think so," McCandless said. "If I did, she was two hundred pounds heavier. A horse this skinny I'd remember—cuz I'd have given the man riding her a punch to the nose."

He slowed as he approached the mare, speaking to her gently in his lilting Irish way and reaching out to offer her a comforting pat. She gave him a look that seemed both grateful and expectant, and he brought up the bridle and slipped it over her head.

"How often you get visitors up this way on horseback?" I asked.

"Never," said Nurse Rosenkoetter. "McCandless brings up the mail and any arriving patients in the buggy. Delivery wagons come weekly with food. That's it."

"So folks never just pop in to say howdy?"

I'd asked as a half joke. It was received as no joke at all.

"No. No one ever 'pops in' to 'say howdy,'" Nurse Rosenkoetter replied coldly. She looked so sickened saying "howdy" you'd have thought one of the other nurses had waved smelling salts under her nose.

"Nor would we want them to," Swann added. "Outsiders mean excitement. Commotion. Gossip and rumor."

He threw a sulky glance at Old Red. My brother had paused his hobbling to look back at us—probably wondering if I was asking the right questions and fighting the urge to shamble back and ask them himself.

I fought the urge to give him another shoo—or just start throwing snowballs.

When he noticed Swann and me watching him, he got started toward his cabin again.

"It's extremely disruptive to our work," Swann went on. "Fortunately, that work doesn't encourage neighborliness. Most people have the good sense to leave us alone."

McCandless began leading the horse toward the barn.

"Come along, girl," he said soothingly. "I've got hay and grain for you right over this way. You can say hi to Hippo-Crates. He'll be pleased to meet you."

The mare didn't need any coaxing. It was unclear how she'd feel about Hippo-Crates, but she was eager to make the acquaintance of that hay and grain.

"When the weather clears, we'll send McCandless down to talk to the constable in Idaho Springs," Swann said. He drummed his fingers against the uppermost of his double chins. "My guess is the horse was stolen from town and abandoned when the thief got…" He stopped tapping and started shrugging. "Wherever he needed to go. Speaking of which…"

He turned away abruptly and headed for the main entrance to the big building. He knew where *he* needed to go. Nurse Rosenkoetter went with him.

"Come on, come on," Swann said, waving for me to follow.

"Breakfast is being served, Mr. Pycroft," said Nurse Rosenkoetter. "The cooks don't leave food out between meals. This will be your last chance to eat until luncheon."

I hurried to catch up. The food the day before had been about as tasty as a newspaper sandwich, but I was hungry.

"Doctor," I said, "something you mentioned has got me thinking."

"Oh?"

Swann sounded skeptical as if he didn't believe *anything* could get me thinking.

"You said the locals aren't inclined to be neighborly," I said. "Just how unneighborly do they get?"

"There's a standoffishness, that's all. We're too valuable to them for anything overt."

"Valuable how?"

"Valuable in terms of our value," he said testily.

Very helpful.

"Tuberculosis sanitoriums are cropping up all over Colorado, Mr. Pycroft," Nurse Rosenkoetter explained. "The climate here is perfect for the Brehmer/Dettweiler treatment. That's the method we use."

Swann raised a finger. "With innovations of our own."

"With innovations of our own," Nurse Rosenkoetter repeated mechanically. "The point being that most people aren't happy about having consumptives for neighbors, but they will most happily sell the institutions serving them food and coal and oil and services."

"Ah," I said. "'Value.'"

Meaning, of course, "money."

"So don't expect any invitations for dinner in Idaho Springs," Swann said. "But you don't have to worry about anyone throwing rocks at you either."

Maybe I jerked my head his way or widened my eyes a bit, I don't know. Swann didn't seem to notice my reaction, but Nurse Rosenkoetter did. She was eyeing me intently as I smoothed the surprise from my face.

Swann had hit it on the head—almost literally—without even realizing it.

I'd been wondering if someone from town might dislike the TB patients enough to ride up and clobber one on the noggin. It wasn't much of a theory—why would this hypothetical lunger-hater set his horse loose rather than ride back down again?—and I knew what Old Red would have to say about it.

In a word: "Feh." So I let it drop and turned my attention to more important matters.

"What's for breakfast?"

The answer turned out to be "more of the same." Not that it was literally boiled chicken and potatoes again. But it was food so bland it would make a saltine cracker seem like a bowl of Texas chili. There was globby-thick oatmeal (hold the sugar) and scorched toast (hold the butter) and heaping bowls of hard-boiled eggs (hold the salt and pepper). If not for the pitchers of orange juice, the spread would have been utterly devoid of color as well as flavor.

I didn't let any of that stop me from piling up a plate, though. I've been on cattle drives with cooks who think undercooked beans and moldy biscuits are a feast. If I were a picky eater, I would've starved somewhere along the Chisholm Trail.

As I turned to go to the staff table—where Dr. Swann and Nurse Rosenkoetter had already headed with their own not-quite-so-loaded plates—I found my way blocked. Apparently, young Miss Johansen was returning for seconds...though to look at her, you wouldn't have thought she'd been able to get through five bites of her firsts for months.

"We meet plate in hand again," I said. "If we're not careful, people are going to talk."

Beyond her, I could see two-thirds of what I assumed to be "the Welcoming Committee"—hatchet-faced Phillips and snow-white, patchy-haired Foster—smirking at me smugly from among the male patients. Their young friend Breckinridge, seated with them, had the decency to look ashamed. But for all I knew, he'd been chief roach wrangler.

"Oh, they're going to talk regardless," Miss Johansen replied. "As I see it, since it's a foregone conclusion one may as well give them something to talk *about*."

She favored me with a smile that would have been sultry on another young woman. But with her sallow skin and sunken eyes and all-around emaciation, "sultry" wasn't quite in her repertoire anymore. That wasn't going to stop her from trying, though.

"But if you prefer privacy, perhaps you could escort me on my morning constitutional," she went on. "That would give us the opportunity to get to know each other better without an audience."

"An excellent suggestion," I said. "And speaking of our audience, I should cut this conversation short before my oatmeal gets colder and Dr. Swann gets hotter."

Indeed, the good (or was he?) doctor was glaring at me from the staff table.

"Of course," Miss Johansen said. "I hope you enjoy your oatmeal...and can tolerate Dr. Swann."

"I'm more worried about him tolerating me. Until later, miss."

I gave her a little bow.

"Au revoir," she said.

She moved past me to help herself to more food she didn't want.

I headed for the staff table. One of the nurses was leaving just as I reached it, so I slipped into her spot beside Dr. Holly. He wished me a good morning and asked about the mare—her mysterious appearance outside had been the talk of the sanitorium apparently—then gave me a small, sympathetic smile.

"I understand that wasn't the only unexpected visit you've had from the animal kingdom since arriving," he said.

"Ah. Yes. My little roommates. Did you hear about them from gossip through the grapevine or me hollering through the walls?"

"Gossip through the grapevine."

"Good. I've been told I scream like a girl and I'd hate to have folks here know it."

"I wouldn't blame anyone for screaming under the circumstances. It's a cruel prank. A bit of a tradition here, though, unfortunately."

"Oh? You get a visit from the Welcoming Committee when you were new?"

Holly shook his head. "They don't subject the medical staff to such things. Even me. Something we do could mean the difference between life and death for them. Why make enemies of us?"

I looked over at the young doctor. He was gazing ruefully at the half-eaten bowl of oatmeal before him. The food was certainly enough to inspire gloom, but it was obvious that wasn't what was bothering him.

"'Even you'?" I said.

"I'm not popular with patients like Mr. Foster and Mr. Phillips."

"Because you treat the charity cases?"

"Partially. I also have ideas they consider…radical."

I remembered the conversation I'd had with Foster and Phillips over dinner—and the notion that had brought a shiver to each man's bony shoulders.

"Like admitting black patients," I said.

Swann was two seats from me, on the other side of Dr. Holly, with Nurse Rosenkoetter to his right. Up to then, he'd been giving the peeling of hard-boiled eggs all his attention. But now he froze, the latest egg still half-shelled in his pudgy hands.

"Yes. Like admitting black patients," said Holly. "They used to call tuberculosis 'the white death' because of the supposed pallor of those it consumes. But did you know, Mr. Pycroft, that the mortality rate for tuberculosis per capita is twice as high for Blacks as for Whites?"

The egg in Swann's hands was crushed into white-yellow crumbles.

"I did not know that," I said.

"Well, it's true," said Holly. "And it seems to me that any institution for the treatment of TB that claims to have a charitable mission shouldn't willfully overlook the very people the disease hits hardest."

Swann cleared his throat.

"And it's not just a matter of ethics," Holly went on. "There's the scientific side to consider."

Swann cleared his throat again.

"We shouldn't just be treating tuberculosis here," Holly continued, either oblivious or obstinate. "Every guest represents an opportunity to learn about it. Yet there's much we aren't learning. Why are Blacks so susceptible to the disease? Is it environmental or physiological? Just a handful of black guests might be enough for us to—"

"A-HEM," Swann said, turning to glare at Dr. Holly.

Simply clearing his throat hadn't been doing the trick, so he had to make it more plain: "I AM CLEARING MY THROAT AND IN CASE YOU DON'T GET IT, THAT MEANS SHUT UP, YOU YOUNG FOOL."

"—make a breakthrough," Holly muttered.

Swann picked up his napkin and began wiping the shattered shell and crumbled yolk from his fingers.

"It would also be enough to bankrupt us," he said under his breath.

"I'm sure it wouldn't go that far," said Holly.

Swann snorted. "I'm sure it would."

He'd turned away to look out at the patients, scanning the long tables for any sign that the conversation had been noted. No one seemed to be watching us particularly closely. But the nurses and orderlies at the staff table had all gone stiff and silent in a way that made it plain every ear was turned our way.

"One of your own charity cases has been so scandalized by the idea of Blacks here that she refuses to see you anymore for even suggesting it," Swann said quietly. "Do you really expect our paying patients to be more welcoming?"

"The guest in question is from the South," Holly replied, his voice low as well. "Feelings on such matters tend to run more strongly there."

He moved his gaze to our left, letting it settle on a patient sitting sullenly at the end of the women's table. To my surprise, it was the very woman I'd spoken to in the sanitorium cemetery earlier that morning: the redhead from Mississippi, Miss MacGowan.

"Feelings on this particular subject run strongly everywhere," Swann said. "Which is why the Board of Trustees chooses to avoid it."

"That's the board," Holly said. "We're doctors. Surely we shouldn't let anyone's backward *feelings* come between us and our oaths."

Swann stiffened in his seat. "I could be in Hartford, Connecticut, making twice as much money treating insurance executives for gout and the clap."

Far off to my right, one of the nurses gasped.

"Instead, I have come into this wilderness to try to heal the doomed," Swann went on. He was still managing to keep his voice down, but it trembled with barely suppressed rage. "So I will not sit here and let some self-righteous whelp lecture me about the goddamned Hippocratic—"

"*Doctor*," Nurse Rosenkoetter said.

"No. I will not be shushed. I am sick of this sanctimonious posturing over—"

"Doctor," the nurse said again. "Miss MacGowan."

She nodded to our left.

The redhead was walking our way.

"Oh. I see. Yes," Swann said. He leaned toward Holly. "If you insist on having this discussion again, we can do it later. *In private*."

Holly said nothing. He was watching Miss MacGowan come closer.

She was *not* watching him. Quite the opposite: Her eyes were resolutely locked on Dr. Swann.

"Yes, Miss MacGowan?" Swann said blandly.

She came to a stop before him.

"Doctor…I was wondering if we were going to be allowed to take our walks today, given the weather. Some of the other patients are saying this might be our last chance to go outside for a week if the snow doesn't stop."

Swann sat back and tapped a finger against one of his round cheeks. "That could be true. Hmm."

"The way it's accumulating out there, Doctor…it might be too strenuous to walk through," said Holly. "We want our guests to get exercise, not give themselves aneurysms."

The unsolicited advice from his young colleague made up Swann's mind. To do the opposite.

"Filling the lungs with cold, clean air is one of the corner-stones of our treatment, *Doctor*," he said. "I can't imagine a better day for it. Those who wish to walk this morning will be allowed to do so." He turned back to Miss MacGowan and gave her a patronizing smile. "But you shouldn't overdo it or wander off far."

Miss MacGowan didn't return the smile.

"Of course, Doctor," she said stiffly. "Thank you."

She started to go, her gaze whipping away from Swann so as not to linger for even a second on anyone seated near him. But then she stopped and turned back.

"That stray horse," she said. "Do you have any idea who it belongs to?"

"None whatsoever," Swann said. "Stolen from town, we think."

"Have *you* seen it before?" I asked the lady.

The question seemed to startle her. Her eyes widened—though she didn't point them my way.

"Certainly not," she said. "I was just curious."

She turned away quickly and stalked off.

"Odd duck, that one," Swann muttered. He seemed disappointed that she hadn't be more grateful to him for overruling Dr. Holly on her behalf.

"I wonder if you should transfer her care back to me," Holly said, leaning closer, voice low. "I'm not sure it sets a good precedent letting guests pick which of us they see. I mean, what would you say if someone under your care insisted on coming to me instead? Several someones even?"

Swann's jowly face flushed so pink it could've been a big ball of county fair cotton candy set atop his suit. He opened his mouth and whipped around to face Holly fully. But whatever he was about to say he swallowed when he looked past his colleague and saw me watching.

He swiveled back to his right toward Nurse Rosenkoetter.

"I'm going to my office," he said.

"Yes, Doctor," said the nurse.

"I'll be...catching up on correspondences during morning activity time."

"Yes, Doctor."

"I am not to be disturbed."

"Yes, Doctor."

He rose and stormed off, leaving his dirty plate and half-empty glass at the table.

"Seems to me he's disturbed already," I whispered to Holly.

He didn't take the bait.

"I'll be in the laboratory," he said to Nurse Rosenkoetter. "Let me know if there's any change in Miss Blum's condition."

He stood, cleaned up both his own mess and Swann's, and left.

Nurse Rosenkoetter watched him go, then let her gaze settle on me. There was a hint of fire behind her usual ice, as if the friction at the breakfast table had been my fault.

"Uhh...what's this about a 'laboratory'?" I said. "I don't remember you pointing that out on the grand tour yesterday."

"It's not in the main building. It's behind—near the barn," Nurse Rosenkoetter said.

"Out of sight, out of mind," said one of the nurses beyond her.

Nurse Rosenkoetter shot her a quick glare, then turned back to me.

"You know our idealistic young doctor is given to euphemisms to spare the feelings of our 'guests,'" she said. "He's also found one for 'the morgue.'"

"Ah."

"He may be soft-hearted, but he is an excellent doctor. Brilliant, even."

The nurse returned her attention to her oatmeal, which she began eating with a remote, mechanical diligence. Food was fuel, that's all, and she'd need to stoke up with some if she was to get through another long day remotely, mechanically, diligently tending to the dying.

I picked up my own spoon...then put it down unused. Damn it if I hadn't gone and lost my appetite again. Another week at Echo Lake and I'd start to look as scrawny as that half-starved horse...or even my brother.

"Guess I'll go put my hat and coat on again," I said. "Someone's gotta keep an eye on the patients who go out for a walk in this weather."

Nurse Rosenkoetter and the other nurses and orderlies just kept eating. The message: No need to announce what *you're* doing. No one cares.

I left.

I took my time getting ready to head out again. Partially to give Miss Johansen the chance to beat me outside. Another part of it was pure dawdling, though. I wouldn't say it was cozy inside the sanitorium—in fact, it was downright frigid away from the fireplaces and stoves. But it was warmer than shivering out in the snow, which I'd already had my fill off that morning.

Nonetheless, I was back at it again twenty minutes later. And I wasn't alone. Word about going outside must have been spread through the patients one way or another because when I walked out there were maybe thirty of them visible here and there around the grounds. Most were in little slow-moving clusters of two or three sticking close to the main building. But a few, further afield, had struck out on their own. One—a splotch of vibrant gold visible through the swirl of still-falling snow—was headed down the long slope to the lake. Whoever it was paused to look back my way, then carried on.

I followed her. For a "her" it was, I could see now. And I had a good idea which one.

She stopped when she reached the edge of the lake, lingering with her back turned but no doubt knowing I was coming. I got a good look at her long velvet coat trimmed with fluffy lamb's wool as I approached. When she finally swiveled to face me I saw that her dainty hands were stuffed into a matching muff. Very stylish. What the most fashionable female consumptives were wearing that season, I could only assume.

"Why, Mr. Pycroft," Miss Johansen said, smiling. "I'm so pleased you could join me."

"The pleasure is all mine."

I gave her the sort of appreciative look she clearly expected, then gazed out over Echo Lake. Not that you'd have known there was a lake there at the moment. The blue-gray ice visible when Old Red and I had arrived was totally covered in snow now, leaving what could have been a long oval clearing at the foot of the bluffs to the east. Still, it was a lovely scene…so long as you didn't picture the bloodied body that had tumbled down from those bluffs not so many days before.

I cupped my gloved hands to my mouth and bellowed out a "Halloo!"

A "Halloo!" bounced back to us off the distant rocks.

"Trying to start an avalanche?" Miss Johansen asked.

"Testing for truth in advertising," I replied. "There really is an echo."

"You couldn't take it at its word?"

I shrugged. "It pays to be skeptical in my line of work."

The young lady gave me—ironically enough—a skeptical look.

"Clerks encounter a lot of liars?"

"Not until the bills are due. Then half what we hear are fibs."

I forced myself to chuckle at my little bon mot…while cursing myself for my carelessness.

You are Albert Pycroft, clerk and fuddy-duddy, I reminded myself. *Don't be so danged interesting!*

Hiding your light under a bushel can be quite the challenge when it burns as bright as mine.

"Well, you won't hear any fibs out of *my* family when it's time to pay the bill," Miss Johansen said. "Though I can't promise you won't hear complaints about its size."

She threw a glance over her shoulder.

"It's as I feared," she sighed with a pouty frown. "Your hallooing was noticed."

I looked back, too.

One of the other patients—a man in a long Ulster coat and Scotch cap, a scarf wrapped around his face—was heading down the snowy slope toward us.

"Would you mind if we carried on?" Miss Johansen said, nodding along the shore to the south. The trees picked up again about forty yards off, blocking the view of the lake—and anyone walking along it—from the main building. "I am supposed to be getting in some exercise, you know."

"Of course."

I almost forgot where and who we were and offered the young lady my arm.

Stuffed into her muff along with her hands, I had to assume, was her little blood bucket.

Walking arm in arm would not be a good idea.

I held a hand out to the south instead, and off we went side by side.

As we strolled, Miss Johansen began asking questions about my background and upbringing. It was only fair, she said, since I'd asked so many of the same questions of her the day before.

I told her of my idyllic childhood in the suburbs of Omaha, my large and loving family, my recently completed studies at the

University of Nebraska, my desire to seek out my fortune further west, and the classified ad that led me to apply for a job at Echo Lake. All of it bullshit. Yet (despite my efforts to keep said bullshit boring) all of it fascinating to judge by the rapt attention with which Miss Johansen listened.

When she shifted to questions about how I was settling in—giving me no opportunity to shift to questions of my own—I told her of my visit from the Welcoming Committee the night before.

"Yes. I heard about that," she said. "Disgusting. I assume from now on, you'll be keeping your door locked."

"Well, I surely would if I could. You need keys for that, though."

"You mean they haven't given you any?"

"Nope."

Miss Johansen looked deeply disappointed on my behalf. Or perhaps not on my behalf.

"Apparently my predecessor was careless with his," I went on.

"Hmm. Yes. Mr. Turner was the forgetful type. Forgettable, too." Miss Johansen gave me a sly smile. "Unlike you."

I grinned back at her.

"And you," I said.

If she could lay it on thick, so could I.

Our mutual mooning was interrupted by movement up ahead. A path emptied out of the forest near the shore, and from it stepped a slim figure in a black mackintosh.

It was Miss MacGowan. She froze when she saw us approaching.

"Oh," Miss Johansen said flatly. "Her."

She spun the other way…and immediately stopped.

"Oh," she said. "Him."

The man in the long Ulster—young Breckenridge, it turned out—had followed us down the shoreline. He'd reach us in a couple minutes.

Miss Johansen sighed.

"Let's just admire the view for a moment, shall we?" she said.

She turned to face the lake, and I did the same.

"You don't seem pleased to see Miss MacGowan or Mr. Breckinridge," I said.

"I'm not."

Miss Johansen left it at that. Or tried to anyway.

"Oh, come now—don't hold back," I said. "If we're going to be friends, that means we share gossip."

The young lady peeped over at me. She still looked displeased to find herself trapped between two people she clearly didn't want to see, but a little hint of her smile returned.

"All right," she said. "Miss MacGowan has been my bed neighbor in the women's ward since she arrived a couple months ago. At first we were on friendly terms. But then a month or so ago, she...changed. Or perhaps simply revealed her true nature."

"Which is?"

"Thief. And packrat. Or so I suspect. I haven't been able to prove anything yet. But many times I've seen her skulking through the ward when no one's supposed to be there or sneaking around at night. And things have been disappearing lately. Odd things. Gloves and scarves from the cloakrooms, bedding, an iron of all things. I've even been victimized by it myself."

"Something of yours was stolen?"

"Yes. A...uh...personal item. Nothing worth reporting. But I'm sure I didn't misplace it."

I was about to ask what kind of "personal item," but Miss Johansen rushed on.

"Why, even the most notable thing about Miss MacGowan— the very thing you in particular might admire—is false."

I put on a quizzical expression to show that I'd taken the bait and allowed her to change the subject.

She reached up and took one of her blonde locks between her fingers.

"Tuberculosis can cause baldness," she said. "Men like Mr. Foster don't bother hiding it. But we ladies can be prone to vanity."

"Are you saying that red hair of hers...it's a wig?"

"You didn't hear it from me," Miss Johansen said...nodding as she did so.

I leaned back to get a look at Miss MacGowan and her (I now knew) phony hair. The lady was gone, though.

Miss Johansen, meanwhile, leaned forward to look past me in the opposite direction—toward the approaching Breckenridge. He was maybe fifty yards off now. And apparently, Miss Johansen didn't want him any closer.

"Let's carry on, shall we?" she said, already moving off.

Before I turned to join her, I gazed out across the frozen lake one more time—realizing only then that we'd probably been "admiring" the exact spot where Wroblewski had tumbled to his death (or had tumbled already dead). That reminded me of a promise I'd made to my brother. A question I had to ask...though I couldn't for the life of me think of a smooth way to get at it.

"Lotta traffic for such a secluded spot," I said. "It's a wonder you were the only one around when that Wroblewski fellow...met with his misfortune."

"I suppose."

Miss Johansen shot me a look of the "Why the heck would you bring that up?" kind.

I forged on regardless. I knew what kind of look Old Red would give me if I didn't. What's more, what he'd say...and maybe even throw at me.

"The splash you heard that day—how would you describe it?"

The "Why the heck...?" look changed to a "Have you lost your damn mind?"

"I would describe it as a splash. What else could one say?"

"Depends on the splash."

I tried to remember the examples my brother had used. And utterly failed.

"Umm...you know. Was it ka-sploush or a splishy-splashy or a...I don't know. Something else?"

"It was the sound you hear when something falls into water. I'm afraid I'm not enough of an expert on that subject to give you a more specific classification. Perhaps if I were a sailor, I could be precise enough for you."

Miss Johansen looked over her shoulder, and for a second, I worried that my (or my more like Old Red's) dumb question had changed her mind about who she should be strolling with. But rather than peel off from me to go join Breckenridge, she swung left onto the trail Miss MacGowan had stepped out from a few minutes before.

"I wonder if I should feel insulted," she said as I joined her in the forest. "Here we are out for a pleasant stroll together, and you insist on asking me about splashes."

"I'm sorry. Let's talk about…"

Now, Casanova I am not. (Yet—give me time.) I have enough experience with young ladies like Miss Johansen, though, to know that "you" was the right way to end that sentence. I even started to say it. But some part of me—probably the part that was still picturing my brother's reaction to the meager "data" I'd managed to squeeze from the conversation so far—couldn't get the word out. I'd spend the next who-knew-how-many-minutes hearing about her exciting (or more likely not) pre-TB life in Evanston, Illinois, while learning not one thing Old Red would care to know.

So I said something else. Something I hoped would make up in results what it lacked in subtlety.

"…who hated Wroblewski enough to kill him."

"*What?*" Miss Johansen gasped.

"We're trading gossip, remember. And I can't imagine anything juicier around here lately than a patient getting himself murdered. And given how the man died, there must have been *some* whispers."

"Well…"

It was dark there on the path, what with the tall, snow-topped trees looming up all around us. But despite the dim light, I could see an eager gleam in the lady's eyes.

This *was* the juiciest gossip at Echo Lake.

"There's been talk, yes," Miss Johansen said. "But no one hated Mr. Wroblewski so far as I know. He wasn't a very sociable man, apparently, but I don't believe he had enemies. I do have a theory that wouldn't require hatred to inspire murder, though. In fact, the inspiration would be *love*."

I rubbed my gloved hands together and fired up a matching gleam in my own eyes.

"Do tell."

Miss Johansen gave me a self-satisfied smile.

"The waiting list," she said.

"The waiting list?" said I.

Miss Johansen nodded. "The waiting list."

"The waiting list…for getting into the sanitorium?"

Miss Johansen nodded again.

"For charity patients?"

Miss Johansen kept nodding.

"Which might have current patients' brothers or sisters or mothers or fathers on it?" I said.

Miss Johansen kept on nodding.

"And someone might've decided to open up a spot at Echo Lake without waiting for tuberculosis to do it?"

The young lady gave me one final, firm nod.

She'd let me talk my way through the whole "theory" myself. Old Red would have approved.

Of her technique, anyway. Her theory, I figured, not so much.

I made the point he would've had he been there.

"But I heard Wroblewski was getting better. He might've left in a few weeks anyway. Why risk killing the man when Dr. Holly was getting him out of the way through good doctoring?"

Miss Johansen frowned—also very Old Red—and some of the gleeful gleam faded from her eyes.

"Yes. There is that," she said. "Sometimes I think I'd be better off if *I* were a charity case. They seem to get more 'good doctoring' than those of us who actually pay for it."

I was about to follow up on that thought—ask again if there was a paying patient so resentful of the charity cases that he'd do something about it—when I noticed how ragged and shallow Miss Johansen's breathing had become. The gray vapor of her breath

was coming out quick, like little puffs from an engine firing up for
its run.

The path wound up an incline, so we'd been walking uphill.
What's more, I'd kept the young lady talking the whole time.

"If I were from…the South Side of Chicago…rather than
Evanston," she panted, "perhaps I'd be…home already."

"Oh my goodness, Miss. I shouldn't have let you overdo it like
this," I said. "Let's stop and let you catch your breath."

Miss Johansen did indeed stop with me—but only for a
moment. The crunching of footsteps in the snow pulled our gazes
back toward the lake, and there was Breckenridge following us. He
was still a ways off, so it was hard to make out his expression in the
murky shade of the trail. But there was something about the way
he tramped uphill toward us that suggested grim, dogged deter-
mination.

"On my heels like a puppy," Miss Johansen muttered as she set
off again.

"He make a habit of this?" I asked, carrying on with her.

"Well, he doesn't do it every day. Just most."

"How about the day Wroblewski died? He trailing you then?"

Miss Johansen thought it over a moment, then laughed. Or
tried to laugh. She ended up coughing instead.

"I didn't see him that day," she said once the hacking passed.
"But if you're suggesting Leslie Breckenridge had anything to do
with Mr. Wroblewski's death…well, that's just ridiculous. The
boy's harmless."

She threw a glance back at him.

"The boy"—who was about her age, same as me—was still
following us up the trail.

"Annoying but harmless," she added.

"I'm sure you're right, Miss. Still…following a lady around like
this. Practically stalking her like a wolf. It's not proper."

We'd almost reached the end of the trail by then. It emptied
out onto a clearing I recognized.

Up ahead were rows of low, snow-covered mounds. Grave
markers. I stopped and gestured toward them.

"I hope you won't mind going on without me," I said. "I think I should have a word with Mr. Breckenridge about his behavior. Just him and me."

"Oh, no. Please," Miss Johansen said. "Don't do that on *my* behalf."

Those were her words anyway. The smirk that came to her face said something very different.

She was delighted.

There was going to be a confrontation between two young men. Over her. What could brighten another dismal, dull Echo Lake day more than that?

"I insist," I said. "We can resume our conversation later...with even more privacy."

I gave her a smirk of my own.

"All right. Thank you, Mr. Pycroft." She gazed past me toward Breckenridge again. "But please be gentle with him. He's just a sick, lovestruck child."

"I shall be firm but kind."

There was something about the way Miss Johansen nodded that told me I didn't have to be *too* kind—and that she would've enjoyed lingering to see just how firm I'd have to be. Yet she turned and continued toward the graveyard alone.

I headed in the opposite direction—toward Breckenridge, who was a mere forty yards off and getting closer by the second.

"Thank you for waiting for me, Mr. Pycroft," he said grimly. "I wanted to have a word with you. Man to man."

"Of course," I said, though there was no "of course" about it, of course.

I'd assumed what was on his mind was more man-to-woman, if you know what I mean. That's what I'd meant to talk to him about. Not to chide him, actually, but to see just how besotted with Miss Johansen he was...and whether that made him prone to the kind of jealousy an infatuated young man might act upon.

We both stopped when we were a few feet from each other on the trail. The wind had picked up again, sending clumps of snow falling from the high branches here and there as it whistled through the trees.

I spoke first.

"So…what did you want to say?"

Breckenridge took a deep breath. Or tried to. He got halfway through it when the frigid air or his crumbling lungs or both pierced him with pain, and he winced and coughed before replying.

"That I'm sorry."

"About what?"

"The box left on your bed. That was vile." Breckenridge looked down, shaking his head. "'The white death'…it almost seemed romantic to me once. Doomed young poets simply fading away. Dying translucent and beautiful. Then I came here and saw the reality."

He lifted his sunken, hollow eyes to meet mine again.

"Walking corpses hacking their insides out while catching cockroaches."

"Oh," I said. "Well. Thank you for the apology. I wouldn't want you to feel too bad about it, though. As you say, this place isn't the most pleasant, so folks have to find some way to get through the days. It's a shame cruelty's what some choose. But I assume my little gift—or gifts, more like—weren't your idea."

"No. It wasn't my idea. I could've said no, though."

I shrugged. "Yeah, but you're saying sorry now. That counts for something. If your friends want to leave me a box of rats tonight, *then* you can say no. Please."

Breckenridge nodded and gave me a tremulous, relieved smile.

Asking for forgiveness had taken some guts, and I respected that. I also meant to exploit it to the fullest.

"So whose idea was it?" I said. "Phillips and Foster?"

Breckenridge nodded again, though warily this time.

"Don't worry—I won't let on you told me," I assured him. "Though they probably want me to know anyway. Makes for better gloating. They ever pull that same gag on any of the charity patients?"

"Yes. But the other male 'guests' told them to stop. Not that they didn't find it amusing. They just don't like seeing so many roaches released so close to their own beds."

"Charming."

Breckenridge shrugged. "Like I said—dying slowly doesn't make you poetic. Or nice. I've learned that lesson."

"Yeah, but some end up un-nicer than others. Like Phillips and Foster. Why do they hate the charity patients so much?"

"I don't know. I used to think it was bitterness. That they needed someone to blame for where we've ended up. What's become of our lives. But the more I've gotten to know them…" Breckenridge gave me another shrug, this one noticeably wearier than the last. Even the effort to lift his shoulders was starting to take a toll. "It's just who they are."

"I understand. It's a condition I've seen often enough. Diagnosis: just plain mean. How far do they take it? Is it just practical jokes and nasty talk? Or do they ever want to do…more?"

"What do you mean?"

"They ever kill anybody?" seemed a bit blunt, even for me. So I had to come at it a different way.

"Well, I was just talking to Miss Johansen about Dr. Holly, for instance. How he's actually got a better record healing-wise than old Swann. But I know Holly's got ideas that don't sit well with everybody, too. Like bringing in black patients. I know how Phillips and Foster feel about *that*. Makes me wonder."

Breckenridge's expression turned quizzical, bemused. He was wondering, too—what my point was.

"Maybe they wouldn't want Dr. Holly's record to be so good," I went on. "Wouldn't like him having too much sway with the Board of Trustees. So…you know…would they ever do anything to…reduce the number of Dr. Holly's patients who go home cured?"

"Oh my god," said Breckenridge, quickly going from confused to incredulous. "Are you actually asking me if they've murdered anyone?"

I guess I should've just come out and said it after all. Or skipped the topic entirely.

"Now I didn't say 'murdered,'" I said (knowing full well I'd implied it, of course). "I'm just trying to figure out how far they'd go with these pranks of theirs...especially if they had more of a reason for it than boredom and spite."

"They wouldn't push a man off a cliff if that's what you're wondering. They're nasty, not insane."

Breckenridge stepped around me, headed up the narrow, shadowy path toward the graveyard.

"I think I'd better be going," he muttered.

"I didn't mean to offend you."

"They *are* my friends, you know," Breckenridge said without looking back.

There was much more I'd meant to ask him, if I could've figured out how to twist the conversation this way and that. Were Phillips and Foster part of the baseball game when Wroblewski died? How smitten was he with Miss Johansen—and what did he make of her goings-on with Turner? Did he know anything about the thefts Miss Johansen had mentioned or Miss MacGowan's supposed nighttime wanderings?

But now Breckenridge was leaving in a huff, and if I wanted to ask anything else I'd have to make it quick. So I did.

"Why?" I said.

That brought Breckenridge to a stop. He didn't turn to face me again, though. He just threw a glance back over his right shoulder.

"Why what?"

"Why are you friends with a couple bastards like Phillips and Foster?"

"Maybe I'm a bastard, too."

"I don't believe that."

"They do. They've accepted me. Befriended me. When everyone I knew before will have nothing to do with me. I don't even get letters anymore. They probably burned the ones I sent unread so they wouldn't have to touch something that's been tainted by me."

"That's too bad about your old friends. But it's not too late to make better ones."

Breckenridge faced forward again.

"Isn't it?" he said.

And he trudged on up the trail.

I didn't want to head the same direction he was—he was moving so slow I would've overtaken him in a dozen strides, which would've been awkward—nor did I fancy just standing there in the cold any longer. So I went in the opposite direction, back toward the lake and the bluffs beyond it. That was the scene of the crime, after all. (If there'd even been a crime, other than clumsiness on the edge of a cliff. It was still unclear to me.) As long as I was nearby, I may as well get another look at it.

The day's thick clouds must have been darkening even more, for as I walked the already dreary forest grew even grayer. The wind was picking up considerably, too, whipping down the trail from the west to push like insistent hands against my back. At first there was no sound other than my own footsteps and breaths and the growing moan of the gusts through the trees. But then I heard what sounded like the snap of a twig off to my left. I saw nothing that way but forest, though, and I dismissed it as a branch cracking under the weight of new-fallen snow or the random passing of a surprisingly pudgy squirrel. Or perhaps my own imagination, stoked by the overwhelming gloom of the sanitorium and its grounds (and occupants).

Then I heard it again.

Still I saw nothing. I looked back in time to see Breckenridge exiting the trail at its other end. The noise hadn't come from him.

I thought again of Mrs. Goldman and her skulking Indians. It was hard to believe any Utes or Arapahos could still be roaming free here so many years after their tribes had been dragged off to the reservations. But someone seemed to be shadowing me, and I didn't think it was the squirrel.

I was just thirty yards now from the lake-end of the trail, and I quickened my pace and put my hand to the Webley Bulldog in my coat pocket. The last time I'd gotten the creepy feeling that I was being followed I'd nearly plugged a hole in my brother. But he'd stick inside his little cabin till darkness fell, I figured, so it could be anybody out there with me—with any kind of intentions. Whoever it was, I wasn't going to let them catch me unprepared.

"You shoulda asked if Phillips and Foster was at the baseball game," Old Red said as I stepped out of the woods.

"Glurk!" I cried, jumping away from him.

My brother shook his head. "You do make the silliest sounds when you're startled."

I sucked in a deep breath of painfully cold air and put my left hand to my chest. It felt like my heart was pounding louder than the bass drum in a marching band.

"*Bang*—how'd that be for a sound?" I said. "That's what you're gonna hear the next time you surprise me like that! Good god—it's like you're *trying* to get shot."

"I thought you knew I was there."

"I knew *somebody* was there, but I didn't reckon it was you. You're stubborn but not usually stupid. What are you doing out and about in the light of day? You're bound to be spotted."

"Had to take that chance." Old Red jerked his chin into the cutting wind. "Ain't just a little snowfall now. Got us a blizzard blowin' in. Might be days before I can get a look at anything again."

"So wait days!"

Old Red gave me a sour look that told me his answer to that without words.

I don't wanna.

I forced myself to let go of my Bulldog. I wouldn't *really* shoot my brother just for being a jackass. But then again why put myself in temptation's way?

"Anyway," I grated out, "I *know* I should've asked about Phillips and Foster and the baseball game. I meant to, but I didn't get the chance. If you were close enough to eavesdrop you heard how Breckenridge reacted to even a hint that his pals are killers. He stomped off before I could double-check any alibis."

"Feh," Old Red grunted. "I woulda figured a way to get it out of him."

"Oh, sure! Cuz you're known far and wide for your persuasiveness and sparkling conversation!"

"When I want to know somethin', yeah!"

I started to swipe a hand at him—a favorite gesture of his when dismissing something I've just said. But the wind was so strong and cold now I changed my mind and wrapped my arms around myself instead.

"You're so damn sure I'm gonna 'booger things up' you booger 'em up yourself," I said. "Well, I won't fight it anymore. Here you are. Do whatever you want." I started to dance from foot to foot in a vain effort to warm up. "But you better do it quick before you freeze solid."

My brother muttered something I couldn't hear over the squall —probably "Dammit" because he knew I was right—and turned toward the lake. His gaze moved beyond it, to the bluffs overlooking the eastern shore. Where Wroblewski had died. Long, steady streams of snow were gusting away from the high cliffs. A fellow going up there would only find whatever clues might be around—and most likely himself—taking off like a kite.

"Dammit," Old Red said, loud and clear this time.

He looked this way and that, then turned and limped off toward the bluffs.

"Don't tell me you're actually gonna try to get up there in this weather," I said as I followed him. "And why go anyway? You told me you got a look up there yesterday."

I had to practically shout now to be heard over the wind.

Old Red didn't bother shouting back. He just pointed down.

There were tracks in the snow ahead of us. Not the ones Miss Johansen and Breckenridge and I had just made. Those came from the right, back toward the slope down from the sanitorium. These swung left.

My brother swung left, too.

I shivered and grumbled and cursed myself for a fool.

And swung left, too.

Afternoon

It was hard to make much of the tracks. With the wind whipping and more snow falling they were less footprints than shallow dips in the solid blanket of white. But it was clearly a single set—one person circling along the lake headed east.

I eyed the trees to our left as we tromped along. Here was Old Red right in front of me now, but the little pit of dread in my stomach—the unsettling sense I was being watched from the woods—hadn't left me.

"You sure there couldn't be Indians around here still?" I said.

"No," my brother said unhelpfully. "But it's damn unlikely."

"But did you notice with that horse? No bridle, no saddle."

Old Red shot a scowl over this shoulder.

Did I notice? the look said. *Feh!*

Of course, he'd noticed.

"Did *you* notice its tracks?" he said, turning back to the ones we were following along the lakeshore.

"No," I admitted. I was too damn cold to sigh, but I felt like heaving one. I was in no mood to have my nose rubbed in a missed clue. "What about 'em?"

My brother stopped and lifted his right foot a few inches off the ground. He stood there on one leg for a moment, grimacing, as he gave his sore foot a rest.

"That horse is shod," he said.

"Ah. So not an Indian horse. Not if we're talking the free-living roam-the-range kinda Indian anyway."

"Which pretty much don't exist anymore."

I looked left again, at the thick forest of pines and firs and junipers. The general dreariness of the day darkened the already deep shadows between the trees, so much so that I could hardly see fifty feet into the woods. Anything could be back in here. Anybody.

"But like you say," I said, "we can't be sure there ain't a few Utes or whoever still about here and there. And maybe more here than there, if you know what I mean. That horse didn't come up the mountain to take the cure."

Old Red set his foot down and started hobbling off again.

"So what's your theory?" he said. "A Cheyenne brave stole that horse and rode it up here for fun…then just let it go cuz he got tired of it?"

"'It is a capital mistake to theorize before one has data,'" I pontificated. "'Insensibly one begins to twist facts to suit theories, instead of——'"

"Oh, shut up!"

That gave me my first real smile of the day.

If I wanted to get under Old Red's skin, all I had to do was hit him with one of the Holmes quotes he so loves throwing at me.

We'd been talking loud to be heard over the wind, and my throat was going scratchy from all the bellowing in the frigid air. So I gave my mouth (and my brother) a break as we carried on around the lake.

The ground had begun to tilt upward sharply, building to the bluffs, and Old Red's already less-than-speedy pace slowed even more. If he got any slower he could be outrun by a rock. The longer we followed that trail, the greater the odds I'd have to carry him back to his cabin like a babe in arms. Which I could probably manage, but I didn't think either of us would enjoy it.

Just as the incline got so steep I started wondering if Old Red could continue, the tracks cut left, into the trees. My brother followed them dutifully (if sluggishly). I did so reluctantly. I was chilled to the core, and it was taking more and more fortitude to keep putting one foot in front of the other when we were headed *away* from shelter.

After maybe a dozen steps into the woods, Old Red finally stopped. The tracks led to a dead ponderosa pine lying on its side, then carried on deeper into the forest. Rather than keep following, my brother knelt by the rotting, snow-topped trunk, cocked his head, then rose and stepped over it. He crouched down on the other side, cocked his head, and reached down to root around beneath the tree.

He said something the whistling of the wind carried away, but I could read his lips plain enough.

"Hel-lo."

He lifted his right hand. In it was a small, white oval.

"Did you lead us all the way out here to start a snowball fight?" I said, surprised and irritated.

Throwing snowballs wasn't Old Red's style—it was mine. And here I'd let him get the drop on me.

"It ain't a snowball," Old Red said. His tone added "ya idjit." "It's an egg."

He reached down with his left hand and pulled out another.

"Oh," I said. "So we've been following a goose?"

That was a joke. The eggs my brother was holding up were half the size of what a goose would lay. And these weren't just smaller. They were familiar. I'd seen them—or ones just like them at any rate—at breakfast that very morning.

Hard-boiled chicken eggs. Not the sort of thing one usually finds just lying around in the woods.

Old Red put the eggs back and rummaged around some more under the tree trunk.

"Four eggs in all," he said.

"Any coffee?" I slapped my arms and did another little jig of the sort that never really warms you up at all. "If so, I'd love a cup."

Old Red ignored that like he'd ignored my crack about the goose.

"Nice little hidey hole," he said, standing up. "If not for the trail in the snow there'd be no way to know it was here."

He turned to look at the tracks carrying on deeper into the forest. Whoever had dropped off that food had done some circling through the woods before heading back toward the sanitorium—

BLACK LIST, WHITE DEATH 169

if indeed that's where they went. Maybe they were still out with us
for the finding. *If* we kept looking.

"Oh, hell no. We're done," I was about to tell Old Red. "If
you haven't noticed, we're in the middle of a goddamn blizzard."

The person behind me spoke up first.

"What do you two think you're doing?" she barked at us.

"Twerb!" I cried.

I really do make the most embarrassing sounds when startled.

I pivoted to find Nurse Rosenkoetter glaring at us from a
dozen paces away, her long tweed coat fluttering in the wind.

"Mr. Melas was breaking quarantine again," I told her. "And I
was chastising him for it." I shook a pointed finger at my brother.
"Now you come along, Mr. Melas. Any more of this rule-breaking
and you're liable to get sent back to Boise."

"Yes, sir. Sorry. Won't happen again," Old Red said. He had
to say it loud—as if speaking to our deaf old landlady back in
Ogden—to be sure the nurse could hear it.

She scowled at him skeptically as we started toward her.

"I hope you didn't come all the way out here looking for *us*," I said.

"As a matter of fact, I did. Only a few patients—and one staff
member, Mr. Pycroft—were foolish enough to be wandering
around in this." Nurse Rosenkoetter raised a gloved hand, indicating the wind, the clouds, the heavy snow coming down over the
lake beyond her. "We had to make sure everyone came in."

"Who else is still out?" Old Red asked.

"No one now. I sent the last couple in before following your
tracks up here."

My brother's mouth clamped tight, as if he was biting back a
"Feh."

She'd managed to answer his question without telling him
what he really wanted to know.

Who had *we* been following?

Nurse Rosenkoetter was watching him closely as he limped
out of the woods.

"What were you doing back there?" she asked him.

"Explorin'. I get awful bored in that little chicken coop you stuck me in."

"I would think you'd appreciate the opportunity to rest." She glanced down at his right foot. "You seem to have an injury."

"Oh, this gimpy thing?" Old Red said, pointing down at his boot. "Been like that for years. Stepped on by a cow."

The nurse didn't look convinced.

My brother remembered to cough. It didn't help.

"Who are you really?" Nurse Rosenkoetter said.

She hadn't moved from her spot on the incline leading up to the bluffs, and we stopped before her and did our best to look sincerely puzzled.

"What do you mean?" Old Red said.

"I've seen hundreds of TB patients. Probably thousands," Nurse Rosenkoetter replied coolly. My brother and I had to prac- tically yell to be heard, but not her somehow. She was able to send her words slicing through the squall through sheer, steely will. "I know the signs and symptoms like the back of my hand. And I'm insulted that anyone could think I wouldn't spot a phony."

I popped my eyes wide. "A phony? Mr. Melas?"

The nurse shifted her frosty stare over to me. Snow had been building up on her shoulders, yet she didn't bother brushing it off. It looked like she had the world's worst case of dandruff and didn't care who knew it.

"Both of you," she said. "Dr. Swann knows, doesn't he?"

I threw my brother a quick, questioning glance. The woman had seen through us. Should we just come clean and hope she could help us?

Old Red looked tempted. But after a second of indecision he said, "I don't know what you're talkin' about."

"Me neither," I added lamely.

If anyone ever saw through one of Sherlock Holmes's masquerades, Doc Watson never wrote about it. So we didn't know what to do other than try to bluff it out like a couple kids caught with their hands in the cookie jar: "Who? Us? Oh, we were just dusting."

"Fine," Nurse Rosenkoetter said. "Carry on with your ridiculous charade. I'll work out the truth eventually. And if you're here to cause trouble for the sanitorium or Dr. Holly, you'll find you've made a formidable enemy."

She spun sharply on her heel and began marching off down the hill.

"Ain't here to cause trouble! We're here to end it!" Old Red called after her. "We don't gotta be enemies!"

The nurse stopped like she'd hit a brick wall. She stood there a moment perfectly still, as if considering my brother's words. When she finally spoke, she didn't spin around to face us —just turned her head and sent the words out over her shoulder.

"'We *aren't* here to cause trouble.' And 'We *don't have to* be enemies,'" she said. "If you're going to lie to me, at least do so grammatically."

And off she went again.

"Dammit," my brother said.

"It's a wrinkle, all right," I told him. "And all because someone couldn't stick to the plan and leave the detecting to me one more day."

"Is that an 'I told you so'?"

"Well, if you gotta ask, I guess I need to be more clear about it." I cleared my throat. "I told you so."

Old Red really did look mad enough to start whipping snowballs at me now. But instead he just shambled off down the hill.

I followed—though I kept a little distance between us just in case he did decide to scoop up some snow and aim for my face.

It was slow going back to the sanitorium. After five minutes we were still plodding along by the lakeshore even though Nurse Rosenkoetter had already disappeared into the woods ahead, up the trail that ran past the cemetery.

I could've been right behind her. Hell, I could've sprinted past her, making for the coziest corner of the sanitorium building. Which wouldn't have been that cozy, of course, but it would've beat trudging at turtle-speed through a whiteout. If my brother was going to get turned into a snowman, I wouldn't let him do it alone, though. Damn him.

When we finally stepped off the trail past the graveyard and got the sanitorium in view again, we saw no sign of Nurse Rosenkoetter. She hadn't hung back to make sure we made it in out of the storm, heading inside instead to warm someone else's day with her sunny ways.

But we weren't alone. A little party was emerging from the back of the main building: a tall, broad-shouldered, scarf-wrapped man—Dr. Holly, most likely—leading two orderlies carrying a stretcher between them.

The stretcher had a passenger. One with a sheet pulled over her head and no need for blankets to ward off the chill. She was going to go cold no matter what.

"Damn," I said. "I bet that's Miss Blum. One of the patients. She took a sudden turn for the worse yesterday."

"I guess she took another," Old Red said. "The worst kind."

The group angled off toward the squat, featureless building Dr. Holly had called his laboratory and Nurse Rosenkoetter called the morgue.

"Anything odd about the way she took ill?" my brother asked as we tramped toward them.

"Not in the slightest for somebody with TB. Started hacking up blood and got hustled off to the infirmary. Given where we are it'd be odd if someone *didn't* do that while we're around."

Old Red made a noncommittal noise—a grunt that either acknowledged I had a point or conveyed his annoyance that he hadn't been inside to see all the clues I'd most likely missed. Or probably it was both.

Dr. Holly was unlocking and opening the door to the morgue now, and as the orderlies stepped past him with their cargo, he glanced over and saw us. He held up his left hand in greeting—his right clutched something close to his chest—and headed toward us.

I groaned as the young doctor approached. Thirty paces from a doorway—and relief from the cold that had me feeling like I'd been stowed in an icebox beside the butter and leftover ham—and now we had to pause for more chitchat.

"Gentlemen," Dr. Holly said, "I'm glad to see you decided to rejoin us."

"Yeah, well…we'd had our fill of sleddin' and ice skatin', so we decided to call it a day," said Old Red.

Dr. Holly nodded, chuckling.

It wasn't like my brother to toss off such a joke—that, like snowballs, was more my speed—and I noticed him eyeing the young doctor intently as the three of us gathered up close.

Nurse Rosenkoetter had beat us back by maybe ten minutes. If she'd told Dr. Holly about us being fakes, he was a good enough actor not to show it.

The wind picked up fiercely for a few seconds, building into the kind of cutting gust that makes you feel like your blood's freezing to ice in your veins. We all winced and squinted, and Dr. Holly put his free hand to the folder he was holding.

"That Miss Blum's patien—…I mean guest file?" I asked when the wind died down again.

"Yes, unfortunately. She succumbed not long ago." Dr. Holly shook his head. "Just twenty-three."

"So she stays out here till the ground thaws enough to bury her?" Old Red said. "Or is the body gonna get shipped off to wherever she hailed from?"

The doctor jerked his head toward my brother, taken aback by his morbid curiosity and bluntness.

"The young lady was one of my patients," Dr. Holly said stiffly. Meaning she was a charity patient. "She'll be put to rest here when the weather permits, as you say."

It looked like my brother was going to follow up with another question—no doubt one in even worse taste than the last—but the doctor cut him off and changed the subject.

"And how are you doing, Mr. Melas? I hear it's hard to keep you in quarantine. Are you that anxious to join the rest of us, or have you changed your mind about being here at all?"

Old Red shrugged. "I'm just prone to gettin' antsy."

"He's promised me this is his last escape attempt," I added.

Dr. Holly looked past us at our trail through the snow slanting off toward the woods.

"It seems you've had a remarkably vigorous walk for a man in your condition, Mr. Melas. I look forward to getting to know you better tomorrow."

When "Mr. Melas" was out of quarantine, he meant—ready for the examination that would surely make it plain he didn't have TB at all.

"You should have fresh food waiting for you in your cabin," the doctor went on. "Please, eat and rest…and do your best not to 'get antsy.'"

"Sure, doc. I'll try," Old Red said.

The orderlies had left the morgue by now. They hurried toward the back of the main building, the stretcher between them on its side, empty.

"Well…duty calls," Dr. Holly said. "I would wish you a good day, but I think this hardly qualifies."

"See ya tomorrow," my brother said as the doctor turned and walked away.

As much as I wanted to make the last dash through a door at last, the way Old Red lingered I knew he wasn't through. So I lingered (shivering), too.

"'Duty calls'?" my brother grumbled when Dr. Holly was out of earshot. "What's his duty to a dead woman?"

"He's gotta fill out the last part of her file. Time of death and all that," I said. "Might even have to do an autopsy. You heard what Dr. Swann said yesterday. The county coroner leaves all that to them."

"Don't seem like you'd need an autopsy to know what killed a lunger."

I shrugged. Or maybe just shivered extra hard. It was getting hard to tell the difference.

"Bureaucracy," I said. "And until they invent a machine that lets doctors see inside patients without opening them up for look-see…well…"

"Sometimes they're gonna open 'em up for a look-see."

Dr. Holly headed into the morgue. I didn't envy him his destination, but he certainly had the right idea about getting in out of the storm.

"All right—I'm done," I announced. "You can keep standing here waiting to get snowed over if you want. I'll be thawing out inside like a sane person."

I started toward the main building.

"Almost don't seem worth it to keep up this 'Mr. Melas' hogwash," Old Red said. "Holly's sure to see through it tomorrow."

I didn't stop to give my answer. Instead I just turned around as I carried on, walking backward. Nothing was going to stop me from warmth now.

"Yeah, probably," I said. "But that still gives us another full day to snoop with only Dr. Swann and Nurse Rosenkoetter any the wiser."

"Gives *you* another full day to snoop. Gives me another full day sittin' on my ass."

"We been tromping around all morning gathering clay for you," I said. "So hunker down and make some goddamn bricks."

And with that, I finally—*finally!*—darted through a door and escaped the wind and snow (and my brother)...

...into a dark, chilly mudroom lined with boots and hanging coats and cloaks. It wasn't much cheerier when I moved on into the sanitorium building proper. Though everyone but Old Red and Dr. Holly were supposedly inside now, it was even more quiet and subdued than usual. I heard a low murmur of voices as I drew closer to the main lobby, and I followed it around a corner to the parlor in the men's ward. It was identical to the women's parlor—tall windows, plush chairs and settees, writing tables, a fireplace—except that the art along the wall had a more manly bent to it. Mighty ships at sea and "The Surrender of Lord Cornwallis" and such. Yet the men gathered there—all the male patients in the place, it looked like—were busy with something that didn't seem very manly at all.

They were hunched over the longer tables together, colorful tissue paper and crepe spread out before them. Many of the men were cutting away with scissors. Others were fashioning the material into bunting and oversized bows. It looked for all the world like they were getting ready to decorate for a Fourth of July picnic.

My surprise must've shown on my face, for much to my chagrin my least favorite patients looked up and grinned at me. Even more to my chagrin, the two men—Phillips and Foster, of course—whispered to each other and stood and headed my way.

Though Breckenridge had been sitting with them he stayed where he was, refusing to look at me after a first cursory glance. I guess he'd had enough of me for a while. Or enough of Phillips and Foster's idea of fun with me.

"Are you here to help us get ready for the party?" Phillips asked me. He tilted his head as he spoke, and with his narrow face and big, beak-like nose he reminded me of a raven eyeing something shiny.

"Party?" I said warily.

"Well, ball," Foster corrected. "A spring ball, for those who can appreciate the irony. Young Dr. Holly's idea. I assume it's supposed to lift our spirits and distract us from *that*."

He jerked his balding, splotchy head at the nearest window and the snow still coming down outside.

"And from what 'young Dr. Holly' is doing this very moment out in our Chamber of Horrors," Phillips added.

"Ah. Yes. Miss Blum. Very sad," I said. "Did you know the young lady well?"

Phillips and Foster looked at each other and laughed.

"'The young lady'?" Phillips scoffed. "No, we didn't associate. I think she was from Hell's Kitchen."

"By way of Warsaw," said Foster.

"Well, no more kitchen for her. Just hell."

Foster's patchy eyebrows shot up. Phillips's joke was so mean it even caught *him* by surprise.

Then Foster laughed again.

Phillips smiled proudly, reveling in his own loathsomeness.

I turned back toward Breckenridge and the other men snipping away with their scissors. If the subject didn't get changed fast I was going to smack somebody.

"So…you're in charge of the decorations?"

Foster nodded. "And the women are preparing refreshments and picking the music."

"I do hope they let the *ladies* among them lead the way," Phillips said. "I'm not partial to boiled cabbage and jigs."

"Yeah, well…it's a strange day for a spring social, but I suppose they've gotta find something to keep you occupied," I said. "I mean, it's not exactly baseball weather."

I was already gritting my teeth just talking to these two, and now I gritted them even harder.

This was going to be a painful transition, but I had to make it while I had the chance or my brother would give me hell.

"Speaking of which," I said, "did you two play in that game a couple weeks ago?"

Foster and Phillips didn't seem to mind the sudden swerve to a new subject. It was one they were eager to talk about.

"I should say so," Foster said. "I pitched six innings."

"And I played first base," said Phillips. "Batted a thousand, too. A double and three singles."

"We were co-captains of our team."

"Of course you were," I said. I nodded toward Breckenridge. "And he was your catcher, I assume. Or was he your batboy?"

"Neither," Foster snorted. "He had better things to do."

"Mooning over Miss Johansen again," Phillips said. "She was on one of her long walks with Turner, and the puppy dog had to stay on her heels."

I thought back to what Miss Johansen had told me of that day —and the walk she'd been on when Wroblewski fell from the bluff. She hadn't mentioned Turner or Breckenridge being around.

"You know that for sure," I asked, "or is that just an assumption cuz none of them were at the game?"

Phillips and Foster's perpetual sneers turned to looks of puzzlement.

"What a very probing question," said Phillips.

"Why are you so interested in who did or didn't play that day?" said Foster.

"Oh, I'm a baseball fan myself, so I'm thinking of fielding my own team. It'd be good to know who my prospects might be."

The puzzlement turned to skepticism.

"Interesting…given that Turner's gone and Miss Johansen hardly seems like shortstop material," said Phillips.

"You're right. Skip them," I said. "How about the rest of the men here? Any other notable absences from the game?"

Phillips shook his head slowly. The skepticism wasn't going away.

"Notable? No. Most of the male patients were there. Much of the staff."

"McCandless was our umpire," Phillips added.

"I would've thought it'd be Swann," I said. "He's the main authority up here, and I heard it was him who gave permission for y'all to play."

"He had pressing business elsewhere," said Foster.

He and Phillips smirked at each other.

"What do you mean?" I asked.

Foster started to answer.

Phillips stopped him with a hand on his arm.

"You want to see for yourself?" Phillips said to me. "Go down in the cellar."

Foster nodded knowingly. "Ahh, yes. The cellar. Look in the northwest corner."

"Behind the Wall of Death," Phillips intoned ominously.

I took a moment to review what my ears had seemingly heard.

Was it "behind the furnace"?

Behind the coal chute?

Behind the pickled beets?

Behind the croquet mallets and old paint cans and that busted bicycle your uncle keeps saying he's going to fix one day?

What else do people keep in a cellar?

And what the hell could sound like "the Wall of Death"? Other than "the Wall of Death"?

Before I could repeat it back, Phillips looked over at Foster and said, "I think we should get back to our streamers, William."

Foster nodded. "I agree, Harold. We wouldn't want the other fellows to think we're shirkers."

They started back toward their table.

"Happy hunting," Phillips said to me with a smile.

Well, what's a self-respecting detective supposed to do after that? Or even a detective like me? There might be a murderer about and there's *definitely* a lot of weirdness going on and somebody tells you there's a big secret something hidden in the cellar behind "the Wall of Death"…? You don't have a choice, do you? Even if you're on your own because your partner's stuck elsewhere staring at the walls.

You go down in the cellar.

Of course, you have to find it first. I went to the office and—after noting Dr. Swann's closed door—grabbed a pencil and a folder of random files so I could look official while I poked around. My poking took me up and down the main hall, into various closets, along the men's and women's wards, and through the dining hall. Just when I was about to give up and conclude that Phillips and Foster had got me again—the gag this time being that there was no cellar at all—I found what I was looking for.

It was around the corner from the kitchen and larder: a door that opened onto utter darkness. The cooks were busy whipping up another meal of toasted cardboard and boiled rags, or something equally tasty, and their clanging and chopping and chattering covered the sound of the squeaky hinges and my footsteps on the creaky stairs. I trailed my fingers along the wall to my right as I descended—there being no wall on my left to touch—and I felt rough plaster but, at first, nothing more.

Then there it was. Sweet salvation.

A light.

A simple brass bracket for gas, to be exact. Which meant I

wouldn't have to follow up my hunt for the cellar with an even longer hunt for an oil lamp or candle.

I turned on the gas and fired it up with a match, then closed the cellar door and started down the stairs again.

The underworld's a mighty warm place if you believe the preachers, but that wasn't the case here. With each step, the air around me grew colder and danker. It got darker, too, for the gas fixture on the stairs only gave off so much light, and there wasn't another one down below. Not that I'd have been able to light another one anyway: The match I'd used on the stairs had been the only one on me.

I could make out just about everything down there once my eyes adjusted, though. The wall carried on for another forty feet or so beyond the bottom of the stairs before cutting left and left and left again to form a perfect box beneath the sanitorium building. Ahead of me, I saw shelves laden with crates and cleaning supplies—scouring powders, bleach, flat irons, and such. To the side was a long line of steamer trunks and portmanteaus and valises and grips stacked up on pallets.

When I reached the bottom of the stairs and took a step toward the luggage, I could make out something else in the shadows beyond it—something I'd taken at first glance for the far wall. For a wall it seemed to be, though I could see now that it was only chest high and didn't run the full length of the cellar.

I walked around the trunks and bags to get close, seeing as I did so that the "wall" I was approaching was simply more trunks and bags. I hadn't exactly been thrilled about facing a "Wall of Death" down there, but realizing it was just a Wall of Luggage still felt like a letdown. Then I noticed what was written on the tag hanging from the shabby valise atop the far end of the pile.

J. WROBLEWSKI

CHICAGO, ILL.

A tag dangled from the Gladstone bag next to the valise. I reached out and turned it around and saw this:

L. PALOMARES
CLEVELAND, OHIO

I looked down the long row of trunks and bags—travel gear for dozens of people who'd never go anywhere ever again. They'd all reached their final destination. The cemetery hidden in the woods.

I was facing a Wall of Death after all. Swann's secret—the "pressing business" Phillips and Foster hinted was in the cellar—was supposedly behind it.

I stepped to the side to look along the real wall running behind the baggage. There was just enough space for someone to walk into the shadows obscuring the farthest corner of the room. The northwest corner—where Foster had told me to look. So I started walking.

Black shapes darted away up the wall and under the luggage. They weren't just stray members of the Welcoming Committee—some were too long and thin for that, with an undulating, zigzag way of running I found both repulsive and familiar.

Centipedes.

I heard skittering on the other side of the cellar, too. Where there's bugs, there's rats.

I tried not to think of what I might step on or bump into as the darkness before me deepened.

There was a shape on the wall, I saw as I grew closer. A square low to the ground, a different shade than the bricks around it.

It was a door, waist-high. An entrance to another chamber. A cellar within the cellar.

The door was secured with a hasp latch with a small brass padlock through the staple. I squatted down before it and gave the padlock a tug. Maybe I'd get lucky and it'd just pop open.

I didn't get lucky. The lock stayed locked. I'd come all this way only to learn that there was something more I couldn't learn. Unless…

I still had the folder I'd been walking around with as I'd searched upstairs. In it were the files for several patients. Each individual's records were held together with fasteners in the upper-left corner—metal triangles with arms you could bend around to pinch the paper. I didn't even know what the little things were called: When I'd been a granary clerk as a boy, we'd tied files together with string. But these little brass doohickeys could do more than keep people's paperwork apart, I hoped.

I opened the folder, slid out one of the fasteners, and straightened one of its arms. Old Red had learned lockpicking from the descriptions in detective magazines. He wasn't any master cracksman, but he could get us past locked doors most of the time. Maybe now I could do the same.

Not that I knew what I was doing. I just poked the metal up into the keyhole at the base of the padlock and started fiddling.

I don't know if it was a cheap lock or I'm just a lucky SOB—probably a little bit of both—but it worked. After a few seconds, the body of the padlock popped away from the shackle, and I was able to take the padlock off the latch and pull the little door open.

Before me now was what felt like a tunnel, two feet wide and three high. I say "felt like" because I couldn't actually see it. There wasn't enough light for that. So I was really looking at a box of blackness two feet wide and three high. With no more matches on me there was only one way to tell what was inside that black box.

I reached inside.

I felt nothing but cobwebs and the cold roughness of brick along the left side of the tunnel. But when I tried again on the right, my hand hit something solid about halfway down. I probed at it gently with my fingers, finding I could wrap my hand around it and lift it up. As I did so, I heard a *clink* as it bumped against something sitting beside it.

I scooched back and stood and lifted the thing in my hand up into the dim light coming over the "Wall of Death." And I laughed.

It was a bottle of Gordon's gin. Full, unlike the ones Old Red had found under the floorboards of one of the cabins.

I squatted back down and patted again along the wall, deeper back this time, with less trepidation. As expected, I felt bottle after bottle after bottle.

Some men have wine cellars. Apparently Dr. Swann had one for gin.

I was so relieved it wasn't something more macabre down there I felt like popping open the nearest bottle and taking a celebratory swig. Given Foster and Phillips' sense of humor I was a little surprised they hadn't steered me into a septic tank.

I (reluctantly) put back the bottle I'd pulled out and got ready to close and relock the little door. I paused with my hand on the latch, though, pondering.

Swann kept his liquor supply under lock and key and could do his drinking in his office or upstairs in his private rooms. So how did those empties end up outside underneath a cabin?

Foster and Phillips knew about Swann's secret stash, so others probably would, too. But would those others be as good (or as lucky) at lock picking as me?

There was a simpler explanation than that. Keys. Dr. Swann said Turner had a full set of duplicates that he'd "lost." But if he'd really given them to Miss Johansen, as the doctor and Old Red suspected, why did she seem so intent on wheedling her way to a new set? I mean, I know I'm a charming son of a gun, but it was obvious she was trying to get *something* from me. I thought back to my conversation with the young lady that morning, sure there was some connection I was overlooking—a link to the questions I was asking myself now.

If Old Red had been there, he'd have probably seen it straight off. He would've scolded me for missing it, too. And maybe he'd be right to. "'You know my methods. Apply them,'" he'd told me again and again, quoting Guess Who. Yet I'd never managed it. Now here I was trying to be his eyes and ears even though where it really mattered—brains—I could never fill his shoes. (Not that brains wear shoes, but you know what I mean.)

Every new word my brother learned to read was one less he needed me to tell him. And once he'd truly mastered reading— and that probably wouldn't be long, now that he was really working at it—what good was I going to be? Unless he got shot in the foot on a regular basis. Which wasn't entirely impossible given his talent for pissing people off. But that was hardly a fitting hope to pin my future on.

Maybe I should become a shoe salesman.

I shook off this random thought. Deducifying properly might not be about brilliance. Perhaps it's more about focus. Which I had clearly lost. If I could just think everything through one more time maybe answers would finally come to me...

There was a sudden, nerve-jangling screech, like nails on a chalkboard.

It was the sound of rusty hinges. Someone was opening the door to the cellar.

I was still crouched down behind the wall of trunks and bags, one hand on the little door's latch. So I couldn't see who was at the top of the stairs. But I could hear them moving to the first step...and stopping.

For what felt like minutes but was probably seconds, the only sound I heard was my own shallow breathing and the thumping of my heart. I thought about popping up and playing it casual—"Oops...I was looking for the privy and somehow ended up down here!"—but why reveal myself if I didn't have to? Maybe whoever it was would come down to collect the can of Bon Ami or whatever they were after and then turn around and head right back up, none the wiser.

Or maybe whoever it was wasn't after Bon Ami at all.

The cat was out of the bag with at least a couple people that Old Red and I weren't who we seemed. Perhaps more knew...and now the very person we were hunting was hunting me.

My Bulldog was still in my coat, which I'd hung up in my room after coming inside. If someone was coming for me with evil intent I'd have only my fists and wits to ward them off. Which Old Red would say left me with fists.

All the more reason to remain silent and still and hope I wasn't noticed.

That was the plan, anyway. But it's hard to stay silent and still

—impossible even, I'd say from experience—when you feel legs start crawling across the back of your hand. And I did. Lots of legs, moving fast toward the cuff of my shirt and the arm beyond it.

I managed to stifle the "Gurp!" or "Blarg!" or whatever ridiculous syllable wanted to explode from my mouth. But I couldn't keep my hand from instinctively jerking away from the door and flapping to rid itself of the centipede intent on taking up residence somewhere inside my clothes. And I couldn't keep *that* from throwing me off balance.

I pitched backward, coming down hard on my rump. It's well-padded enough to absorb the shock, so I still didn't cry out. But there was enough of a *thump* to reach the top of the stairs.

I expected to hear "Who's there?" Or "Come out where I can see you." Or "Oh, get up offa your ass and tell me what you're doin'." (That'd be if Old Red had got antsy again and came sneaking inside this time.)

Instead the silence stretched on a little longer…until I heard a creak, then another, then another on the stairs.

Whoever was up there was coming down, slowly but steadily. Another few steps and they'd be far enough down the staircase for me to see who it was. Assuming I worked up the nerve to get to my feet and take a peep over the Wall of Death.

The footsteps continued.

I started working on my nerve.

"…god forbid we should use garlic!" I heard a woman laugh in the distance, and suddenly the footsteps were twice as loud and twice as fast and going in the opposite direction.

The person on the stairs was hurrying away.

"Just once I'd like to take a bottle of Tabasco," another woman said, coming closer, "and empty it in Swann's bowl of… oh."

Again I heard footsteps—echoey ones from the hallway connecting the kitchen and the larder and the cellar. The steps stopped at the top of the stairs.

"Dr. Swann?" the second woman said. She let a quiet moment go by. "Caitlin? McCandless?"

I should've popped up to try my "Hi—got lost on the way to the john!" line. But I guess I'd grown accustomed to cowering in the shadows, and I was still thrown by the need to cower at all.

Who had that been on the stairs before…and what were they coming down to do after they heard me?

"It was probably Swann," the first woman said, her voice just above a whisper. "Restocking."

"Yeah, probably," the second woman said. "And if he caught *me* leaving the lamp on and the door open he'd sack me on the spot."

And with that, what illumination there was winked out, and I heard a jangle and a squeal and a rattle.

The woman had turned off the light and closed the door. Locked the door, too, it sounded like.

"Shit," I said. And worse. I cussed a blue streak wider than the Mississippi, in fact.

I was trapped in a pitch-black cellar with rats, roaches, centipedes, and spiders for company. And the only person who knew I was down there might or might not come back to see about visiting some kind of mischief upon me. And my gun was two stories up in a coat pocket while my brother rode out a blizzard a hundred yards away, none the wiser.

How do you become a shoe salesman anyway? I resolved to find out. If I ever got out of that goddamn cellar.

I turned and picked up the file I'd been toting around and started groping my way along the Wall of Death with my free hand. Moving as fast as I dared, I shuffled through the blackness until I reached the end of the luggage. There I turned again, headed for the stairs (I hoped), utterly blind and with nothing to touch to guide me. My hand was stretched out before me now, and eventually my fingertips bumped into something ice cold and metal hard. I probed it a moment and found it had a tip up top and a blunt body and a handle on one side.

It was an iron. I'd drifted off course in the dark and ended up walking into the shelves near the bottom of the stairs. The steps would be a few feet to my right. I started turning that way then froze, fingertips still resting on the iron's steepled tip.

When Miss Johansen had listed off stuff that had been stolen from around the sanitorium lately, she'd included "an iron, of all things." Apparently the spares were kept down here in the cellar, under lock and key. Which might mean something...

I'd literally bumped into a clue.

I gave the iron a little pat, then moved on to the stairs. Those I discovered with my right toe. I went up slowly, left hand trailing along the wall, until my knee hit wood. I was at the door at last.

I found the knob and gave it a try. It was locked, like I thought.

There was only one thing to do. Knock...and hope whoever answered wasn't a murderer.

I rapped on the door. It took a while—and a *lot* of rapping—to get a response. Who expects company to come calling from a locked cellar? But eventually I heard voices out in the hallway, and someone stepped up close to the door and said, "Who is that?"

"It's Albert Pycroft. The new clerk. Would you mind letting me out?"

There were murmurs on the other side of the door—the two women from the kitchen I'd heard earlier, it sounded like. No doubt they were whispering something to each other along the lines of "What the hell...?" or "Is he nuts?"

"I'd be happy to explain if you'd be so good as to open the door," I said.

There were more murmurs, but I heard the jingling of keys, too. The lock rattled, and the door swung open.

The two women—both plump and short and dressed in identical blue dresses and white aprons—stepped back to let me out. I'd promised an explanation, so I smiled and gave them one.

"Went down looking for a pencil and lost track of time."

I didn't say it would be a *good* explanation.

"A question for you, ladies," I said quickly before the women could ask *me* anything. "I hear a hand iron was stolen recently. You know anything about that?"

"Not really," said the woman holding the keys. "We're kitchen staff."

"Of course. But it's just the general details I'm wondering about. When did it happen and where was the iron taken from—the linen closet or the cellar?"

"It was taken from down there," said the other woman, pointing at the darkness beyond me. "A week or so ago."

"At least that's when they noticed it was gone," the cook with the keys added.

"Ah. So this would've been *after* the big baseball game."

The cooks furrowed their brows and looked tempted to take another big step back.

"Yeeeeess," the woman with the keys said slowly. "What does that matter?"

"Oh, it might not matter at all. I just thought I should note it." I held up the file in my hand and gave it a little jiggle. "For a report I'm working on. How about food? You ever notice any of that getting pilfered?"

"All the time!" Key Woman huffed. It looked like I'd hit upon a pet peeve of hers. "You never know what you're going to find missing come morning!"

"Any idea who's doing it?"

"Well…"

Key Woman stopped there, obviously not sure she should let her guard down around this strange, inquisitive man who'd just stepped out of the basement.

Fortunately, the other cook was the trusting type.

"Erin thinks it's Swann," she told me, nodding at her friend.

"Molly!" Erin exclaimed.

"Oh, you don't have to worry," I assured her. "My report's not for Swann. It's for the board. You can tell me anything. You won't get in any trouble."

"Well…," Erin said again. This time she let herself go on. "Dr. Swann has habits. Appetites. If anyone was going to go into the pantry in the night and steal a hunk of cheese, it'd be him."

"Because of his 'appetite' for cheese?" I asked innocently.

I knew now his appetite was for Gordon's gin. And that said appetite would make some folks prone to sudden irrational hungers in the middle of the night (which they would probably regret when heaving into their chamber pot soon afterward).

"I've said too much," Erin said, shaking her head.

"All right. That's fine. We don't have to go on about the who. Just give me the when and the how. "

"There's always been some thieving," Molly said. "Patients trying to make off with salt or something else they're not allowed to have. But it didn't get bad until a couple weeks ago. That's when we noticed food missing from the larder."

"Which you need those for at night?" I asked, pointing at Erin's keys.

She nodded. "That's right."

"So again...*after* the baseball game."

Erin scowled at me. "Why are you so fixated on what happened after that dumb game?"

"Oh, that's what my report's about. The destructive influence of baseball." I shook my head disapprovingly. "Swann should've never let a single patient put on a glove. It's a wonder this place is still standing. Thank you, ladies."

I pivoted and marched off down the hall. I had no doubt the second I was gone Erin and Molly would go down into the cellar to see what I'd been up to. They'd find the door to Dr. Swann's gin crypt open. I hoped they'd just lock it up again—after perhaps helping themselves to one of the bottles.

They might feel obligated to report it to the doctor instead, though. I didn't mind him knowing I'd been sniffing into his ways —surely he knew that already. I just wouldn't want him hearing I'd got myself locked in the cellar. Heck, I'm surprised I'm telling *you* about it. If anything like that ever happened to Sherlock Holmes, Doc Watson had the good sense not to mention it.

Now that I was out from underground I could hear the wind

blowing harder than ever outside. I meant to find a window looking out on the cabins to assure myself that Old Red's hadn't blown away. But another sound—an eerie, ethereal, unexpected one—caught my ear and drew me elsewhere.

It was music. A full orchestra playing a concerto inside a coffee can.

That's what it sounded like anyway. Both grand and cramped. I followed it out into the lobby then around into the dining hall.

There was no orchestra and no coffee can, of course. But there was a phonograph perched on a little side table, a wax cylinder spinning round and round beneath its brass horn. I didn't recognize the tune it was playing, but it sounded like the kind of thing fancy folks in tuxedos and fox furs try to listen to at the Metropolitan Opera House without falling asleep.

The long dining tables had been pushed to the back of the hall to create a makeshift dance floor...which only one gaunt, ghostly couple was using. They spun in slow circles as the moaning of the wind competed with the thin, tinny sound of the phonograph to be their accompaniment.

The Echo Lake Tuberculosis Sanitorium Spring Ball was underway.

Evening

Predictably, Breckenridge seemed to have swooped in on Miss Johansen to claim the first dance, and—slightly less predictably, but not exactly surprisingly—she hadn't said no. For it was they who circled the hall withered arm in arm while the other patients —men clustered on one side, women on the other—stood around watching.

Various staff members, Dr. Swann and Dr. Holly and Nurse Rosenkoetter among them, formed their own cluster at the back of the room. On one of the tables near them was a punch bowl and a big platter of cookies, and I made a beeline for it, lunchtime having long since come and gone while I was out wandering the frozen wastes with my brother. As I passed the dancers, I briefly locked eyes with Miss Johansen, and she opened hers wide, signaling for me to cut in.

I pretended not to get the message. I had a date with some sugar cookies.

The cookies were there, but the sugar broke the date. There wasn't the slightest hint of sweetness. I forced myself to finish the flavorless white disc I'd picked up, washing it down with a gulp of "punch" that seemed to be little more than watered-down orange juice and skimmed milk colored red.

"Not very refreshing for refreshments, are they?" someone said.

I turned to find Phillips and Foster coming my way. It was Phillips who'd spoken, and he stepped up close and picked an empty cup up off the table.

"Did you happen to bring anything with you from the cellar?" he said. "Something we could use to zip this stuff up, perhaps?"

He began pouring out a serving of punch using the ladle in the bowl.

"Sorry. No zip from me," I said.

Phillips lifted the ladle high, frowning at the crimson liquid as it poured down into the cup.

"They should've gone for green coloring. This is supposed to be a spring ball, after all," he said. "This looks like it belongs in someone's blood bucket. Speaking of which, if you'll excuse me..."

He returned the ladle to the bowl, turned his back to me, and hunched over hacking.

"But you *did* go down in the cellar, didn't you?" Foster asked as Phillips kept coughing.

"I did. You didn't happen to go to the cellar, too, did you? To see if I was down there?"

Foster furrowed his brow. As with the top of his head the hair there was patchy and wispy and white. He looked like a bald man who'd walked through cobwebs.

"Why do you ask?" he said.

"Oh, I just thought I noticed someone poking their head down while I was having a look." I nodded at the male patients bunched up along the dining hall wall. "All you gents together since I last saw you?"

Foster smiled. "Your questions get stranger and stranger."

"And your answers never seem to be answers."

Phillips finally finished his horking and turned toward us again. Somehow he'd managed to not spill a drop of the punch despite practically heaving up a lung.

"No, Foster and I didn't go to the cellar. And no, the men weren't always together," he said. He'd done a good job hearing me over the cacophony of his own coughs. "We practically live in each other's pockets, but even so we weren't always in sight of each other as we got cleaned up for the 'ball.' Now if you'll excuse me, I have an act of gallantry to perform."

He went striding off toward the female patients.

"What's he up to?" I asked Foster.

"You'll see," he said.

He widened his grin, taunting me.

His answers *still* weren't answers.

As I watched Phillips walk across the room, I caught Nurse Rosenkoetter and Dr. Holly watching *me*. The nurse seemed to be whispering something to the doctor, who was nodding gravely. When they saw me looking, Holly turned his gaze away and took a bite of one of the oh-so-delicious flour-and-baking-soda-flavored cookies. He managed not to gag.

Nurse Rosenkoetter kept on staring at me, though. It was meant to be an intimidating *I've got your number* kind of look. And it worked. I knew she had my number, and I was intimidated.

I took to watching Dr. Swann instead. He was standing a few feet from her, swaying to the music. Which interesting, because the music had stopped. I guess Gordon's gin can give a man so much sway he doesn't even need musical accompaniment for it.

"Let's try something a little more lively," said Mrs. Goldman, who was manning the phonograph with her friend Mrs. Kowal-ska. "A waltz!"

There was a smattering of applause but no rush of patients from one side of the room to the other in search of dance part-ners. In fact, the only couple on the dance floor looked like it was breaking apart: Breckenridge was speaking earnestly to Miss Johansen, who shook her head and pointed my way, clearly saying "Mr. Pycroft asked for the next dance." Never mind that I'd just walked in.

Beyond them I could see Phillips presenting the cup in his hands to a dour-looking Miss MacGowan.

"I didn't think you two would be friendly with Miss MacGowan," I said, surprised. "Her being a charity patient and you being the cream of society."

"Occasionally we make exceptions," Foster said. "She's a special case."

"Because she dislikes Dr. Holly's ideas about admitting black patients as much as you do?"

Foster shrugged. "She and I have much in common."

"Then why aren't you the one bringing her punch?"

"Because she finds me loathsome."

"Ah."

At last he'd given me a straight answer. One I could relate to, as well. It meant Miss MacGowan and I had something in common.

"I'm not blessed with luxurious crimson locks, like some people," Foster went on, his eyes flicking up toward the top of my head—and the thick red hair there. "It makes it hard to impress the ladies these days."

"Yeah, that's what it is. If only you had more hair…"

Mrs. Goldman and Mrs. Kowalska fired up the phonograph again, and as promised it began bleating out a waltz. Miss Johansen was determined to make use of it, too. She came striding up to me, snatched away the file I'd been carrying around, walked over and gave it to the nearest nurse, then swept back and grabbed me by the hand.

"Uhh…would you care to dance?" I said as she dragged me to the middle of the room.

"Why, yes. Thank you for asking."

We passed Breckenridge, who was slinking over to take my place by Foster, then Miss Johansen spun around to face me, and suddenly we were dancing.

"I just love a good waltz. Don't you, Albert?" the young lady said as she spun me around the dance floor. (Yes, she was leading.) "I may call you Albert, mayn't I?"

The first response that leaped to mind was, "Why the heck would you want to do that?" Then I remembered.

Oh, yeah. That was my name.

"But of course…Ingrid," I said.

Miss Johansen smiled.

I actually haven't waltzed much, but it's easy enough to pick up on. You just circle the room in little three-step spins—*one*-two-three, *one*-two-three—and pray you don't plow into anybody. So with some gentle pressure to the lady's hand and waist and a small change to our gait, slowing our swooping and guiding us across the floor toward the female patients, I was able to take the lead.

"It was a *kersplash*, wasn't it?" I said.

Miss Johansen cocked her head, still smiling. "Excuse me?"

"The noise you heard in the lake just before Wroblewski rolled down into the rocks. It wasn't the *plip* of some little thingamajig sinking or the *plip-plip-plop* of something light skipping across the surface. It was a big ol' *splash*. The kind you get when a heavy object hits the water and—*blorp*—goes right to the bottom."

As I spoke, the young lady's smile wilted, and she looked away from me and shook her head.

"Why would you ruin the moment by bringing this up again?"

"Because it's been an awful long day, Ingrid, and I'm tired of fooling around. And I think there might be good reason to figure this out fast. Now whaddaya say? *Kersplash* sound about right? Or will I have to write to my predecessor, Mr. Turner, to ask what *he* heard that afternoon? Or perhaps I should ask Breckenridge."

Miss Johansen jerked her face toward me again but kept her mouth shut tight.

"He was following you two that day, wasn't he?" I said. "Just like he followed us this morning. History repeats itself. Well... except that nobody got their head stoved in today. Maybe it was too cold for that."

"You're horrible," Miss Johansen said softly.

"Only when I have to be. That's more than some folks around here can say."

Inspired by the sight of us, a few of the male patients had worked up the nerve to walk over to the women in search of partners. To my surprise, I saw as Miss Johansen and I swept past, Phillips was still standing before Miss MacGowan, his long, thin arm now stretched out toward the dance floor in invitation. The way she scowled at him you'd have thought a slug was asking her to dance.

"How has she seemed today?" I asked, nodding at her.

Miss Johansen glanced over at Miss MacGowan and, seeing Phillips before her with his arm out, scoffed.

"Even more fidgety and peevish than usual," she said. She looked relieved that I'd changed the subject to something as amusing as sniping and gossip. "I guess they don't get blizzards in Biloxi. She's been staring out the window so much you'd think she'd never seen snow."

"Well, certainly not in April she hasn't. You said earlier she took something from you. 'A personal item.' Something you hadn't reported before. What was it?"

Miss Johansen's expression darkened again.

"It's really nothing that...well, would you look at that!"

I followed her gaze. Which wasn't easy when you're spinning in circles. I had to look over one shoulder, then over the other, then switch back to the first.

But I saw it: Miss MacGowan and Phillips stepping out to join the dancers.

Phillips was smiling. Miss MacGowan wasn't. It looked like she was gritting her teeth and doing what she had to do to rid herself of a pest. Except instead of slapping the skeeter on her arm she was about to dance with it.

She and Phillips began whirling around together just like me and Miss Johansen and the half dozen other couples out on the floor.

"Phoebe and Phillips," Miss Johansen marveled. "I never would've believed it."

"She dislike him as much as she dislikes Foster?"

The young lady scoffed. "What's there to like?"

"Good point."

At that very moment we danced past Foster and Breckenridge by the refreshments table. Breckenridge was eyeing us with a doleful, hangdog expression. Not only was he not trying to hide his heartbreak as he watched Miss Johansen in my arms, it almost seemed like he was reveling in it. He was a jilted suitor *and* he was wasting away from TB He got to be a doomed romantic twice-over. His moist, moony eyes and sallow skin and slender, slumped shoulders practically screamed *Quick...someone write a poem about me!*

Foster, on the other hand, was focused on Phillips and Miss MacGowan with a leering, eager keenness that made me swing my head around for another look at him after we'd reeled past. There was something unsettling about the way he stared at the couple twirling around toward him. He was like a batter at the plate watching a pitch float in right where he wanted it. He thought he was about to hit a home run.

Phillips steered the lady within a few feet of him, and Foster took his swing.

Foster stepped forward, reached up, and caught hold of the long red hair that swirled behind Miss MacGowan as she looped by. All Foster had to do then was stand in place and let the lady carry on.

Her wig jerked free in his hand, leaving her with nothing atop her head but a skull-hugging mesh cap. The scalp beneath it wasn't covered with thin, patchy hair, like Foster's. It was shaved smooth clear down to the skin.

There were gasps and, I'm sorry to say, a few laughs.

"Oh, for Christ's sake," I spat.

Miss Johansen and I jerked to a stop. So did Miss MacGowan —though Phillips waltzed on alone a few steps for (in his mind anyway) comic effect.

"I *am* sorry," Foster said to Miss MacGowan. "I was trying to cut in."

He offered her both the wig and a taunting grin.

I couldn't see the expression on the lady's face. Her back was to me. But I could see her shoulders tremble and her fists clench. And I could see Foster's face—and the way the grin went sliding off it as he realized what was about to happen.

With a shriek of fury and despair, Miss MacGowan flung herself on him. He stumbled and fell backward, and she came down on top of him. As she flailed at his face, she unclenched her fists—so she could claw at his eyes and ears, still screeching.

"Good lord!" I heard Swann cry.

"Stop her!" said Holly.

Yet none of the nurses and orderlies near them took a step. If anything, they cringed back, horror on their faces. So I started toward Miss MacGowan—and Miss Johansen grabbed me by the arm and pulled me back.

"Albert, don't," she said, still holding tight. "The way they're screaming…you can't get close."

She was right. Miss MacGowan was shouting words as she scratched at Foster now—ones no publisher would dare set in print—while he howled and kicked his feet and pleaded beneath her. If I got between them, one drop of their spewed spittle might be enough to kill me. Not instantly, of course. Slowly, over the course of years, as I wasted away to nothing like the man I'd been trying to help. A man who wasn't worth helping.

"Dammit," I said.

If anyone was going to pull Miss MacGowan off Foster, it was going to have to be one of the patients.

It was Breckenridge who overcame his shock and stepped in first.

"Miss MacGowan, please stop," he said with surprising gentleness as he moved toward her. "That's enough."

Somehow she heard him over her own ranting and Foster's wails and the waltz still blaring out of the phonograph. She stopped tearing at the face of the man beneath her and began raining down halfhearted slaps instead.

"Stop it, you crazy bitch!" Phillips snapped, and he started charging toward her.

I figured a punch to his nose would be more dangerous to me than to him. So I just stepped into his path and shoved him back on his bony ass instead.

I know I should probably feel bad about doing that to a dying man. But at that particular moment he wasn't dying fast enough to suit me.

"She's stopping," I said, hoping that the firmness in my voice would convince *her* it was true.

I don't know if it was what I'd said or the comforting way Breckenridge put a hand on her shoulder rather than grab her or if she was just tiring out. But Miss MacGowan stopped hitting Foster and crawled off him and began to sob.

I could see Foster's face now—and the bloody scratches and gouges that covered it. He still had both his eyes, but Miss MacGowan had pulled out clumps of what little hair he'd had left.

He rolled over on his belly and wriggled away from her like the snake he was, leaving a smear of blood across the floor as he went.

"Let's get them to the infirmary," Holly said to Nurse Rosenkoetter.

At the sound of the young doctor's voice Miss MacGowan stopped crying and jerked her head around to look at him. Her face contorted with a contempt she couldn't hide, yet she tried to wipe it away like smoothing out a skirt.

"I'm fine now," she said with exaggerated calm. "I am sorry. But I'm all right. I don't need to go to the infirmary."

Her wig was lying nearby, where Foster had dropped it, and

she snatched it up with blood-covered fingers and re-covered her shaved head.

"Really. It was just the surprise," she said, sniffling and trying to smile. "It won't happen again. And I don't think I hurt Mr. Foster *too* badly."

Foster, a safe distance away by the refreshments table now, offered a reply so obscene it made Mrs. Goldman and Mrs. Kowalska gasp.

"We will discuss it in the infirmary," Holly said firmly.

"No, really!" Miss MacGowan said, voice rising again. "I won't be any more trouble! I swear!"

Holly turned to three white-jacketed orderlies clustered up trying to look inconspicuous behind him.

"If you please, gentlemen," he said, holding a hand out toward Miss MacGowan and Foster.

"I'll just go back to my bed and stay there, all right?" Miss MacGowan went on, her begging just a hair's breadth from hysteria. "You don't have to worry about me! I'm fine now!"

The orderlies didn't move.

Nurse Rosenkoetter harrumphed and started marching toward Miss MacGowan herself.

"Come along," she told the woman in a flat, hard, "No more nonsense, now" tone. "Let's go."

A couple nurses peeled away from the rest of the staff, headed for Foster.

"Really…," Miss MacGowan said, voice trembling.

She began crying again but allowed Nurse Rosenkoetter to draw her to her feet.

The other nurses, stepping carefully so as not to slip on the blood-smudged floor, huddled in around Foster and began helping him up, as well.

As they left—Nurse Rosenkoetter and a still-weeping Miss MacGowan out front, Foster and the other nurses following at a discreet distance, Dr. Holly bringing up the rear—the other patients watched them go, frozen and silent. In fact the only sound in the place for a long moment were footsteps and the whistling of the wind outside.

Dr. Swann had been motionless, impotent, throughout the whole thing. But finally he stalked over to me and leaned in so close I could tell his punch had a lot more punch to it than anyone else's. The kind a healthy pour of Gordon's gin supplies.

"Make sure you mention in your report to the board that the ball was Holly's idea," he said under his eighty-proof breath.

"And you make sure somebody keeps a close watch on that woman tonight," I replied. "And that somebody else keeps a close watch on the somebody."

Swann just beetled his brow and scowled at me a moment. Then he brushed past, turned toward the pasty, emaciated faces peering at us from around the dining hall, and stated the obvious.

"The party," he said, "is over!"

Day 3: The Void
After Midnight

I heard the storm end. I was lying on my cot trying to sleep—and trying *not* to imagine little legs scurrying across me again—when I noticed the change.

The sharp, steady whining of the wind around the sanitorium walls had already died down to a wheeze that rose and fell, rose and fell for over an hour. Then at last it simply fell and stayed fallen. The wind was there, then it wasn't. It was over.

I wouldn't be the only one to note it, I knew. I was sure Old Red was out there in his little hut seething over the fact that I hadn't braved the blizzard to bring him news from the big building. Never mind that there was no way to do it earlier without being noticed or that the storm had gotten so bad for a while I might have gotten lost in it two steps beyond the door. (That had actually happened to a farmer we'd known as boys back in Kansas. He'd stumbled into the blinding white gale to check on the animals in his barn and didn't get found until three days later, a hundred yards in the wrong direction and so frozen in place his family had to chisel him out with picks.)

No, Old Red wouldn't want excuses. He'd want data.

Well, I had it for him. In spades.

I had the whole thing figured out. Who did it, how they did it, why they did it.

All right, maybe I didn't have it all deduced through. There were loose ends. But I was saving those for my brother to tie up. I didn't want him to feel *totally* useless this trip.

As long as the storm was past—and I wasn't sleeping anyway —I figured I may as well see about slipping outside to throw Old Red his bones. Maybe he'd actually be grateful if I didn't make him wait till dawn for an update on the doings since last I'd seen him. Probably not, but it was worth a shot.

I went slinking down to the first floor slow and quiet. If anyone spotted me, the jig was up, as I'd bundled myself up for the snow. It was cold inside the sanitorium, but I didn't think anyone would believe I'd put on my coat, hat, muffler and gloves for a trip to the water closet.

I did pause for a long, hard listen at one point as I crept along the lobby wall. I was outside the door to the infirmary, and I didn't know who might still be inside. I'd seen a bandage-wrapped Foster heading back to the men's ward before I'd supposedly turned in for the night. But the last I knew of, Miss MacGowan was still in the infirmary so the staff could keep an eye on her.

That suited me fine, so long as she and the staff didn't get an eyeful of *me*. Later—when my brother and I took action on what I'd learned—remaining incognito would no longer matter. But for now, better that everyone think Albert Pycroft, milquetoast clerk, was up in his shoebox fast asleep.

When I slipped out the front door a moment later, I found myself stepping into a big, cold bunch of nothing. Above was a solid ceiling of gray. Below was more of the same. Thick snow covered everything, turning the world into one big, smooth, shape-less plain that seemed to carry on forever under a starless, moonless, cloud-shrouded sky. I wasn't raised Catholic so I don't know much about Limbo, but if the place exists I figure I know what it looks like. If I end up there after I die at least it'll be familiar. I'd still want someone to pray me out fast, though.

I made my way slowly through the gloom, having to navigate more by memory than sight. The cabins just looked like especially large mounds in the snow, but I remembered which my brother was in and headed for the door. As I got closer I could see (barely) a wisp of smoke curling from the black chimney pipe. I quickened my pace, sure that my brother would be frosty, but his fire at least warm.

Just as I reached the cabin, my left toe clunked into something hard on the ground in front of the door. The snow there had drifted up over my knees, and I reached down and sifted through it. Almost instantly I felt something solid, and when I brushed away more snow, I saw what looked like the top of a big, glass candy jar—the kind storekeepers put licorice whips and lemon drops in.

I knew I couldn't be *that* lucky. I go stumbling through the freezing darkness and end up finding a stray jar of peppermint sticks?

This wasn't candy, and it wasn't stray. Someone had left it here.

I started digging around the thing. It was indeed a big glass jar, that much I could see pretty quick. But there wasn't enough light to tell what was in it. As I dug around it some more, I heard footsteps inside, coming closer.

"Don't open up yet," I said loudly. "You got something on your doorstep."

"You mean other than you?" Old Red replied from the other side of the door.

"Yes, other than me. And it ain't the morning paper."

"Well, hurry up and bring it in! I been sittin' out here waitin' for news so long I started thinkin' you forgot I was here at all!"

"Yeah, yeah," I said, still sifting through the snow.

It was just the reception I expected. For a moment, I considered packing up a nice little gift for my brother—a patty of snow just the right size to slide down the back of his shirt—but I decided I was too professional for that. Unless he kept griping. Then any snow in his clothes would be his fault.

After a few more seconds of digging, I could get my fingers underneath the jar, and I lifted it up. It was heavy and cold, with a chill to it I could feel through my gloves. But to my surprise, it wasn't solid. Whatever was inside it sloshed.

I tapped the door with my toe, then stepped back. "All right. Open up."

The door swung open, and I hustled inside as fast as I could lugging what felt like a bucket of ice-cold water with no handle. I carried it to the cabin's little black stove and plopped it down on the floorboards in front of it.

"What the hell is that?" my brother asked.

"You got me. Maybe the milkman came by…?"

Old Red ignored that, of course. Despite the hour, he was fully dressed. He wasn't in the oversized suit he'd worn as "Mr. Melas," though. He was back in the hickory shirt and Levi's and boots he prefers. He hadn't put his Stetson back on—he'd reluctantly left that at home in Ogden, a ten-gallon hat not being something you can just slip into your carpetbag—but I'm sure he would've if he could've. He was done with masquerades.

He stepped up to the jar, hunkered down before it, and peered at it, keeping the light from the stove behind it.

"Funny that whatever's in that thing isn't frozen solid," I said. "It was buried under the snow natural. From snowfall, not someone piling snow on top of it. So it must've been out there for hours."

I was proud of this little bit of ratiocination—not exactly up to Mr. Holmes's level, but at least my brother couldn't accuse me of seeing and not observing.

"There's a reason it didn't freeze," Old Red said, leaning in close to the glass like a kid picking out the gumballs he wants for his penny. "That ain't water in there."

"How can you tell?"

My brother was blocking my view of the jar, and I stepped to the side to see past him.

There was a dark shape floating in the liquid, its edges outlined by the fire behind it.

"Jesus," I said when I recognized the shape.

I grew up on a farm and worked the cattle trails. I've butchered plenty of animals.

I know a pair of lungs when I see them.

"Ick," I added.

Just because I had to gut animals once upon a time doesn't mean I like delivering innards door to door.

"Can't argue with that," Old Red said. He pushed back from the jar, going to his knees. "You see any tracks?"

"Oh. Right. I guess I kinda forgot to look. I was in a hurry to get in out of the cold, then this came as a surprise. But if there'd been anything obvious I would've seen it."

"Yeah," my brother said skeptically. "Maybe."

He stood, snatched his coat up off the bed, and headed back toward the door.

"So you reckon that stuff in the jar didn't freeze cuz it's alcohol or formaldehyde or whatever they'd use for pickling... that," I said.

"Yup. And it's obvious where *that* came from when you look at it up close."

I glanced down at the jar again.

"Oh?" I said without getting any nearer.

I had a hunch I knew what my brother was going to say. And if he already had it figured out for sure why should I get up close and personal with someone's lungs?

"There's scars on them lungs," Old Red said. "Spots where it looks like holes healed over."

I congratulated myself on making a good decision.

"So they're from someone who had TB," I said, heading over to join my brother by the door. "A patient here who didn't need them anymore."

"Most likely."

Old Red put on his coat and opened the door.

It was cold in the cabin, but compared to outside it was practically balmy, and the icy night air hit me like a slap.

My brother stepped out into it and hunted around the front of the cabin for tracks.

"Can't see squat tonight," he said, throwing an irritated look up at the lightless sky. "And the way the snow was comin' down and the wind blowin'...."

"No trail. Like I said."

"Oh, there's a trail...if I could just see to find the damn thing."

Old Red kicked the nearest snowbank.

"We can find it in the morning if you want," I said. "But it doesn't really matter, does it? We know where it leads."

My brother looked at me sharply. "Oh, we do?"

"Sure. To that little morgue shack—they ain't gonna keep lungs in the barn—and from there to the main building."

"Because you're assumin' *who* brought them things over here?"

"Phillips and Foster, of course. It's another one of their gags. I got 'the Welcoming Committee,' and you got this."

"So you think a couple lungers snuck out in the middle of a blizzard, picked the lock on the morgue door, lugged a forty-pound jar of formaldehyde over here, then snuck back inside again? Without bein' seen or coughin' themselves to death doin' it?"

"Oh. When you put it like that..." I said. "And there's something else, now that I think about it."

I was recalling the shape Foster was in the last I'd seen him. It was hard to imagine even as big a bastard as him heading out into the driving snow for a prank with a scratched-up face covered with fresh bandages.

"Now that you're finally thinkin', *what?*" Old Red prompted me.

"Well, first thing I'm thinking is why the hell aren't we having this conversation inside by the fire with the door closed?"

My brother harrumphed, limped inside, and slammed the

door shut behind him. (God forbid I should ever get a "Good point" out of *him*.)

"So?" he said. "Somethin' happen in the big building you ain't told me about?"

"A whole lotta something."

The surprise on Old Red's doorstep had thrown me—organs running around loose will do that to a person—but now I remembered what I'd been coming out to say.

"So much, in fact," I announced, drawing up to my full height and trying (and no doubt failing) to keep the self-satisfaction off my face, "I think I know who killed Wroblewski."

Usually, "Who?" would be the expected thing to ask after such a statement. But doing the expected isn't my brother's way (unless you're expecting him to be testy—and you should).

Instead he opened his eyes wide and began pinwheeling his hands in the air.

"Come on, then—tell me everything," he said. "*Everything.*"

That was easier said than done, of course. "Everything" to most folks isn't everything to Old Red. I could talk till dawn and still leave out a dozen little details he'd think weren't little at all. ("Why didn't you tell me there was a ball of lint under the couch and a kitten with a whisker missin'? Dammit, Otto—that there's the key to the whole thing!") But I figured this time I had it all covered. Or mostly, anyway.

I filled him in on the preparations for the "spring ball," Dr. Swann's not-so-secret stash of gin, the somebody who may or may not have been stalking me in the cellar, the missing iron, the dance, Phillips and Foster's cruel trick on Miss MacGowan, and—most importantly of all (I figured)—the wild, violent way the woman had reacted to it.

"Now, remember—Miss Johansen said Miss MacGowan's been stealing things, including something 'personal' from her," I said. "Well, what could that be but the keys she'd either wheedled from or stolen from Turner herself? She'd been using them to help herself to Swann's booze out in that other cabin, most likely. But Miss MacGowan had something else in mind. She was either

helping one of Mrs. Goldman's 'Indians' out in the woods—
leaving warm clothes and food for 'em, like those eggs—or she's
deluded enough to think she was. And when Wroblewski saw her
at it, she stole an iron from the cellar, used it to bash his brains
out, then threw it in the lake."

I spread out my hands in a "Case closed" sort of way.

"Ker-splash," I said. "Fortunately, now she's in the infirmary
with doctors and nurses and orderlies to keep an eye on her
through the night. And in the morning, we can tell Swann what
we know and get the rest of the story out of her and get the hell
out of here. And collect our fee—which I mostly earned this time
while you had a nice little holiday with your magazines and your
McGuffey's."

I folded my arms over my chest and waited for Old Red's
reaction. Applause would've been nice.

What I got was a "Feh."

"What?" I said.

"Why?" said Old Red.

"I just said why. Wroblewski was known to take long walks in
the woods alone. So he saw something Miss MacGowan didn't
want him to see, and she reacted like she did tonight at the dance.
You heard what she did to Foster. Practically tore his ears off...not
that I blame her. But still—the woman's got a crazy side."

My brother hit me with another "Feh."

"She got pushed too far. That don't prove nothin'," he said.
"No—we still ain't got it all."

"Do we *need* it all? We know Miss MacGowan's a thief
capable of attacking a man. The why could be a lot of things—it
doesn't have to be that Wroblewski saw something. Maybe he did
something mean to her, like Phillips and Foster. Or maybe she
was jealous that he was heading home. Or maybe it wasn't about
him at all but Dr. Holly. We know she hates the man cuz he
wants to bring in black patients. Well, maybe she thought one
less cured lunger would give him that much less sway with the
board."

"Maybe maybe maybe," Old Red groused.

"But we *definitely* know she had the temperament for it and a way to do it. The rest is just a loose end."

My brother looked like he wanted to heft up the big jar in front of the stove and empty it over my head.

"A loose end? *A loose end?* We got so many loose ends I may as well be lookin' at a bowl of Chinese noodles! Palomares! The horse! The damn *motive*! Not to mention that!"

He jabbed a finger at the jar.

"Well...not everything has to tie up neat and tidy," I said lamely. "There are such things as coincidences, you know."

Old Red's jaw dropped.

Now I'd spoken sacrilege.

"Forget I said that," I added before my brother could go back to bellowing at me.

He clamped his mouth shut and shook his head silently for a moment instead.

"Do we even know for sure," he grated out, "that Miss MacGowan wasn't at the baseball game?"

"Ah ha!" I said. "She was not! Told me that herself yesterday morning. Said she was out for another of her long walks in the woods. And if you'd seen her when she went after Foster, you'd know the woman's unhinged. I'm telling you, it was an unnerving sight—her screaming and clawing like a wildcat but her head shaved bald as a cue ball. I've never seen the like of it."

My brother shook his head again, looking skeptical. Then suddenly he froze.

"Hold on," he said. "What do you mean 'shaved bald as a cueball'?"

"I mean shaved bald as a cueball. What else could I mean?"

"Her head, you're sayin'? When the wig came off? You could see it was sheared down to the skin?"

"Well, I can't speak to the rest of her, but yeah—her head."

"Completely smooth-scalped?"

"Good lord, how many ways do I have to say it? Yes! She didn't have a hair on her head! It happens to some TB patients. The hair goes. That's why Foster looks like a corn husk doll that's lost half its silk. If you're a lady, I guess you get to throw a wig on over it."

"And where'd you say she was from? Mississippi?"

I nodded. "Biloxi."

"Biloxi...."

Old Red's gaze dropped away, drifting to the room's darkest corner. It stayed fixed there while he absently brought his right hand up and ran his fingers over his stubble-covered chin.

"And shaved. Not scraggly," he muttered. "Cuz maybe...yes. Which might mean...yes. So also...yes. And that would explain... yes."

"Do *you* want to explain why the lady's haircut is so danged important?" I asked. "Cuz I'm only catching half of this conversation, y'know."

My brother just carried on talking to himself.

"And assumin' that's the case...yes. So the only way to figure it would be...yes. And yes again. And if *that's* what's happenin'..."

Old Red moved his gaze again—this time back to the jar glowing dully before the fire, its contents two black silhouettes.

"*No,*" he said.

He spun around to face me again.

"Where's she at?" he asked.

"The infirmary. Hopefully strapped to a bed. I told Swann to keep her under lock and key."

Old Red's bushy mustache puckered in a familiar way. Under all the bristles, he was frowning.

"That your Bulldog?" he asked, nodding down at a bulge in my coat pocket.

I patted it. "It ain't a butter churn."

"Then let's go."

My brother bolted for the door.

I didn't. Not right away. I was still trying to make sense of it.

"Bald from Biloxi?" I said. "That was the key?"

"Yup!" Old Red cried.

He yanked the door open and went limp-running out into the

snow, his tender right foot giving him a little hop that popped him in the air with every other step.

"Miss MacGowan's in danger!" he shouted as he bounced away toward the main building. "It's time the truth came out! It can't stay hid no longer!"

"Yeah, well…if you say so…," I muttered. But I was thinking *Bald from Biloxi? Really?*

If it had been anyone but my brother I'd have figured cabin fever had cooked their brains. But it was Old Red, so…

I ran from the cabin and tried to catch up. He was moving surprisingly fast for a man hobbling through the snow, though. By the time I was by his side he was bursting through the front door into the lobby.

"Where's the infirmary?" he asked, whipping his head this way and that to take in the long, dark hallways stretching off to either side of us.

"Over here."

When he saw which door I was headed for, he lurched past me and threw it open.

On the other side were two long rows of beds. Only one bed was occupied.

Miss MacGowan lay stretched out under the covers, eyes closed, wig still off, one sleeve of her white cotton gown rolled up.

Nurse Rosenkoetter was leaning in over her with a syringe, the needle gliding in toward the lady's exposed arm.

"Stop!" Old Red roared.

The nurse jerked her up and glared at him, the needle now hovering inches from Miss MacGowan's skin.

"What are you doing in here?" she snapped. Then, without waiting for an answer, she added, "Get out!"

My brother limped toward her.

"Don't do that," he said, pointing at the syringe.

"How dare you?" Nurse Rosenkoetter sneered, and she turned her attention back to Miss MacGowan.

The needle started moving toward the lady's arm again.

Miss MacGowan was on a bed about halfway across the room from us—far beyond Old Red's reach.

"Brother!" he said.

Nurse Rosenkoetter was far beyond my reach, too. But I could be more persuasive. Especially with a Webley Bulldog in my pocket.

"Look here, ma'am!" I said (because she wasn't). "We're serious!"

I couldn't even tell if the needle was poking into Miss MacGowan or not at this point, it was so close to her. But Nurse Rosenkoetter did look up at me—and gasp when she saw the gun that was now pointed her way.

"Sorry," I said. "But you really should listen to my brother."

"Your *brother*?" the nurse said.

Oops.

In the heat of the moment I'd forgotten we were still supposedly incognito.

"That's right," I said with all the confidence I could muster considering my blunder and the fact that I was set to shoot a woman for reasons I didn't even know. "Gustav Amlingmeyer of the A.A. Western Detective Agency. Perhaps you've heard of him. The Holmes of the—?"

"Put that thing down," Old Red cut in, pointing at the syringe. "Right now."

He was still limping toward Miss MacGowan's bed. She hadn't reacted to the hullaballoo around her in any way. Her eyes remained closed, her body still.

Nurse Rosenkoetter lifted up the syringe. I was moving closer, too, and I could see that the plunger hadn't been pushed in. It hadn't been used.

The nurse turned and placed the syringe on the empty bed behind her. Then she faced us again with her hands up.

"What's going on here?" someone asked from the far end of the infirmary.

Dr. Holly stepped from a side room there.

At the same moment I heard footsteps behind me, and I

glanced back to see one of the other nurses gawking at me from the doorway.

"Hello," I said with a reassuring smile. "Nothing to worry about here. Just having us a little chat."

She stared at the gun in my hand, whimpered, and fled.

So much for my reassuring smiles.

My brother ignored both her and Holly.

"What's wrong with her?" he asked Nurse Rosenkoetter, nodding down at the still-motionless Miss MacGowan. "Why's she like that?"

"She became agitated again. Violent," Nurse Rosenkoetter said. "So we applied ether."

"I never heard of giving people ether with needles," I said.

Dr. Holly was headed slowly for Miss MacGowan's bed, like Old Red.

"The ether was earlier. That's chloral hydrate. To help her sleep through the night," he said. "Look—whatever's happening here, I'm sure guns aren't necessary."

"I'm pretty sure they are," said Old Red.

I kept my Bulldog pointed at Nurse Rosenkoetter. I didn't care for that much—and from the distressed look on her face, it was obvious she didn't either—but I had to trust my brother's instincts.

"You get that dose of chloral-whatever ready yourself?" Old Red asked the nurse.

"No. Dr. Holly prepared it for me."

"And it was his idea for y'all to give it to her?"

"Yes."

My brother nodded. "I figured. She'd kicked up a commotion. People'd be keepin' an eye on her. Holly couldn't slip in and fake a suicide like he did with Palomares."

Dr. Holly's eyes widened. Nurse Rosenkoetter's eyes widened. *My* eyes probably widened.

The doctor spoke for all of us.

"*What?*" he said.

I didn't know my brother's thinking yet, but all the same I

moved the Bulldog from Nurse Rosenkoetter to Dr. Holly. He didn't stop heading toward Miss MacGowan, though.

"Umm…doc? You wanna hold it right there?" I said.

"Now, really—" he began, still coming closer.

"Yes. Now. Really," I said. I thumbed back the hammer on the Bulldog. "*Stop*. While we talk this out."

Holly finally stopped about twenty feet from Miss MacGowan's bed.

"Have you two lost your minds?" Nurse Rosenkoetter said. She lowered her hands and crossed her arms and narrowed her eyes to skeptical slits.

With the blame—and the gun—shifting, she was quickly getting some of her usual frost back.

"Not losin' 'em. Usin' 'em," my brother said. "We was told Palomares was cured, gettin' ready to leave, when he 'collapsed' and ended up in here. 'Practically comatose' is how I think Dr. Swann put it. Just like that." He nodded down at Miss MacGowan. "I found it mighty interestin' that Palomares managed to wake up and open his veins so quick and quiet and thorough. You ever see the mess people make when they try to slit their wrists? I have—a couple times. It ain't as easy as they think, and they end up sittin' there with mangled wrists wonderin' why they ain't dead yet. But Palomares suddenly wakes up and manages to find himself a scalpel and get the job done in one go? Feh."

"And from that, you concluded that *I* killed him?" Holly said.

"No. But I *deduced* that a doctor or nurse did it. Someone who could get him drugged up first—ethered, I'd say now—then slip in and finish him in the middle of the night."

Holly and Nurse Rosenkoetter both scoffed.

I didn't join in, of course. I was kicking myself inside for not seeing it all along.

Heavy footsteps echoed in from the lobby, and Dr. Swann popped into the doorway, a paisley dressing gown wrapped around him and his hair sticking out at every angle.

"Good god—it's true," he said when he saw me. "Put that thing away, you fool!"

The nurse I'd failed to reassure earlier peeped in from behind him, gaped at my gun again, then quickly disappeared with another whimper.

I couldn't blame her. That's how I feel about a lot of the situations Old Red gets me in. Only I don't have the option of running off. (Or at least I never take it.)

I did not put the Bulldog away.

When that sank in for Swann, he staggered toward me, his round face flushed. There was a sluggish shuffle to his steps that was more than just the drowsiness of a man roused from sleep. He'd been roused from a drunken stupor, too.

"I said put that down!"

"*No*," I said. "And you stay right there till this is all cleared up."

I gave Swann a look that said I'd be just as happy to point my gun at him if he made me. Ditto for pulling the trigger if it came to that.

This time, my look worked.

Swann came to a swaying stop. He goggled at me a moment, double chins atremble, before finding the wherewithal to speak again.

"What's this all about?"

"What it's about is murder," said Old Red. "Only I don't think the killer looks at it as that. I think he sees it as science."

He looked at Dr. Holly.

Holly shook his head sadly.

"He's sick. Hallucinating," he said to Swann. "I just don't understand why Pycroft is going along with it."

"Yes, you do," my brother said. "Nurse Rosenkoetter told you yesterday, didn't she? That 'Pycroft' ain't no clerk, and I ain't no 'guest'? That's why you decided to cover your tracks."

He nodded down at Miss MacGowan again.

"How could *she* be the 'tracks' to anything Holly did?" Swann said. "She wouldn't have anything to do with him."

"Because she knew what he'd done."

"And how would Miss MacGowan know that I'd supposedly slit someone's wrists?" said Holly.

"I ain't talkin' about Palomares now. I'm talkin' about Wroblewski...when you hit him over the head with an iron you took from the cellar then tossed in the lake."

Old Red threw me a quick glance and a raised eyebrow over his shoulder.

At least I'd gotten the part about the iron right—if not who'd actually used it.

Not that anyone else there was acting convinced. There was so much snorting in disbelief it sounded like we were out in the barn with the horses.

"Why would Dr. Holly murder the people he's here to heal?" Nurse Rosenkoetter said. "Especially the very ones whose recoveries demonstrate his superior skills as a physician?"

Swann switched from disbelieving snorts to affronted grumbling.

Old Red ignored him.

"'Cuz Holly didn't know *why* they got better, I reckon," he said. "What was different about Palomares and Wroblewski? How come they got over TB 'stead of hackin' their insides out like that poor gal who just died? The folks you bury here—Holly gets to open 'em up and poke around inside 'em first. But how do you get a look inside someone who's cured? You don't—unless you make special arrangements for it. The kind that won't do any damage to the bits you really want a peek at."

My brother threw me another quick look, and I gave him a nod of understanding.

The lungs.

I only half understood, though. I got why they were important. What I still didn't know was how the hell they'd ended up on Old Red's doorstep.

"You already knew Holly was willin' to go further than you to understand tuberculosis," Old Red said to Swann. "Him wantin' to bring in black patients, I mean. You just didn't realize he was willin' to go a hell of a lot further than that."

"But that's precisely why Miss MacGowan disliked me. Because I want the sanitorium to admit black guests," said Holly. He turned to Nurse Rosenkoetter. "Perhaps that's why they're trying to destroy my reputation. If they were sent by the board to find a way to fire me—"

"Oh, you're way off with Miss MacGowan," my brother cut in. "She needed an excuse not to have you for her doctor cuz she knew what you did to Wroblewski. Admittin' black 'guests'—why, she'd be all for it if she could be honest."

He cocked his head and gazed down at the woman lying so perfectly still on the bed near him. Even with her pallid skin and hairless head and mouth slightly ajar she was strikingly pretty, with a long, slender neck and an aquiline nose and eyes you could tell were unusually large even though closed.

"You see," Old Red said, "Miss MacGowan *is* black."

"Preposterous," said Nurse Rosenkoetter.

"Ridiculous," huffed Dr. Swann.

"Insane," said Dr. Holly.

I reserved judgment.

"That's why she shaves her head," Old Red said. "Her skin's light enough, and her features white enough. But her hair—that must be the giveaway. So she gets rid of it. Wearin' a wig's got nothin' to do with TB"

"Can we stop listening to this drivel now, please?" Holly asked Swann. "It's insulting."

Swann looked inclined to agree. I think a bottle of Gordon's was calling to him from his room, and he was eager to answer.

"Plus," my brother went on as if Holly hadn't spoken, "there's whoever came up here with her from Biloxi."

"Who what now?" said Swann.

"No one came with her from Biloxi," said Nurse Rosenkoetter.

But I was finally catching on and catching up.

"The food and clothes she was stealing. That was for...whoever," I said. "Someone trying to live out in the woods or at the abandoned mining camp." I snapped the fingers of my free hand. "Mrs. Goldman's 'Indians'! She *did* see somebody skulking around outside!"

Old Red nodded. "Somebody from the Gulf Coast of Mississippi who wouldn't know you can get snowstorms in Colorado this far into the spring. Although I think the livin' was tougher than they expected even before that blizzard blew in. That's why their horse looked as bad as she did—and why they finally let her go so she could find food elsewhere."

"Why would someone come from Mississippi to live in the woods around Echo Lake?" Nurse Rosenkoetter said slowly, as if catching a child in an obvious lie—like that it was the dog who'd cut a perfect slice from the apple pie cooling in the kitchen.

"Because," my brother replied equally slowly, "cold, dry mountain air is supposedly good for TB But he or she couldn't pass like…"

He turned toward the door to the lobby.

Nurse Rosenkoetter and Holly were already facing that way. The nurse gasped. The doctor went stiff and took a step back.

Swann and I turned around like Old Red.

"Whoa," I said.

"Good lord!" said Swann.

A stranger was standing in the doorway.

I'd been too distracted to notice his approach, but my brother must have been listening for him: Unlike the rest of us, Old Red showed no sign of surprise. I thought back to his shouted words as we'd hurried toward the main building a few minutes before— "Miss MacGowan's in danger! It's time the truth came out! It can't stay hid no longer!"—and realized he hadn't been speaking to me. He'd been calling to the somebody he figured was riding out the storm in one of the other cabins.

The man was tall and gaunt and wrapped in several layers of ill-fitting winter clothes.

He was also black.

He gazed past my brother at Miss MacGowan, sunken eyes filled with fear and sadness.

"…your…wife?" Old Red said.

The man certainly didn't look like Miss MacGowan's brother or cousin or some other blood relation. Not with skin so much darker than hers.

He gave Old Red a curt nod, then hurried forward toward his wife.

"Is she all right?" he asked Nurse Rosenkoetter as he passed a stunned Swann.

"Yes. Fine. Just unconscious," the nurse replied stiffly.

The man hustled around my brother and dropped to his knees by Miss MacGowan's side. As he gazed down at her, he took a ragged, trembling breath—the strained gasp of a lunger or of a man fighting to hold back tears or probably both.

"Are you Mr. MacGowan?" Old Red asked gently. "Or is that name fake?"

The man pulled off his gloves and ran a hand down Miss MacGowan's cheek.

"Fake," he said. He had a stronger Southern accent than his wife—so strong I could've guessed he was from Mississippi or thereabouts even if I hadn't already known. "We had to make up all that MacGowan business to get her in here. Our real name is Butler. Norris and Phoebe Butler."

"And you've really been living out in the woods?" Swann asked, incredulous.

Butler took in another deep, obviously painful breath, then nodded.

"In an old shack I found about a mile from here. I didn't know if Phoebe would ever make it back to Biloxi…or if I'd still be there when she did. So I came, too. We thought I could get by with what I brought up and some hunting. But I'm no mountain man, and it's been colder than we figured. So poor Phoebe…" Butler stroked his wife's cheek again. "She had to find ways to help me. Keep me alive."

"Like hiding food for you on the bluffs by the lake," Old Red said. "Which is how you came to see what Holly did to Wroblewski. And why you used the key your wife had passed you to get into the morgue—his 'laboratory'—and pull something out that would point me and my brother in his direction."

Butler wiped tears from his eyes, bowed his head, and nodded. "I couldn't come forward or Phoebe and me might both be sent away. But I was up there by the lake again yesterday when you two were talking to Nurse Rosenkoetter. I heard what she said about you not being who you pretended to be. And I'd seen you both poking around like you were searching for something. The truth maybe. So I couldn't keep it to myself anymore, no matter what."

Butler raised his head and locked his gaze on Holly. I couldn't see his expression from where I was behind him, but I could sure hear the contempt in his voice when he went on.

"Not when there was a killer here pretending to be a healer."

Swann and Nurse Rosenkoetter gaped at Holly in shock. For a moment. I could see the certainty sink in for both of them—the disbelief turning to terrible, horror-filled acceptance.

There was a witness. Dr. Holly was a murderer.

Holly saw it sink in, too.

"Herman," he said to Swann. He looked over at Nurse Rosenkoetter. "Frieda. You're going to believe these ravings? Because that's all this is. The fantasies of a half-frozen, half-starved, half-dead negro and two clowns throwing around accusations and waving guns. There's no proof of anything."

"Oh, there most certainly is," my brother said. "We won't be able to dredge up that iron until the lake melts, but it's out there, I'm sure. And there's something else, too. Something that'll prove the truth about you right here and now."

"What are you talking about?" Swann said.

He didn't sound angry. He sounded weary and nauseous like he just wanted to get all this over with before he had to throw up.

"Holly must've suspected that Miss MacGowan—Mrs. Butler, I should say—knew something, what with her refusin' to keep him on as her doctor," Old Red said. "And with me and Otto closin' in, he had to make sure she didn't tell us nothin'. So when her nerves were finally shot thanks to worry about her husband and the storm and then what Phillips and Foster did, he saw his chance and he took it. Had her knocked out with ether, then moved in to finish her. And he wouldn't have to worry about anyone bein' the wiser afterwards, because he's the one who does the autopsies."

"I still don't understand," said Butler. "What's the proof? And what did Phillips and Foster do to Phoebe?"

There'd been no one to tell him what had happened at the dance. And he'd come inside after Old Red and I burst in and forced Nurse Rosenkoetter to put down the syringe.

The syringe, I realized, that was still sitting on the bed behind her.

My eyes went to it…just as Holly sprinted toward it.

My Bulldog was angled down toward where his knees had been a second before—*you* try holding a gun on a man through all of a ten-minute conversation—and by the time I had it swung up toward him again, he was on the other side of the bed, careful to keep himself behind Nurse Rosenkoetter. There was nothing I could do but shout "Stop!" as he snatched up the syringe.

"No!" Butler cried, throwing himself over his wife to protect her from the needle.

He needn't have bothered.

"I'll give you proof," Holly said. "Proof that you've grievously wronged me."

And he jerked up the shirt and coat sleeves over his left forearm, stabbed the needle into it, and pushed down on the plunger.

"Dr. Holly, don't!" Nurse Rosenkoetter cried.

But it was too late.

Holly pulled out the emptied syringe and threw it to the side. It shattered against the metal footrail of one of the other beds.

"Now you'll see a maligned, misunderstood man—a good man—get very drowsy and go to sleep," he said. "And you'll be sorry."

I've heard the phrase "color drained from his face," of course, but I've never seen it so literal. It was as if somebody pulled a cork out of the man and all the pink in him—all the life—started gurgling out.

"I *am* a healer," he said to Butler, who was peering up at him now, arms still stretched out over his wife. "Everything I've done has been to help."

A blankness had come over his features like a white curtain coming down, and his breathing was growing rapidly heavier, more labored. Foamy spittle formed at the sides of his mouth, and his eyelids fluttered.

He swayed, put his left hand to his stomach, and sat down hard on the bed behind him.

Nurse Rosenkoetter moved toward him, but he shoved her away with his final bit of strength.

"The world could have had...so much from me," he wheezed. His head lolled, and he lay down on his side. "But now...you will all get...nothing."

He grimaced, then shuddered, then went still.

Nurse Rosenkoetter knelt in over him again, and Swann staggered to his side. But I knew it was pointless. I'd seen the way his eyes had gone glassy, focused on an emptiness far beyond anything in the room.

Holly was dead.

Noon

The sanitorium had a sleigh in addition to a surrey, and despite the height of the snow that had been dumped on the mountain McCandless was confident he and Hippo-Crates could get me and Old Red back down to town without too much trouble. Which would suit just about everybody fine. My brother and I were itching to go, and Dr. Swann and Nurse Rosenkoetter were itching to have us gone.

The nurse glared her goodbye to us as we crossed the lobby with bags in hand. From the cold loathing on her face I took it she blamed us for how things had turned out. The only hint of warmth I'd ever seen in her was for Dr. Holly, and now that was snuffed. All that remained was efficiency and ice. And, for us, resentment.

We went to Swann's office to take our leave of him—it seemed like the professional thing to do though he'd never want to see us again either—and found him waiting with the door open and a bottle of Gordon's on his desk. I guess there didn't seem like any point in hiding them anymore.

He sat there glum and motionless as we told him we'd be heading down to inform the authorities and send a telegram to the board.

"Well," he said when we were done, "as long as you're still working for the sanitorium, technically speaking, you can do one more thing for us on your way out."

He took a quick swig from a coffee mug and heaved a gin-tinged sigh.

"Escort the Butlers off the premises," he said.

"What?" said Old Red. "In the shape they're in? You'd kick 'em out when she's barely awake and he's weak as a baby and they both're liable to cough themselves to death any second?"

"It's policy! They're not allowed here!" Dr. Swann snapped back, sitting up straight. He had no heart for his job anymore, but the chance to yell at us still gave him a little lift. "They are tres-passers who need to leave—*now*—and if you don't like that you can take it up with the board!"

My brother did not like that. He did not like that one bit. And he was about to say so. About to say how much he didn't like Swann, too. Say it loudly. And profanely.

"Brother," I got in first. "If I may put in a word...?"

He glowered over at me a moment, then nodded.

I thanked him with a nod of my own, then turned to the red-eyed, puffy-faced, drunkard waiting none-too-patiently for us to speak our piece and leave him to his bottle.

"Dr. Swann, let's just lay it out there," I said. "We are about to get you fired. We gotta report what we gotta report, and that's gonna be that for you here. There's no way around it. So I'll understand if you wanna tell us to go to hell. But that's no reason to say the same to Mr. and Mrs. Butler."

Old Red bugged his eyes a bit in surprise. I guess he'd been expecting me to spread out some kind of honey-sweetened bullshit instead of acknowledging the obvious.

Swann puckered his lips and leaned back in his seat and took a long sip from his mug.

"There's nothing I can do for them," he said. "Especially with my time in charge here about to end, as you say."

"But that's exactly why you *can* do something," I replied. "It'll be days before the board acts. Probably more like weeks, slow as some wheels turn. And in the meantime, the Butlers could be here. Resting. Healing. Who knows? Maybe the board'll even decide to change its policy after they hear from us, and they'd be welcome to stay. Or the board itself could get tossed out on its ear, and who'll be in charge after that? And what policies will they believe in? And what good could you do while it all gets sorted out? I won't pretend to know the Hippocratic oath, but I've heard the gist of it, I think. 'First do no harm.' Isn't that it?"

Swann just stared at me silently. His hand was still on his mug, but at least he hadn't lifted it to his lips as I lectured him. He didn't give me a nod or tell me I was right either. He was listening, though.

"I guess Holly forgot that. Or the meaning of it never sank in for him in the first place," I said. "But you've got a chance to show you do understand it. That you do believe it. I don't know— maybe it's even your last chance. Would you really want to pass that up just 'cuz you're mad at *us*?"

Swann's stare had turned into a seething scowl by now. His pudgy fingers went white around his mug, gripping it so tight it was a wonder the porcelain didn't crack.

I expected a bellow. An expletive. *Lots* of expletives.

But when he finally spoke, the words he grated out were quiet and controlled.

"Go on," he said, moving his gaze from me to the bottle on his desk. "Get out."

"Uh…just the two of us, you mean?" I said.

"Just the two of you."

He snatched up the bottle and began refilling his mug.

Old Red and I looked at each other. I jerked my head toward the door.

We got out fast, before he could change his mind.

McCandless and Hippo-Crates were all set for us out front. This time, unlike the ride up, my brother and I both climbed into the back seat and settled in side by side. McCandless had thoughtfully brought out a bearskin rug for us, and we pulled it up over our legs as we went sliding away.

I looked over my shoulder to see if anyone was watching us go. Two people were. They were standing there as motionless and pale as white curtains in separate windows.

Miss Johansen was in the women's ward, Breckenridge in the men's, forty yards of snow drifts and wood and glass between them.

I gave them a cheerless little wave. Neither waved back.

As we moved further from the main building, I saw more people, though they weren't paying any mind to us. Two orderlies in heavy coats were carrying another loaded stretcher out to the morgue shack. I didn't know where Holly would wind up in the end—if he had a family that would still want him after what he'd done. But for now, before he got planted somewhere for good, he'd get a little more time out in his laboratory with the specimens and experiments and files and notes he'd found more important than anything.

I faced forward—toward our long ride through miles of seemingly lifeless white.

McCandless didn't say anything for a while. I think he was saving up his many questions until he had more distance between himself and Nurse Rosenkoetter.

Old Red was quiet, too. Which wasn't entirely a surprise, him being him. I'd been expecting a little ribbing, though. Some jabs about how I'd been his eyes and ears the past two days yet had been mostly blind and deaf. Even shunted to the side with only hearsay to go on he'd been able to see it all clearly. I'd still be in the dark even when in the full light of snowy-bright day.

What use was I to a detective agency? What was I good for other than blundering and pointing a gun while my brother got the job done?

"I wanna know things so bad," Old Red said out of the blue, surprising me. "Gotta figure 'em out or go crazy. But have you noticed it don't always make things better? Sometimes it even makes things worse?"

I nodded. I had noticed that. Solving mysteries doesn't always solve problems.

"But what you managed to do in there just now?" Old Red went on. "With Swann?"

He surprised me again by doing something unheard of for him—reaching out from under the bearskin to pat me on the knee.

"You done good, Brother," he said.

I nodded again. It took me a few seconds to get the "Thanks" past the lump I suddenly had in my throat.

My brother gave me another pat, and I felt a little warmer in spite of the frigid wind that blew over us as we wound our way down and down and down to whatever we'd face next. Together.

A LOOK AT: HOLMES ON THE RANGE
HOLMES ON THE RANGE MYSTERIES
BOOK ONE

SHERLOCK HOLMES MEETS THE OLD WEST IN THIS THRILLING MURDER MYSTERY ON A KILLER RANCH.

It's 1893, and wandering cowboy brothers Big Red and Old Red Amlingmeyer are down to their last few pennies. When a job becomes available at a ranch run by a confident and enigmatic foreman, neither brother can say no.

Although the work is tiresome and their boss is bad-tempered, they have a welcome distraction—the Sherlock Holmes stories Old Red has come to love so much.

But when someone discovers a dead body on the ranch, a menacing game is afoot. Old Red is determined to catch the killer using Holmes' infamous methods, and Big Red is dragged along for the wild ride—whether he likes it or not—while his brother tries to deduce his way to the truth.

Can Old Red and Big Red solve the mystery with stampedes, rustlers, Holmes-hating aristocrats, and a cannibal named Hungry Bob standing in their way?

AVAILABLE NOW

ABOUT THE AUTHOR

Steve Hockensmith's first novel, the western mystery hybrid *Holmes on the Range*, was a finalist for the Edgar, Shamus, Anthony and Dilys awards. He went on to write several sequels—with more on the way—as well as the tarot-themed mystery *The White Magic Five* and *Dime* and the *New York Times* bestseller *Pride and Prejudice and Zombies: Dawn of the Dreadfuls*. He also teamed up with educator "Science Bob" Pflugfelder to write the middle-grade mystery *Nick and Tesla's High-Voltage Danger Lab* and its five sequels.

A prolific writer of short stories, Hockensmith has been appearing regularly in *Alfred Hitchcock* and *Ellery Queen Mystery Magazine* for more than 20 years. You can learn more about him and his writing at stevehockensmith.com.

Made in the USA
Coppell, TX
20 December 2023

26726084R00139